Praise for Tom Stewart, *Immortal North*, and *Under Big-Hearted Skies*

"I'll be thinking about *Immortal North* for a long time. Some of the passages are just so exquisitely written. A lot of emotion and setting the scene—it was just so vivid. Excellent read."

"*Immortal North* broke my ̣ ̣ ̣ only to shatter it again and ̣ ̣ ̣ ̣ ̣ ̣ ̣ would keep going back for more. Tom Sṭ ̣ ̣ ̣ has this exceptional way of transporting his reader to the very center of his bookly world, immersing you in the cold unforgiving *Immortal North*. I will truly miss the trapper's northern refuge."

—Heather Hays Reed, BookSirens

"Tom Stewart lives a foreign life to me, but only in the details. This man's heart is large and utterly relatable."

— Kitty Purdon, Goodreads

"Tom Stewart's short life-stories combine for an outstanding memoir that sets it apart from the pack. This memoir delivers a punch. The stories within are also written in a way that makes for great conversations with those more adventure savvy. While this may, at first glance seem like a book for adventurous individuals, I assure you the content within will be enjoyed by all."

— Jill Rey, Reader Views

Books by Tom Stewart

Under Big-Hearted Skies

Immortal North

Lucky Dollar Media
British Columbia, Canada
luckydollarmedia@gmail.com
Page design, layout and typesetting: AtriTeX
Cover design: Marko Cerovac
Paperback ISBN 978-1-7772211-2-6
Ebook ISBN 978-1-7772211-3-3

IMMORTAL NORTH

A Novel

Tom Stewart

Dedication

To the North

Do you believe in the chance that you could be changed by something as timid as a word?

— Tobias Wolff

Listen. There are Northern sounds. *Across still water a loon is calling. Back in the deep timber a grouse flaps wing feathers against its swollen chest like ritual drumbeat. Under the night's dancing aurora, honking geese are V'd up, flying airpaths millennia old, and had those paths been travelled over land they'd have looked so deep you'd swear a river cut them into the earth.*

An eagle circles high above. Trees talk through tingling roots under the moss of the forest floor. A crow in a snag tree turns its head.

Welcome to the North.

1

In that predawn steel light the trapper turned, he bent down, he raised and placed a single finger across his lips. He spoke to his boy.

"We're close. Softer than whispers now."

The boy nodded.

"What do we think about the animals?"

"We respect them and love them."

"Do we hunt like the wolf?"

"No."

"Why?"

"They hunt in packs and run their prey down."

"Do we hunt like the bear?"

"No."

"Why?"

"They're loud when they kill and scare the forest."

"How do we hunt?"

"Like the owl."

"Tell me why."

"It hunts by stealth. It's the quietest predator."

"How does it kill?"

"Swift and without remorse."

"How do we kill?"

"Swift and without remorse."

The trapper nodded.

The boy nodded back about as grave as a boy's ever nodded, and the man almost smiled at that. He turned back around to the trail ahead and a forest gradually revealing its details in the slow dawn light. Tree leaves and root stumps, animal tracks and trails emerging like first sounds at the start of a growing crescendo eventually to be taken up by all.

There's language to the woods and it's speaking to those capable of listening, to ears taught to decode meanings mild or malignant. Geese flying, bees buzzing. Howl of a wolf, height of the clouds, face of the moon, colour of the night and the morning sky, movement of game, snowfall heavy or light—things mostly lost on most people. Where others heard the winds in the maples, the trapper smelled the sap on the breeze. A wind veered northerly and where another might think the evening cold, he knew frost was coming early and the temperatures would stay cold for a week and the bears would feed heavily before the berry bushes died and the deer would be more active at dusk, at dawn. Inflections of the forest, cadence of the wilderness, language of the North.

A stilled, uneasy forest can give a predator away. When the boy was even younger a cougar once stalked their path and the trapper had sensed it there before he turned to draw. The mute alarm of absent sirens is loud if you're listening and the tension in the woods can feel like the skin of a snare drum. Big moving animals—which most hunters are—quiet the woods. His every step with thin leather soles like fox footpads felt the ground for whatever might break under his weight. Twigs unsnapped. Thin ice uncracked over a moose-print puddle. Between steps he watched silently like one of the trees.

A mind ten thousand hours at the task recognizes patterns not visible to common eyes and he's a whole life lived in wild lands beyond that, raised under the tutelage of a heritage of straight killers with the stakes of hunting to feed families or starve trying. He's hearing fingers hit the keys before others would hear the notes. An intelligence, and that's what it is, fitted to those wilds and perhaps too so is his version of moral conduct—and why wouldn't it be? Leave a person to the isolate woods mostly separate from other customs and that person may start to embody the particular standards of those surroundings: accountings and reckonings.

"Dad," the boy whispered pulling at his coat, and so the man turned around. The boy had his arm outstretched with a hand palm up. "I get to carry one," he whispered.

The trapper unclipped an arrow from the side-quiver of the bow and handed it to the boy.

"Don't let it—"

"I know."

The dawn glow gilded the forest as if the trees were of gold leaf and all within it coloured the same, and he looked at the boy cast in this golden hue. When she left she had entrusted their boy to his care and he saw her in him and he saw his own self in him too and he saw things that were neither of them. And all of it marvelled him—marvelled him and terrified him. In his forty years he'd had encounters with wild animals that people in a small town a bushplane flight away still talked about. He'd been lost a dozen times alone in the woods in the night and even when he was a boy himself that just didn't phase him much. He'd gone hungry and been injured and maybe he was just built a little differently 'cause he never winced never wilted. When she passed and he knew this boy was entirely under his care, that in very fact he lived or died based on his decisions and protection and planning and that some of it would just be up to luck and outside of his control, he was absolutely terrified. Felt it in his stomach, his heart. At times it kept him up in the night like he'd been entrusted to safeguard a star. But it drove him.

And out of that long predawn with the forest light changing from silvered to golden, he looked at the boy looking back at him, and the trapper did smile. He closed a fist, and a nine-year-old boy clenched his own small hand and bumped it back.

He turned to the forest. They moved quietly in the waking forest.

2

In a small-town bar near that trapper's remote cabin, which was not all that close given no roads connected the two, making it a floatplane trip or canoe with portage or snowshoe trek over the frozen lakes of winter, sometimes when bottlecaps were popped off beer tops his name was mentioned. Just sometimes. Stories that made him into something he wasn't quite, but wasn't entirely not, either. People like the drama. Take some liberties with the details, pull at the seams a little. How else do legends get made? Take some bare truths passed around in the old oral tradition where tales are living things growing and changing from one mouth to another's ear. A detail is forgotten or a new one swapped in or something added for a little impact, and eventually those living stories fill out. They fatten. Give them years of long winter nights and pour those truths a drink. But they always start somewhere.

Maybe a story about a knife became an axe. Maybe a six-foot leap over a gap in the rocks running from a bear became ten feet after a round of shots. On a good night by the time they heard last call was for sure fifteen leapt over a chasm where I heard they went back after and dropped a pebble in and couldn't hear it hit bottom. Loose little details build tall tales. But not all stories are liable for embellishment, not if the first ears that heard it found it hard enough to believe as it had arrived. If even repeating it as it was told was liable to make the storyteller accused as a liar, a bullshitter, that story was more likely to be unchanged or even tamed, rather than wilded up.

When they said he pulled her by snowshoe in the sled three days and three nights with the little boy on his back that he had given water to and fed over his shoulder with food from his pockets trekking without sleep, only stopping if he had to care for the boy, stepping snowshoe tracks in front of the sled he pulled behind him, rails sometimes sticking to the ice, sled belly sometimes sunk in heavy snow, when they said he went three days and he would have gone more, purely wasn't capable of quitting, wasn't in his makeup or the assembly of his brain parts, his heart parts, when they said that they got that right. Some said that on that long trek he wore the full lengths of his feet down to raw bone entire and when he walked into the hospital you could hear his feet through the thin leather of his worn boots clicking on the polished hospital tiles like skeleton feet, click click click, they said. That wasn't true. But the same sled he brought furs in, same sled his dad and his dad's dad had too, lay empty on the winter street outside the hospital doors, and people in town saw that and people in town talked.

He had carried her inside with the boy on his back, then stood beside her bed for hours until they stabilized her. The hospital staff that gently took the little boy from his back to care for him pleaded with the man to let them treat his feet. He didn't look down to his feet nor did he meet the eyes of those speaking. He did not look away from her, not once. Who'd believe that? Their words might not have even registered to him. When he did see her sleeping safely and that she had stabilized and they told him it'd just be better for her to rest alone, he turned and looked away from her for the first time like he'd only just heard them. Maybe he had. They led him to the care ward and then someone mopped up the floor where he had stood in a red puddle of melted snow.

If you asked the doctor who had seen to the man's wife in the emergency room and who then tended those ragged soles and first looked to the nurse, then to the feet, then back to the nurse, then to the feet and applied the balm and wrapped the bandage, if he happened to be in that small-town bar and you asked him about it, he'd say he'd never seen anything like it, never thought feet like that could support standing weight, never mind trekking the night with a child on his back while pulling a sled shuttling a woman. That same doctor in days to come said there was nothing more he could do for her and that he was sorry. That he was beyond sorry, he said. And if you asked him about it that was about as much as the doctor would say.

One night not long after she died that doctor was sitting at the bar and someone else's friend that no one seemed to have a direct tie to, a guy who had emptied a few Coors Light past cordial civility, was sitting next to him. Buddy wouldn't quit asking him about the man with the stories, about the trapper, as some people in town called him. The doctor told him no more than the few details he'd tell anyone else who asked about it. Said it was a sad thing and he wished he could have done more for her. He said that then looked away, looked back ahead to the bottles on the shelves and to drinking his own.

But the drunk man there wouldn't quit.

The doctor ignored him, his feet on the barstool footrest, his fingers laced around the back of the bottle. Him having to listen to this guy. This guy leaning in occasionally slurring his words. Who kept on with it.

Eventually the doctor turned and looked at him, gave a small headshake, then looked past him to a room about as quiet as it'd ever been on a Friday evening—in fact the jukebox must have been between songs too. Somebody coughed. The bartender who had already told buddy just to ease up there was towelling the inside of a clean glass and you could hear the squeak of it. That quiet.

The man leaned in a bit closer to the doctor. He said something crude and baseless, just to liven things up a bit 'cause it was Friday evening and the beers were feeling warm in him and he just felt like getting a reaction 'cause he was feeling really good with the beers in him, so he said a few words that insinuated a little something about the doctor and the trapper's wife.

That actually made the doctor smile. Like he was impressed about something. After the man said that he leaned back on his stool smiling too, them both smiling. The beer smell on his breath didn't lean away with him though, he left that with the doctor.

Then he said to the doctor, "Oh that's it then isn't it? Yeah," he winked, "that's it."

The doctor finished his beer 'cause he didn't want to get it on the floor too, and then he felt bad about the glass on the floor. The doctor helped the man up and he helped him across the street and then he sutured up the man's bleeding head.

Had the police inquired to the room full of customers they'd likely not have encountered a single witness. But they didn't inquire.

3

The trapper and his boy continued walking a gametrail in the fall morning of northern boreal lands lit by light yet to warm that which it brightened. A rustling vole scurried under fallen leaves and tree frogs croaked and there were happy tunes from chirping sparrows. A red squirrel ran up the backside of a pine tree next to the trail, sounding its tacky grip over the bark then bounded out on a limb to gnaw at the stems of cones, dropping them thumping on the forest floor. One whizzed past the boy's ear, narrowly missing him, and he looked up with his brows bent at the squirrel returning that gaze. The boy had long before declared them enemies and this offense only strengthened that conviction. Another cone gnawed and thumped.

Brown pine needles hung from branches by thinnest bonds and with the morning's own whisper lighter than breeze, needles fell about the pair like slender rain. One snagged in a cobweb glinting with dew-beads, until the next draft dislodged it and one more needle fell to the forest floor already thatched with needles that quieted the steps of these two hunters searching the woodland for game.

In the distance came a heavy droning sound. In years past that wasn't so uncommon but now it stopped them in their trek. They looked up in the direction of the motor's sound, but the tall forest canopy thick overhead prevented them from getting a visual. The volume and vibrations from its big nine-cylinder engine storming towards their forest world like that engine's own military roots. Then high up between the branches in blue pockets of sky the man saw a yellow Beaver floatplane. Its path was slightly to his left and he could just make out the pilot in the front and a passenger in the aft seat beside the cargo door. That big motor beating down heavily. When he was about the boy's age an overloaded floatplane was about to take off in marginal weather and the seasoned pilot had said that's all the flying he'd ever known up there, just another day at the office he said. The young trapper standing on the dock had watched the plane screaming down the lake taking off into a strong headwind that would give that heavy load a quick lift. The pontoons lifted from the lake and the plane was gaining altitude, until that headwind veered hard, dropping the plane half the height it'd climbed. Never cleared the trees. He'd seen the plane take off that day and he'd seen it snapping treetops as it crashed that day. His grandparents raised him after that day.

The trapper and his boy watched the yellow plane as it flew out of sight, its aft docking rope flapping in the air behind a pontoon. Its motor quietening at a greater rate than warranted from its growing distance told its power was being reduced and the plane was starting a long and angled approach to water. The only body of water large enough in that area to land it, the trapper thought. The same water that an overloaded plane had one day taken off from. As if its yellow fuselage stained the air, this new plane was an unwelcome foreign presence. Perhaps for a man who considered himself a keeper of stars, a father at constant vigil, he was inclined to interpret the signs in the world around him and the boy as more threatful than they inherently were. This plane now one more concern among many: weather, predators, food, the boy's health. But he preferred to keep that concern to himself, so when he turned to the boy he kept his face stoned over like a bluff on the river. Saw the boy had been watching him. And why should that surprise him when he's trying to raise an owl. The kid's own face told nothing of what he saw in the man's.

4

The yellow Beaver floatplane was starting its descent for the lake beside the hunting lodge. Dave sat in the aft seat and Jacob up front beside the young pilot. Jacob requested through the headsets for them to circle a flyover. The pilot eased the controls back and touched the power up to make a slow pass just above stall speed following along the lakeshore.

Seeing the fall colours and the cabins and the cold blue of the lake below them, Jacob turned around to Dave. "Damn," he said. "That is somethin' beautiful." Last spring Jacob and Dave along with the two investors who had backed them to buy the lodge, all came up to check it out. Now Dave and Jacob were seeing for the first time what it looked like in fall. Dave sitting beside the cargo door of the WWII-era bushplane smiled back to his joint partner. Then went back to taking it all in from the window of the plane banked in the slow turn. The big lake calm with no ripples, bordering outcroppings of grey bedrock, green treetops of pine and spruce in the otherwise orange and yellow and red forest. Eight grey roofs below them.

The first time they had talked about owning a business together was sometime in high school. Ten years later Jacob was a hunting guide and had worked at more than one operation and casually floated the idea of them running a small hunting outfit together.

"You keep your eyes open," Dave had said. Easy to say when it's mostly just talk. There weren't that many around, fewer for sale, and even the lowest priced operations, the more remote outfits with rustic cabins, were not so cheap. They both had only modest savings.

One afternoon Jacob called Dave and invited him to steaks at the small bar in their small town. Dave knew something was coming but wasn't sure what.

"I found backers."

"What?"

"I found a lodge for sale and I found financial backers." Jacob was smiling like he'd found gold.

Dave lifted his own pint glass. Set it down looking genuinely intrigued. "Alright. I'm listening."

Jacob told him that for the past several hunting seasons on the last day of every hunt while he was skinning out the hide for his rich clients, he'd pitch them the idea of backing him in running a hunting outfit. "You get your own lodge run by your favourite guide," he'd wink while skinning out their moose or bear. "Remote land like this is only going to be in more demand in the future. Call it a savings account that keeps up with inflation, meanwhile you get an incredible place to bring your buddies for free. I bet the charm of an operation like the one I found for sale would itself seal the deal on any future business ventures you're trying to close. Just bring 'em up there, your clients. The place would only put dollars in your pockets, boys, without taking any of your time." Jacob told Dave how Dave himself was the sweetener. "My best friend and finished top of his class in a business degree. Smartest guy I know and a good hunter too."

Dave had a diploma from a vocational college in small-business management that he had taken by correspondence. "My cheeks are red from the Tabasco on this peppered steak not from your motivated flattery," Dave said while grinning and looking down cutting into his steak, "but go on."

"I don't think it's just talk. These two guys have more money than the whole town and I've guided them three years now and they like me. We've always done well on our hunts. I made sure they know this parcel for sale is game rich. A most unique place. I let them know that. They said they want to come up this spring and check it out. If they like it, they'll back us they said. It's been idle for a bit so you and I would have to start fixing it up this year after the deal goes through. Market it over the winter, start running it next year."

"How much is it?"

"Five hundred thousand."

"They're putting a hundred percent of it down?"

"Well here's what I'm thinking and been wanting to hear your thoughts on." Jacob halfway through his meat, potatoes and greens untouched, put his utensils down askew. "Five-hundred-kay is peanuts to these guys. But I'd rather you and me be owners not just operators. Get some skin in the game. Even if we don't have fifty-one percent. Better to be an owner. I have forty thousand in savings and I can get another ten." He drank. "What do you think of that?"

Dave didn't say yes. Didn't say no. "Tell me about the outfit."

Jacob told of the lodge by location and when Dave drilled down on him Jacob told of it by name.

"Bit of a history to that one, no?"

"All the better for marketing. A place with a story. That's just good business." Jacob smiled and then looked for their waitress but he caught the bartender's eyes first. Held up his empty pint glass to him. Set his empty glass down and his hand around it showed a ring finger with a pale band of skin. "What place doesn't have a little history?"

"Is that land unceded? I heard some area around there has claims against it."

Jacob told him there were no claims.

Later, before Dave pitched the idea to his wife, Sarah, after he had made her dinner and washed the dishes and asked her about her day and complimented her hair saying I just like what you're doing with it lately, it's lighter or softer, actually both I think, and said why don't you just lean back and let's just talk and let me massage ya a little, and she said laughing okay what the hell, he had in fact verified the title was clear and there were no claims against the land.

By the end of that winter night in the small-town bar it wasn't official, but when Jacob raised his fresh beer at last call to his good buddy and said, "To new ventures, partner," Dave before raising his own glass looked first at the beer in Jacob's hand, so Jacob said, "Got that under control, my man," and Dave did cheers him back. "Alright," Dave said, "let's do it."

They went up to the property with their investors and checked it out that spring. They were part owners by late summer. Now it was fall. The pilot having met the start of the holding pattern he'd just circled, unrolled the lower wing back up to level flight and looked to his right. Jacob gave a thumbs-up and nodded and the pilot steered for the water and into the wind and reduced power and lowered the flaps. Then finally flared and touched down on the lake water, puttering towards the shore to unload.

5

When the man slowly turned his head to scan the periphery for movement, so turned the boy. When the man subtly cocked an ear to a sound, the boy as well. And now he froze in his step and so too froze the little shadow. The trapper put his hand balled up behind his back with pointer and pinky raised, like horns protruding from a clenched fist. The signal for a deer. A buck.

They listened, both their mouths slightly open to fully port their ears.

Songbirds. Silence. Dew from dripping trees landing to lower leaves like pat, pat, pat. Silence. Then a faint and sporadic rustle. Weight moving over dry and fallen maple leaves—movement in the forest. They both heard it but the boy's young ears a split second first and needing not be told he slowly crouched in place, with the man now mirroring the smaller human behind him like a shadow cast from a trailing sun of which it was.

A whitetail deer sees poorly and its sight is even worse when it's looking into the day-breaking sun, the bright light at the back of a predator. The trapper tried to put small things in their favour and added up they made big things. Take advantages there to be took, he'd told the boy, probably more than once.

Hardcoded in its makeup a deer knows its life depends on being quiet, hidden and alert. But cautious as they care to be and mostly are, the deer make noise like everything else and all animals leave a scent and show a trail and when the squirrels are watching they sound alarm for all without prejudice or favour.

Last year later into the season in nearly the same part of the forest as now, they watched a buck the size of a buck from one of his granddad's stories tending a doe. The doe was wandering leisurely while she browsed vine maple. The buck never once fed himself and never once lifted his eyes from her. She'd take a few steps then he'd follow. Her tail stuck straight out. If they kept watching sure enough he'd breed her. They moved in that lockstep waltz for over an hour but never coming closer than about fifty yards to where he and the boy were hiding in cover. Some bowhunters shoot that distance and some farther yet and he did not. A deer can jump the string when you start reaching for distance and that makes wounding animals more likely. They'd pass on shots rather than risk a long one. Hunt close, kill every time, he'd told the boy.

He'd taken the lives of a lot of animals and knew they had a capacity to suffer. He didn't like either of those facts. And maybe that suffering was not all that different from humans, and if that was the case or if it was even close to the case he wondered just how he could ethically continue hunting them. For an innocent human to suffer was a terrible thing, so why shouldn't that compassion extend to all other creatures that are capable of experiencing significant anguish? Why should it be permissible to take life outside of the boundary of the human species? He thought about this. If humanity values that all things capable of feeling significant pain should not suffer needlessly, then was he being inhumane, being cruel? The progression of civilization is to look back on former times with horror for practises that were then common, crucifixion for rebels, stoning for adultery, amputation for theft. He did wonder if future generations would look back on him as a type of monster for the hunting and trapping he'd done. But he'd seen what happens to wild animals in old age. Losing teeth and starving before being eaten alive by predators. That seemed crueller than a fair chase and quick death from one well-placed arrow. No rabbit lives out its golden years in the company of its family. What awaits is starvation or disease or being pulled apart by a fox. And not so long ago the deer hit a seven-year-disease cycle, and the ice on the lake prevented their casting from shore, yet it had been still too thin to walk on and fish through. They didn't have any luck snaring rabbits and so all they'd eaten was root vegetables and grains from the cellar. And they did not feel so strong. They were weakened. So he taught the boy reverence for their world along with all the life they shared it with and that their own lives were of no greater value than those of the other animals. And he taught the boy to kill quickly as he'd been taught, and in his eyes that made it permissible. The animals were in good numbers and that made it sustainable. Still, taking a life and inflicting suffering gave him thought and came with weight and he tried to impart that significance on his son.

Last year that doe browsing with the buck following fed away from the trapper and his boy and it didn't look like she'd have any reason to turn back towards where they were concealed. They weren't going to be able to close the distance without spooking the animals. If the wind was stronger to cover their sound, if it was raining to mask their footfalls, or if even the ground hadn't been recently overlaid with dry leaves frosted to crinkle at each step, they might have taken off their leather boots and barefoot stalked—*tricks of Granddad*. Maybe. But that day last year was rainless and calm and a forest floor covered with papery leaves that to the listening animals were like landmines waiting to be set off. So he had curled his hands into hollow tubes and placed them end on end then raised them to his mouth. The boy had watched. He lowered his head to relax his throat. As did the boy that day. He drawled out a low grunt lasting a couple seconds, a sound of mock challenge from a rival suitor coming for the doe, for that buck's doe, for his doe, and it was time for him to fight or flee. He followed up that grunt with a second, making a sound that in another language called someone out. Right there in front of his lady. Immediately they watched the spine-line of fur on that buck bristle up mohawk straight. Watched its hide pull tight over flexed shoulder muscles where it stood quartering away. Then it lowered its head slowly, and for the first time looked away from the doe. Swung that big rack on its heavy head to scan towards the sound of the challenger. Its barrelled chest followed that brooding head-turn and its broad shoulders with a white chest-patch squared up to the source. The boy almost screamed. The trapper heard him gasp beside him and looked to the boy and would have scowled him silent but he saw he'd actually put a mitt over his own mouth. Then a second mitt. Mitts the trapper had worn himself as a boy, red ones Gran had knitted, and deer are mostly colour blind so that's okay.

The buck raised a hoof as big as a saucer-plate and hung it in the air a second. Then it stamped the cold ground and they felt it from where they crouched some fifty yards away. It snorted up a mist cloud. Again: lift, suspend, stamp, snort. He'd hunted a hundred deer starting before he was the boy's young age and even that being the case he'd not seen an animal like this. Always thought his granddad was stretching at the seams a little on his stories as he tended to talking them fireside. Get that man talkin'.

Man and boy had stared at this myth buck that had now closed half the distance and the trapper almost drew back his bow without an arrow nocked—a mistake you only make one time. The animal, sensing some-thing, stopped its slow saunter and sniffed the air with flaring nostrils, black and glistening and streaming in morning air trying to catch the smell of what didn't feel right. Then failing to catch it, snorting that air back out. Snorting like he'd be pissed off if he caught that rival's scent and pissed off not to of just the same. Like that buck both woke up and went to bed angry, if it did sleep at all that time of year. In late fall some dominant bucks raged in the forest all hormone crazed and with a bad attitude. Here was one. His massive rack had a chipped brow-tine that was stark white where the other tines were dark brown and every year those racks grow back from scratch—he was no stranger to putting that headgear to serious use in that season, maybe even that same day.

The buck in its search had closed in and stood about fifteen yards from them. Looked for his rival and he wheezed and snorted like he had a few words of his own to say. Raised a hoof to step again, but that hoof never set the ground because a soft dull sound of spent bow-limbs had sent a tri-bladed broadhead honed like a scalpel three-hundred-feet per second to sever its windpipe and the carotid artery and so too its spine in that rut-swollen neck. And a deer head with antlers like a king's crown toppled from a buck that died standing.

Normally the trapper only sent arrows for lung-shots but this deer was nearly walking on them close, nearly died at their feet. He had a follow-up arrow nocked but it would not be required. He looked that day to the boy beside him and the wide-eyed boy removed a mitted hand covering his mouth, then the other, showing his jaw was dropped underneath them and probably the whole time. Then he raised those arms in victory in the fall air.

That was last year.

The foliage that earlier the sun had made golden was now coloured its common browns and greens and greys of no less beauty than gold, and the forest's still collage was broken by motion. Not the hunters'. From where they crouched hidden in the undergrowth they scanned their unblinking eyes trying to decipher out a deer body moving out there in the dense forest. When it froze the deer blended in so well with its surroundings but it gave up that camouflage when it stepped and stopped and stepped again. They tracked its movement with their slow-turning heads, so far the deer only revealing its general shape, still mostly covered. Then the brush opened up enough with the deer now only partially hidden by a few thin paper birch trees and a balsam poplar. The boy's knuckles wrapped around the shaft of the single token arrow he carried were white. The man's wrapped around the bow handle were not.

His arrow already nocked, the trapper drew back like a brushstroke on an artist's canvas, like a virtuoso over violin strings, smooth and deliberate like he had done almost every day of every year of his life whether in practice or pursuit, and the soundless bow flexed its limbs and the mute cams rotated into full draw, the compound bow now loaded and waiting. He slowly tracked the sight-pin to the walking deer still partially concealed by the stand of trees. Then he led the bow farther on ahead of its path to the open forest where that animal would emerge full broadside. He held it there and waited and it wasn't long. Forelegs stepped out clear, then the deer paused, its head behind a branch. It took two more steps exposing its torso. He floated the pin as if the deer leg continued on vertically inside the deer's chest and he stopped halfway up its body: top of the heart, centre of the lungs.

A little lower on the deer's body was the centre of its heart. He knew the precise location of the heart muscle with its oblong shape and he knew where connected the arteries and veins and the location and width of the protective ribs, and his knowledge of a deer's anatomy was in practical terms not so far off from a biologist's or veterinary surgeon's. And he never aimed centre heart. If that arrow is a touch low from an unseen branch or movement of the prey, it's liable to nick the belly or hit a leg. Sends that animal on a miserable path, if it even

25

recovers. Centre that pin for a double-lung shot and it's equally as deadly while the target gets sized three times larger and it's vitals all around. If you miss high it's spine, low it's heart, miss back it's liver—all of it fatal and ethically quick. Heart-shots make for wounded game and hungry bellies and humility fills the freezer. The trapper's left eye narrowed and his dominant eye stared at that target-patch of fur behind the sight-pin. His pulse beat half time. Partial exhale. The boy whispered, "Doe."

"She's a doe, Dad."

His narrowed eye unnarrowed.

"We don't shoot the does, Dad." He spoke quietly while tugging at his elbow outstretching the bow.

The deer lowered her antlerless head to feed. Looked around with a mouthful of fern. One ear turned one way and the other flicked the opposite. She sniffed into the wind and her tail flipped and unalarmed she fed on. One buck can breed dozens of does so it better serves the deer population to hunt just the males. The trapper and his boy could still fish and berries were dried and grains were stored and they weren't going hungry at all and so he drew down the bow.

The kid had caught it and he didn't and that was a first. He turned to him and whispered, "Just making sure you're paying attention," and the boy smiled at that. Concealed as they were and the wind in their favour they watched her feed for a while. That doe took quiet steps with gentle movement. Just a soft presence oblivious to her own grace.

He saw her in the things around him. *Her.* Not every time but sometimes. Not just memories, but those too. Like she and some elements of the forest shared a similar quality. Certain shapes and shades and sounds. Things unconstrained by particular forms. Sometimes the sun bright on the bark of a tree had her same hair colour. And whether bad habit or otherwise, 'cause how do you move on if you call the past to every scene, but fact was those shared qualities frequently recalled her to his thoughts, and then seeing her there reinforced her presence. A virtuous cycle—or vicious one, depending on who you asked. He'd say the former. As she still came to mind even after she had passed, some memories were not exactly from before she left, but had originated afterwards—in thoughts, in dreams—then merged with former times they'd lived together. And it all played with the truth some, augmented and warped it. One time in a section of forest where he and his wife had walked hand-in-hand in days gone by, he didn't turn his head he turned his whole body and looked beside him because he felt her so strongly he could've sworn her there. Looked and saw nothing. The boy had watched it all. Saw his dad turn and saw what his face looked like when he turned. The kid didn't say anything about it, that time.

Right now the kid said in a hushed voice âpiscimô-sis. *Deer*. The boy knew a few Cree words. "She's looking at us," he said.

The doe was staring towards their general area but could not pick out their motionless shapes lost in the surroundings. She seemed to sense something and raised then lowered her head. Turned both ears their way and sniffed the air with her nose that was far better than a bloodhound's and a bloodhound's can smell cancer. But the direction of the breeze told nothing. She stood frozen still with big unblinking eyes. She had all day for this. Again lowered her head then looked away to goad them into moving, snapping back her gaze to try to catch them. Cunning tactics of instinct. But they'd seen that many times before and didn't fall for it. She repeated that inquiring gesture twice more. In her everyday of constant alert such encounters were not so rare and eventually she gave it up, forgot them and with no rush she turned and fed on into the forest.

"See how her tail is down and not outstretched. See how she isn't looking behind her. There's no buck here. Come on."

They walked in the forest's aromatic fall morning, the sweet rot of it. That fragrance lacked the freshness of spring where the melting snow saturating the earth weighted the air with rich scents of soil and budding plants. Woods that lacked the colourful, opulent bouquet of summer's blooming wildflowers in a baking forest of heated scents where berries both decorated and perfumed the woods that sprawled and pulsed with summer. But the fall was his. Nearly called to him. Maybe a type of candor in its increasing openness, fewer places for threats to hide with the dormant trees dropping their leaves, the forest preparing for heavy snow and hard winter. And the deer sensed it too and were feeding heavily and the geese knew it too and were leaving the scene and all the scents made crisp from frosted mornings and the nights were cold so fires felt their warmest and coffee tasted its richest and he slept a little better with the cold that brought clear days where hunting would be good and only getting better—somehow all of it in that fall aroma.

Later into the morning they heard the floatplane flying away in the same direction that had brought it. For over one hundred years his family had owned the land around that lake. There his granddad had built the first cabin for a hunting outfit. But one night the trapper's dad lost the title and there were better ways to lose it than the way he had. The trapper had accepted two decades ago the hard fact that the land and those cabins were not going to be passed down to him. Didn't like it, but he accepted it. So it's not that whoever was on that plane were trespassing—they weren't and he knew it—but for the last several years that hunting outfit had not been running and he preferred its vacancy. If it was going to be back in operation that meant more hunters disturbing the land and spooking game that he and his boy were living off of. Who knows, maybe even wandering up to their cabin, as the distance from the lodge to where he and his boy lived was only a few hours hike if you knew the forest. There's plenty of space if it was managed properly, it just didn't sit all that well with him. He even wondered if the sight of the plane itself was like a shiny lure that might make the boy curious as to what he was missing out on in town. Over these quieter years they had seen the odd plane come and go, and one plane by itself was likely just the owners coming to check in on the place, for whatever reason not running the operation in full. The trapper was looking between the treetops for that Beaver plane. Wanting to see its cargo window. Only caught a flashing glimpse of yellow.

6

Two whisky jacks perched on a tree limb and canted their small heads as they watched the trapper and his boy walk below. Then flapped and rose and wheeled and dipped and lit to a farther branch ahead. And again waited. Then the next. For crumbs, for curiosity. The boy looked up at the birds and they screeched to him so he crooned back and the man watching half expected the birds to reply. The whisky jacks lifted up and the boy, disregarding his father's rule of moving quietly through the forest, flapped once too, chasing them in his mind, or perhaps not entirely sure he couldn't flitter up and give one small turn with them. And whose father would tell him he couldn't do so and what father in a small corner of his own mind hasn't the tiniest wild part of him not entirely convinced the boy couldn't fly up either, if only for a split second or two.

Spiritual is a word with one metric shit-ton of baggage and to say that the trapper was spiritual could be interpreted differently by anyone who heard it. Better said he loved being alive and nature and his kid and didn't take any of it for granted. His wife's death nearly ruined him and he was sad for a long time, but he had the boy and he liked their life and in fact she never felt all that removed from it. He wasn't putting a positive spin on everything like *All suffering is growth* and *Everything happens for a reason including terrible suffering and so it's not really suffering at all.* It seemed like sometimes pain was just pain and worth avoiding. Not all hurt is instructive or retributive or sensical. Seemed like the world could be hard and sad sometimes—full stop. Beyond that was mere speculation. He once believed in a god and now his faith had faltered and she'd played a role in that—mostly her words not her leaving. But he felt no less awe, no less meaning nor profundity in his world and no less moral conviction about how to act within it. He tried to put his focus on things other than himself: care for the boy and live respectfully with the life around them. Show the boy that simply being alive takes incalculable luck, this one little world in a billion empty others, one lucky sperm that outswam the rest, that the world with its gravity and plant life and all the rest even worked at all—that there was even something rather than nothing, and *that* something lit up in the morning every morning, and love existed in all its various forms. If your existence starts when you're born and stops when you die, that's pretty narrow in the whole history of things, and it was really nice that right now wasn't also oblivion forever. Most days it didn't even take much. Coffee early on cold mornings. The woods and the smell of the woods. Even just the birds and the sky. The simple pleasure of a book. He and the boy had a small library in their cabin and though he'd read them all many times over, he'd keep on reading them as who remembers every piece of it. The sound and smell and warmth of a fire. The boy. The boy especially.

Fall is too early for the lakes to be frozen and though snow had fallen by this point in past years, this year it yet hadn't. They walked in the darkest parts of the forest under the heaviest canopy where the snow would last the longest if it had fallen, but it had not fallen. It had rained like a son of a bitch the night before though and the trapper now in passing a small pine tree reached out his bow-limb behind him and tapped the narrow trunk, and the hanging rain-beads dislodged from lower branches and a light shower fell on the boy who had just followed him underneath. He kinda sounded like an otter when he laughed. It sometimes made the trapper laugh.

Their life was reclusive but he'd met various personalities over the years, mostly during his time as a young man guiding hunters at the lodge, both before and after his father had lost ownership of it. And he saw things he liked and things he didn't. And as nice as it would be to say that he loved the shortcomings in people because it took the bad to see the good and imperfections made people complex and that made them more deeply lovable, that would be a lie, a pretty one. There were ignoble traits of humans and capacities for cruel acts even in ordinary people and much of history was abhorrent. But humans had happened and were happening and you couldn't change that.

And he wouldn't want to.

The cruelty that humans sometimes show is just of a piece with all the other darkness and violence in nature, the animals eating other animals alive and diseases rotting living things away. It fits. But their light does not. That stands out. Kind and generous acts are vastly human things and he greatly admired the pockets of triumph from humankind's efforts. Things he'd read about from books and newspapers from fur trading trips to town. Even common things like the light in their cabin and the medicine he'd got from the hospital for the boy.

They edged muskeg swamp staying on the solid ground, and on the low hills they placed careful steps on slick bedrock, him leading, the boy following.

He knew how soft skin was. He'd touched it. How easily it bled. He'd bled it. How it one day wrinkled then died and lay like an old husk. There was an utter preciousness to life and he tried to keep that truth close and sometimes that sounded trite in his head and he knew it and that's not important. *Stop*. Are you listening? He'd ask himself that. The leaves, look at the leaves. Slow your breath just one time. He'd say that to himself. Look into the open forest, the sky. Slow down. *Hey*. Like he was trying to slap his own mind. *This is it.* Take a break from planning conceptualizing expecting fearing regretting. It's almost over. This, this is precious. Your time in these trees won't last. The second it took to realize that, was one more lost to oblivion. Turn your hands over and look at your skin, it's already withering, he'd tell himself that.

If all that taken together means he was spiritual, then he was. And if it doesn't, he was not.

The sun had about hit its apex which was still far from overhead in those northern latitudes. They lowered their packs on a small knoll surrounded by low-growing blueberry bushes. He laid the hunting bow quiver-side up on the ground and the boy carefully laid down the token single arrow he'd been carrying with its three-bladed broadhead on a piece of moss to protect its resting edges from dulling.

They talked sitting on their packs and picked berries and ate and looked out from their little vantage point. A vista showing a puddle lake not far below them bordered by an evergreen forest, the occasional deciduous tree standing bare having lost its leaves, or another still brightly coloured having yet to. Where beyond that vista lies a vast unseen of sprawling forests like this one and replica lakes and near endless country.

From each of their packs they had taken out small bags of dried and pounded venison, salted and enriched with rendered bear fat and sweetened with berries. A nutrient-dense food that preserved for months. The first member of his family to try it was an ancestor that had sailed from Scotland to North America in the late 1700s to work in the fur trade. An industry driven by the fashion craze for hats made from waterproof beaver pelts. He had hopes of owning land and was told by the men who had recruited him that he'd have more of it than he'd know what to do with. That early Scot never trapped animals, he ran a six-man crew on exploratory, mapping, and scouting trips from the outposts of his employer, the Hudson's Bay Company.

On one winter expedition his crew had met with an Anishinaabe tribe. The next morning before they set out, the chief gave—not traded—gave them each a small moose-skin parcel. Said, miijim. Then he said food, as that particular chief in addition to his own native language of Ojibwe, knew some English, French, and Cree. Mostly simple words relating to trade: numbers, animals, weather, navigation, brief civilities. As they'd already eaten together that morning, no crew members opened the little packages. It was agreed to meet again in thirty days. Later on his crew stopped for lunch and took off their snowshoes and sat resting their backs against tree trunks. Untied the thin wrap of hide and unfolded the packages. Four square brown pucks a piece, equally wide as they were deep, about two inches. That food was common for the time, would one day even have a war named after it. First time he had tried it though. Each crew member ate only one square and nobody ate another until well into the afternoon and they looked forward to it and said as much. Flavourful, but heavy like a rock. In the time before his return to that small village the Scot tried another version and it wasn't nearly as good. Made him curious.

On the returning trip the Scot inquired to the chief about that particular food by saying an unparticular word for it. Said the same word the chief had last time used himself. Miijim. The chief must have forgotten what exactly he'd given to him or perhaps he'd sent other traders on their way with different food or could be to him all white people looked alike. The chief took him to a table. Offered him dried fish, berries, nuts, a simple jerky. The Scot declined them smiling and looked for the heavy snack. He tried creative gestures to help his search. Held his hand in front and moved the other behind while saying miijim. *Food before.* The man just shook his head kindly in the miscommunication of it. It wasn't until the Scot held one hand out and then made an unwrapping motion of an invisible and small package then pretended to eat one square of four, laying four fingers against his open palm. Then he rubbed his belly and bent his knees like the food itself was heavy. The man smiled to that. Turned to a few

36

of his friends and family and said, "Nooka'iiwagwaan."
The Scot tried to repeat that word and said nothing very
close and likely that was the reason that word wasn't
said to him the first time, and some of the people there
laughed and so did he. The chief pointed to a woman
nearby and then he walked the Scot to meet her. More
simple words, as well some hand gestures followed:
pointing at the sun, swinging an actual mallet, as she
crudely demonstrated its recipe. From a cache she
showed him dried chokecherries which gave that recipe
its distinct flavour. Them standing there in the friendly
awkwardness of it where their words could have used
better translation but their smiles that day didn't need
it. That early Scot over the years and among different
groups of people frequently saw that food. Sometimes
the meat was sun-dried, other times it had been
smoked. Some made from bison, others from moose
or deer. One time fish even. The type of berries varied
and sometimes there weren't any. More commonly he
heard it call pimîhkân. Pemmican. The root Cree word
pimî meaning fat or grease. Two-hundred years later
the trapper's own boy would try it. Try it and like it. It
had chokecherries in it.

That Scot wouldn't head back to that particular
camp until next winter. In the meantime he'd actually
made some pemmican himself. It wasn't as good but
it wasn't bad. On the return trip he took three packs
with him. One for himself, one for the chief who'd
given it to him, one for the woman who'd taught him
the recipe. Four squares per package like they'd done
and he wrapped them not in moose skin but in heavy
paper and tied them each crosswise with a string. Upon

arriving to that camp they found it deserted. In some cases smallpox killed over half the inhabitants in any given village. They found out later that particular camp had been wiped out entirely save for one boy and one girl who were adopted into another Indigenous community by the members who had found them. That community itself ravaged by disease.

In years to come traditional lifestyles of the Indigenous peoples were almost destroyed. The bison that was integral to food and clothing became nearly extinct. The beaver population dwindled. With the modernization of travel, steamboats replaced paddles and livelihoods were lost. Less money being earned meant poverty increased. Eventually, treaties were signed but often under duress. Many promises made were never kept. Most Indigenous people were forced to move from territories their ancestors had thrived in for millennia, to smaller tracts of land. In cases of noncompliance, the government withheld resources many had become dependent on: starved people into compliance. More injustices followed and with repercussions that carried through to the very day the trapper and his boy were having pemmican for lunch on lands that were part of that history. The acre the trapper owned was not separate from a complicated past and he sometimes thought about that. Right now he was looking over the vista of a beautiful lake and pretty trees, wondered if the very land he and his boy walked on could speak, if every other step it would cry.

That early Scot at the outset of his employment was forbidden by the company to marry or have sexual relations with Indigenous women. That early Scot married and had a family with an Indigenous woman. She was Cree. They never owned land but when the legislation for homesteading arrived, a grandson did. He bought one hundred and sixty acres for the going rate of ten dollars. The acquired land remained in the family, until it didn't. Some traditions from a combined culture trickled down. Pemmican, bannock, preserving hides, certain plant-based medicines, a reverence for the wilderness around them, a rich variety of Lowland Scottish cuss words. Subsequent generations further broadened out into the growing communities of immigrants, most living in town, a few in the woods. With the trapper's late wife being ancestrally English-Irish, all that made the blood of the boy sitting beside the trapper on this little vista a mixed liquid from a melting pot land.

The boy had eaten some of his pemmican then put the rest away in his pack and was holding a carrot they'd earlier pulled from the garden. His dad pinched a small hemlock branch overhead then pulled his fingers along a stem to shear off a little bouquet of needles that he then minced on a log with his pocketknife he kept clipped inside his pant pocket. Unscrewed the cap of the thermos they shared between them and it steamed its contents into the cool midday air. He lifted the wire-mesh bulb hanging inside it and filled it with the needles then screwed the cap back on to steep for hemlock tea. The cap was also a cup and inside that cup was a smaller cup, like a Russian toy egg. After a few minutes he placed the small one on the ground at the boy's feet. The boy held it secure between his boots while his dad poured him his tea, then his own.

They held the smoking cups warm in their hands.

"That was a pretty doe yesterday," he said to the boy.

The kid was swinging around the orange nub from its stalk. "Why didn't that one have a buck?" he asked.

"She will when she's ready. It's still pretty early. Still a few more weeks until the peak of the rut."

"Oh. Did Granddad ever shoot a doe?"

"My granddad or your granddad?"

The kid blew into his cup. "Both."

He was looking at the boy holding his cup, saw his nails at the end of his fingers. Thought maybe he should trim them when they got home. Felt like he just did that. Saw that his hair was starting to get long again too and it being the same dark blonde of his mom's, if it grew much longer it'd have her same length. Him thinking that about the boy while his own hair was nearly down to his shoulders.

"I hadn't heard that they did. Never saw it either. But they would have if they had to. If they got hungry enough." He drank from his tea, its wafting steam lightened by the sun. "Just never had to.

"How's your shoulder?" he asked the boy.

The boy was rubbing his shoulder. Yesterday afternoon when they'd returned from their hunt the first thing he did was go and shoot his daily arrows behind the shed.

"It's a little sore."

"How many arrows did you shoot yesterday?"

"You know how many."

He smiled. "That's how many I had to shoot too when I was learning at your age."

"I know. You tell me that every day."

"We'll go grouse hunting tomorrow. You outshoot me I'll wash the dishes."

"If I outshoot you can we skip school?"

"This is school."

"The other kind."

"You know the answer to that. You ask that every day."

The kid started talking about grouse 'cause he liked to hunt them a lot and he said he'd heard grouse can go four days without eating any worms and on the fifth day they might just eat gravel. And that was just fine by them, the boy said.

The kid had talked to maybe half a dozen people in his whole life, a third of them being him and the kid's mom, a few others on trips to town and not for long at that. The trapper seriously doubted those conversations included grouse. This kid killed him sometimes. He said to him, "That's what you heard, hey?" Then raised one eyebrow up at him. And the boy in trying to mimic that gesture just contorted his face all up and that now confused-looking face befit his suspect bird knowledge. The man said he'd heard that too.

There was no legal requirement to register the boy with the nearest school or contact any governing body of education. No permission had to be sought to raise and educate as the trapper saw fit his boy in those remote lands. But the legality of any practice does not necessarily make it an ethical one. Just because he himself had been raised there and loved the woods more than what he saw on trips to town, didn't mean that in this day and age it was best for his son to follow a similar path. *Raise that child in town.* Of course if opinions were sought, that would likely be the one of most. Bringing up a child in the woods far from a hospital, from socializing among other little boys and girls and isolating him from a rapidly changing culture might be seen by some people as selfish at best, or dangerous and cruel at worst. Valid concerns and they were not lost on him. More often than food or weather or the animals or his late wife or his own self he thought about the welfare of his son. Though the trapper didn't always keep regular hours for the boy's schooling and sometimes lessons were taught under trees on rests amid a hunt or before sunup leaving for one, he was diligent that the boy, in addition to what he was learning from the university of these wild woods, had completed with proficiency the official curriculum for his age. *Raise that child in town.*

Every year the trapper and his boy went to town. Usually just once, before the lakes melted in the spring. You don't trap during the summer or fall, only during the snow season as you want the animals wearing winter coats. His last stop for the past several years after trading furs and buying provisions was the school. A couple years ago they were walking down one of the town's few alleyways taking the most direct route from the pharmacy. Saw some kids ahead leave the alley. They weren't the boy's age but to the trapper they didn't look all that much older. Didn't see them shoot up and didn't see them drop the needle, but there was a syringe on the ground and a couple more cracked and dirty that looked a few days old. The boy said looking down at them, "What are those?" The trapper told him trouble. "Let's go," the trapper said. *Raise that child in town.* He'd heard of gangs that supplied those drugs. *Raise that child in town.* He'd seen the type of food in the vending machines at the school. Heard kids graduated not knowing how to plant a garden. Heard other things too.

If someone was to fault him for how he was raising his boy it might not be met with too much resistance. Some nights when the boy was asleep it was just him and his self-doubt for company. Sat there questioning everything. Everything. Other nights though, he might just tell those opinions to fuck right off. In the end, so far at least, he had weighed the pros and cons, considered the plausible outcomes as best he could, then pushed his chips in. At least the threats from the woods were ones he could recognize. The forest was home and the one his family long knew and for now at least that's where he'd raise his son. Those coming to rescue this poor child from this barbaric man would do better not telling the boy's father they're coming. Either way it's likely one more story afterwards told in town.

That first year they went to the school he tried to time the visit for the end of the day's classes. But that day there were still kids playing outside throwing a football in the trampled down snow. Just unorganized catch. He was holding the boy's hand as they walked to the school and the man had to stop or he'd be dragging him. The boy was just staring, his eyes wide. People his own size. Later the trapper wondered if he had let go of the boy's hand that day if he would have run to them. If he would have come back.

The small school had kindergarten to grade twelve all under one roof. Sometimes three grades combined in one class and still some classes with only single-digit attendance. The teacher who taught the boy's age group was a stout and modest-looking lady appearing to be about seventy and whose name was on the chalkboard in capital letters. Big ones. The trapper had explained who they were and what they'd come for. She said she'd heard of him. She said wait, then left for another room. Came back shortly with a cardboard box in a garbage bag. "Keep the moisture out." The trapper wasn't sure if she was extolling the virtues of the plastic bag or giving him instruction. "Textbooks and test material." He already liked the woman for her brevity. The trapper had put away enough money for the estimated sum and asked her how much.

"That's alright." She was looking at the boy and smiling.

"That's kind of you ma'am. But we'd prefer to pay, just the same." He took out his billfold and there wasn't much to it.

"You don't have to call me that."

He'd seen a slip of paper on her desk with a name that matched the blackboard's. "Thanks just the same, Nancy."

She said, "Don't you be calling me that."

The boy smiled then covered his mouth.

She turned and looked at the trapper who still had the measly billfold out, and the smile she'd had for the boy faded. She said, "Pride goeth before the fall." Then she just stared at him like he should know what to do with that. He didn't. She kept on looking at him through her thick glasses and he still hadn't returned the billfold to his pocket. She kinda pursed her lips then reached out and pushed the chair aside that was just partially separating them. Her forearms looked bigger than his own and one seemed to be tattooed or maybe just birthmarked in the shape of a longsword. He managed to notice from the corner of his own staring eyes that the boy's eyes were also locked on that ink-blot test on her arm. He nudged the kid to stop. She moved that chair and coulda been she was just tidying up at the end of the day, but he kinda got the impression she was straight up preparing to unlegend him right there in front of his boy. It was remarkable how much this lady was beginning to remind him of someone from his past. He narrowed his eyes just a fraction trying to see if that beloved old lady he'd lost long ago wasn't just behind those thick glasses somewhere.

She saw him narrow his eyes at her and figured he was sizing her up. She'd seen it before.

He was doing no such thing and in that short pause he took before he responded, which may have been the longest pause any one's ever taken to answer that brutish educator, he was simply wondering to himself if the farther north you went the harder women got. And if you went sufficiently far enough north you'd just straight up be birthed by a crack in the bedrock and one day wedded to a piece of granite. Because this lady here seemed a stone-cold replica of one of the few older ladies he'd had the pleasure of respecting in his life. And the back of his right hand gave one sharp throb like it formerly had a tendency to do when in the presence of

45

a certain older blood who had a tendency to smack it when he got smart. He almost smiled right then missing that former pang of the sweet lady who used to inflict it. This here is Gran incarnate, he thought. He covered his phantom panging hand with his left and now in the classroom with his hands clasped before this no-bullshit matriarch, he looked the picture of humility. Had he grinned at her maybe she woulda touched him up. And before things got strange he mumbled out in words about as articulate as his oldest known ancestor had once tried to pronounce the Anishinaabe word for pounded meat—ironically in both cases that seemed to be on the menu—he quickly stammered out the name on the blackboard. "Thank you Mrs. Babich." Next year he didn't take so long using it. He put away his billfold. His boy beside him looked about to burst.

To what looked like a forty-year-old man in front of her, she said still unsmiling while pushing up her thick glasses, "Good boy." She moved the chair back. To the boy beside the man, she smiled and said, "You too." That child there was laughing.

As they walked out she said, "I'll have the package ready for you next year. You make sure to come back and get it." They both said, thank you Mrs. Babich. "Or I'll dog sled on up there."

In that jurisdiction the government did not provide funding for homeschooling which therefore meant that teacher giving them the books and course work was breaking the law. Or could be she was paying the minor cost herself. He wasn't sure. Didn't feel like asking her. Either way every year the box was ready and there were crayons and colouring books and extra pencils he'd never asked for. Every year a used book of classic literature she'd put in for the trapper himself. He started bringing her prime cuts of venison backstrap.

***

They had finished their lunch on their little vista and watched an eagle wheeling high above as it slowly circled on a rising column of air. The puddle lake's surface mirrored its surroundings: the bordering trees and the blue sky and somewhere in there the eagle itself.

"How are your feet?"

"They're fine. They were sorer when we started but they're okay now," said the boy.

"More sore."

"Than what?"

"No. It's not sorer. More sore." The man's knowledge of grammar about approximated the boy's knowledge of grouse.

"Oh. They were more sore this morning."

"Well let's not go any further today. Start our circle back here. Give us time to check the snares before dark. And we might see a buck yet. It doesn't have to be peak rut for them to start wandering the day more often. Each day from now on it gets more likely you'll see one during the daytime. They're mostly moving between doe bedding areas, trying to find one coming into estrus. Then after that peaks in a few weeks it'll taper off again and they'll quiet back down and they'll be mostly nocturnal again." He finished the last of his tea. "It's good for us to make this month count and put meat away."

The boy was only half listening. He looked up at him. "Can I swim after lunch?"

"That frigid-looking pond is calling your name or what? It's almost zero."

"I still want to."

"You'll be so cold coming out. Might be warmer tomorrow. The winds are starting to back southerly. Why don't you wait a day?"

"More warm," the boy corrected him.

He looked at this kid. He reached to the boy and poked a finger to the chest of his plaid jacket and said look, and the boy did not look down because you only fall for that once and so the man gave it up and just pulled the kid's toque down over his eyes. "Next week it's back to verbs, wildman," he said to the blinded kid. "Let's sit for a minute, I want to try something. Then you can swim."

"Alright."

"Just relax. Take a breath."

The boy breathed.

"Now close your eyes. Tell me when they're closed 'cause mine are closed too."

"Okay they're closed," he said.

The man opened one eye to see if he was telling the truth. The kid had his eyes closed very hard.

"But relax your eyes."

He softened them.

He closed the one eye he had watching him, said, "Okay. I want you to go one minute just sitting, just keeping your eyes closed and relax and just watch your own mind."

"Watch it?" asked the boy.

"Yeah watch it. Just notice what's going on there."

"Okay."

"And I want you to try and go a minute without having a thought. I'll keep track of time."

"Don't think?" the boy said.

"Right. Don't think. But tell me if you have one."

"Okay."

"Okay go."

"Wait," the boy said. "I wasn't ready."

"Alright. Tell me when you're ready."

The boy kinda wiggled settling down into his seat, folded his hands in his lap. "Okay," he said. "Ready."

The man opened his eyes and just watched the boy. "Alright, starting now."

In a short time the boy said, "Um." And his closed eyes crinkled and his face looked confused. "I think I had one," he said. "How long was that?" His eyes still closed.

"About four seconds."

"Do pictures count?"

"Yeah they count as thoughts."

"Oh. Yeah then I had one."

"Okay. Let's do it one more time. Keep your eyes closed."

About the same amount of time passed and the boy said, "There. A thought. I think. Yeah there, I had one for sure. I saw a squirrel. How long was that this time?"

"About four and a half seconds."

The boy paused. "So what does that mean?" he asked. "That I tried not to think but had a thought anyways?"

"I'm not sure exactly. But that's about as long as I go too."

The boy opened his eyes. Looked around squinting like it'd gotten brighter. Between his crossed legs was a clump of wet mud clinging to the heel of his boot. He poked it. Looked at his muddied finger. Pressed that finger to the back of the trapper's hand beside him. It left a fingerprint mud mark. He looked up and said to his dad, "I think you might be crazy."

"Takes one to know one. Go swim quick."

The kid scrambled up and unbuttoned his jacket then shimmied out of it and flung it down then the toque and his sweater and shirt and kicked off his boots wildly and one hit the arrow lying on the moss and sent it rattling into the hunting bow. It came to rest with the sharp broadhead atop the string. A string that even while undrawn was under high tension from the bent limbs of the bow. He froze. Shirtless, bootless. Stared at the bowstring to see if it would snap. Then he stared at his father.

Their lineage had some hot blood in it. Not just the men either, the elder ladies too, whom you simply respected and there was no doubt in you doing your chores and timely at that and of the language you spoke to them it was ma'am if it wasn't mother. When the trapper was growing up his bare ass was no stranger to a spanking, as well the kitchen spoon a time or two, and he'd never wanted to find out if the rolling pin was an empty threat or otherwise. Some bluffs are not worth calling. As for the men they were brought up well and to be kind and respectful, and though some-times tempers did get raised their hands rarely did and not once to the ladies. Most altercations were seasonal. Sometimes on a trip into town to sell furs a few drinks might be drunk and a game of cards played and a little steam was liable to get let off. But that trait was more one of his dad's than his granddad's. And the trapper himself just came directly home when he sold furs and bought provisions. He knew from a young age the severity of his own temper and was also told it 'cause they'd seen signs that it was likely as wild as any family members' that came before him—likely wilder, they said. Could be because both sides mother and father had some rage in them and therefore it doubled down on him. He avoided certain scenarios: he didn't drink and he didn't overnight in town.

The boy stared at his father who hadn't taken his eyes off the broadhead lying on the bowstring. Things were quiet, things almost hummed. The eagle was gone.

The boy's mouth had hung open and he now silently mouthed the words: "I'm sorry."

The man moved a hand to the arrow. He held his breath and fingers above it before he finally pinched the flat of the upright blade like he was clipping uncertain wires of a ticking bomb. Had he not that task to channel his temper he might have raised a hand to the boy. It would have been the first time he'd done so. He lifted from off that string two edges he'd stropped to razorblades on buckskin leather. Slid the arrow the boy had carried back into its quiver and snapped it secure. He didn't look at him, he just said sit down.

The boy sat.

"Listen," he said speaking slowly. "Some mistakes we can't make out here. Not everything has to be

serious and not all the time but some things are serious.
Weapons are a serious thing. For food. For protection.
Do you understand?"

The boy nodded very gravely as boys who have
their father in their life are capable of nodding.

The trapper was going to ask him to tell him why
it matters but he knew the tears that were welling in
the kid's eyes would have flooded out if he made him
speak. And more importantly than that he knew the
kid understood—the point had been conveyed, no
need to belabour or patronize it. He now looked at the
boy. The boy nodded again more quickly.

"Okay. Okay," the trapper said. "Go swim."

Now very slowly, the boy finished undressing, then
turned for the lake. And once facing away he said, "I'm
sorry." Walked for the lake naked and stooped and
with a raised hand to his face turned away. It wasn't the
admonishment, it was having disappointed his father,
the team, upsetting the flow of the good day.

He watched the kid now a ways off crouch down
to the water's edge. The afternoon sky was still. Then
somewhere out there a loon called. Its song almost
irreverent in the solemn tenor of that moment. Like
wayward beauty, or beauty misplaced. To scold the
boy was to punish his own self and he sat there and
begrudged his sternness. Resented that which he knew
he had to do to make a strong thing. A thing to survive
his absence in harsh lands with pitiless winters. He
didn't like bringing the boy to tears and the dozens of
times he'd done it in the past never made it easier and
he didn't expect the ones coming to be any different.
So be it. He'd do it again and again if he had to if that's

what it took to harden steel that could cut stone when he was gone, if it had to. His eyes looked above the small lake that like a painting held the trees and the sky and the painted boy within it. To the sky he asked if he was too harsh and she said nothing back and he said out loud I don't know.

He unsat his pack and loosened the top drawcord and without looking in the bag reached to the left-side internal pocket and pulled out a small canvas roll tied with a backup bootstring. He laid it on the bedrock. He untied the bootstring and unrolled the small rectangular canvas revealing a coil of monofilament line and three polished fishing spoons: one copper, one silver, one painted a red-and-white devil, all reflecting enough sun they looked to be generating it. He picked the painted one. Tied it to the roll of line he pulled tight with his teeth while wetting the knot then walked to the lakeshore. Made sweeping hand-casts into the calm water. Swept out a cast and then another while walking the lake edge, pausing the pace of his hand-over-hand retrieval, twitching the lure in little jerks, sinking it, climbing it, his hands toward the water to leave room for a hookset. Then cast again.

Crouched drying on the bank blue-lipped and white-fingered under a warming maternal sun sat the boy. And the boy watched all, missed nothing. Like an owl.

7

The boy was still asleep in the loft above. With the iron poker in one hand the trapper eased open the stove door then pushed the glowing log-ends and quaking coals into a little smoldering mound, layered quartered pine logs overtop then blew it gently to flames.

In the morning every morning he brewed coffee with a stovetop percolator and the rich aroma would fill the cabin—almost colour it—and somehow it was a thing that never got old. A simple pleasure that he always looked forward to. He'd sit by the stove in the morning as the fire warmed the cabin and drink it slow and hot and black. Sometimes he'd creep up to the loft and sit beside the boy awhile as he slept. Sit there watching his breaths raise and lower the blankets in the semidarkness. Then come back down quietly before he woke without him even knowing it.

This morning he was looking out the window watching for daybreak, waiting for a world to be coloured out of the dark. Smelling the same aromas of camp-coffee out in the woods on cold mornings of boyhood fall hunts with Granddad. A smell that carried sweetness from the past like those memories themselves were distilled within it.

When Gran and Granddad took over his upbringing after his parents had passed, they had said between them that for a boy who wasn't afraid to show his anger he was remarkably quiet that day. The days following too. It did concern them. Like he hadn't processed it fully or he'd packed it away somewhere. Maybe time would dissolve it. Could be some of those things never dissolve they just calcify and so you carry them all hardened up as some lump within you. Gran continued teaching him what his mom had started, gardening and baking and cooking, schooling and how to read and what's more, to love to read. She said if you can lift the world with a long enough lever, with the right teachers and time you can better understand it. The winters were long and dark early and anyone can be taught anything and get better at anything with enough time and a good teacher. She was a prize, Gran. It was she who saw he gave as much effort to his education as he did his hunting, would simply whoop ass if he didn't. The hunters he would guide in later years were always caught off guard by that—you'd expect him to be a straight killer in the woods given he was raised there and with his heritage. But you wouldn't exactly have expected him to be educated, to have been raised a thinker.

The trapper had loved Gran and still thought about her often. But he loved that old man something special and his time with him was some of his favourite he'd ever lived. Hunting for moose, for deer, even for small game, birds and rabbit, it didn't matter. Showed him how to track. How to move in the forest. How to always be hunting even when you're not 'cause a predator never stops, doesn't punch a clock, his words. Basically taught him how to think out there. In an afternoon of one of their hunts a wolf howled. A sound to make weaker forms of life stop mid-step. The rest of that day and for two days next they tracked her pack through the forest. Granddad pointed out to him over a stretch of sunbaked soil, swept markings across her dusted prints, said her belly dragged low with pups. They continued to track her even over outcroppings of bedrock, she'd mostly lead her kind on a straight line over exposed ground, he said. Later in the evening under the canopy of a red pine Granddad pointed and whispered look and they watched some few blades of matted grass just ever so slightly unbending themselves. Then far off and through the trees they could see her leading her pack of white and grey and black wolves, some mottled and some pure. And those animals did not look back once at them. That was Granddad. He'd never be Granddad.

As a boy the trapper would come down in the morning and see Granddad by the fire with his coffee early, and of course he knew he slept he just hadn't ever seen him do it. The man was a thinker in his own right too. He never wrote anything down and that's a shame. But the trapper carried some of the old man's words with him, some of the old man, too.

Those days were like dreamed things to him now. As if you'd almost need someone you could call on to stand witness and verify that they had in fact actually happened 'cause now they just about felt like they were someone else's story. In fact there was no one he could call on. Growing from a child to an adult, the body is so altered and outlooks change and so does personality along with tastes and pleasures and you're just about rebuilt from the ground up and maybe he couldn't even call on his own self to testify, and perhaps it did in fact make more sense to look fondly on the past as if it belonged to someone else.

But coffee did bring things back, or brought them a little closer, anyways. Maybe itself being immune to the effects of time gave events and memories some point of reference to orient and attach themselves. Those days there wasn't anything more that he wanted than to just come along. Can I go too? Ask and hear no and ask again anyways not expecting any different. And one day a yes you can. Yes you can. Really? Yes. Get your things ready. Oh man. Like dreamed things. And now it was him and the kid. And that's alright too. More than alright.

His granddad had started a hunting outfit and at first it was just two cabins. Over the years a few more and the trapper had helped build a couple. Finally a larger cabin they called the lodge. When Granddad no longer wanted to manage the operation he had passed the title to his son who ran it for the fall months then trapped fur the winter. In late winter his father would make the long trip to town with a sled full of pelts, mink, marten, fox, beaver, pulled by two husky-wolf crosses for supplies and gear. For cooking essentials like grains, oil, sugar, salt. For clothes and hunting supplies. Books and newspapers. A few times his dad took his time coming back. A couple extra days he'd said to get a good price on the furs. One time it was almost a week. It was after that longer trip that he came back and said he had sold the lodge and a parcel of the land and had little to show for it besides what the furs brought in. They could keep their cabin. But their legal plot was now sized like a postage stamp when they once owned the whole letter. When his dad told that to the family he looked at his son, the trapper, and that boy saw something he hadn't before.

His dad had some talent in cards and in fact he was very good, but everyone gets felted now and again and talent runs on short time when that talent's had enough to drink. He was not a bad man, in fact those who knew him would say he was a pretty good one. But he had his vices as most would say most do.

When his father was in town he and Granddad would fish for perch, pike, walleye or trout through a hole chopped in the ice, or walk the trapline to club the animals caught in leg traps, lift the others with bodies stiff and cold, free of the steel-jawed conibear traps that ended them painless and quick as it crushed their skulls in an instant. Things you get used to when you're raised up there doing them from an early age and you don't see them as cruel nor the language of it, just factual. And not so cruel if it feeds you and buys you clothes and is passed down from family and the animals are taken from a forest in an isolated area that can sustain that limited hunting pressure. If it was cruel, as the trapper did start to wonder in later years, it was hard for one raised doing it to recognize it as such. They'd reset all the traps. Some buried just under the snow they brushed smooth with a dragged pine branch to hide the tracks, help mask the scent. Some set in wooden marten-boxes nailed to a tree. Laid a fish head on the trigger pan of another. Granddad showed him how to cut small tree limbs and stand them in the snow to make a little barrier that'd serve to funnel the scattered cottontail tracks that printed the snow. Then hang the rabbit snare's brass wire loop down from a low and angled limb. They'd come home by dark and he'd be dog tired but still excited and Mom would listen to it all where she had dinner waiting, and if she could keep him awake they'd read together.

In poker you only make so many premium hands in your life and when you're holding one you get your money in and if you're beat you're beat and it was still the right move. For some things it's correct to evaluate the process not the outcome, only scrutinize whether your decision-making was good up until the point where you had to put it to chance. And nobody should fault you if your reasoning was valid. Some hands are so rare they're worth going bust over and it's not a mistake. But you put your money in, not your house, not your livelihood. And so three-quarters drunk with a four of a kind, the trapper's father lost their land. A wife and husband couple bought the lodge from the man who had won it that night in town when the river card came a spade and made his straight flush. Nobody sitting at the table that night who saw that fateful river card get turned could believe it, the trapper's father least of all. He was the last one to get up and leave that table. Someone brought him a drink as he sat there. People watched him, talked. The lodge and the one hundred and sixty acres of land it stood on that their family owned since it was first acquired through the homestead legislation of the 1800s enacted to help settle these lands while also taking it from those who had lived there for millennia, never got passed down to the trapper.

When the trapper was a young man he worked for the new owners as a hunting guide. He'd take the hunters who had arrived by floatplane for week-long trips to hunt the unspoiled forests he'd been raised in. Western moose, black bear, white-tailed deer. His style of hunting was immersive: hunt like your life depends on it, as for him during part of the year at least, it did. The most consistent and successful hunters simply hunt a lot and do it thoughtfully and with patience. They're out there before the season starts, or there simply is no offseason for them, not hunting but putting time in the woods understanding the animals and their habits after the rifle or bow had been put away. There's the wind to consider and the moon and the temperature and the coming cold or warm fronts and the precipitation and the stage of the rut and what food was in season and when it last frosted and the other animal signs of prey and predator they'd seen on previous days and prior years. He studied it. It showed in the success of their hunts. Sometimes they spoke his name at the tables back at the lodge when sitting for dinner, sometimes wrote it in office emails down south where the trips were first planned.

The trapper got up from the chair and walked to the stove and poured a second cup of coffee from the metal urn. Sat back down by the grey window.

It was his fourth season guiding at the lodge when at the start of summer a floatplane landed, like they did every other day, and so that alone was not so special. But unbeknownst to him this one carried inside of it a new world. Carried inside of it secrets and proposals and plans and teamwork and laughter and inside jokes

61

and love and love-making and so many types of love. The owners' daughter who had come to clean cabins and serve dinners to the clients for the season stepped down from the plane's cabin and onto the pontoon then the dock and her hair swept by the wind blew dark-gold strands across her smiling lips.

But he didn't see that as he was out guiding.

In the evening of that same day when he was sitting down for dinner with the rest of the small crew, plates were being brought out to the tables. She placed his down in front of him and the first thing he ever saw of her was her wrist. Slender wrist pale with a freckle. He stared at it for a very, very long time, which of course it couldn't have been. His brows bent in slightly. He had raised his water glass to drink but didn't drink from it, just held it there in the air stupidly. Looked at this misplaced thing—a young man seeing that which he was built to want but had never yet known. Slender wrist, pale, with a freckle. As if some platonic form had slipped out of the mind of a dreaming philosopher, some lost ideal, and even if it wasn't real and his mind had somehow just conjured it up like a dream thing, at least he got to see it, even if only for a long second in his mind's eye, 'cause having done so let him know such things could possibly exist at least somewhere in the world if not here, and now knowing what to look for maybe he could track it down. He was good at that. But it wasn't misplaced nor lost nor conjured up at all, rather only his conception of what things ought to be where was ill-conceived due to his young mind whose vision of the world, though oftentimes cocksure of itself, was a narrow one yet. You start as a boy knowing nothing, you get a bit older and think you know most things, then more years pass away and you realize you know much less than you once thought and you're nearly back to where you started, as a boy. Upwards to the inside bend of an elbow. Shoulder covered in a simple red dress. Farther up, that pale skin returned showing her neck with its own freckle, him travelling those curves shaped in the clay for certain.

And when his eyes arrived to her lips he saw she was smiling soft enough to crack stone. And right then she split his heart in two and he felt inside his chest thin bursts of light as apparently he carried within him a pocket of the glowing universe, and as quick as she had severed it, her batting eyes above stitched it back up a size larger. He saw those eyes were smiling back and that was hardly fair. Saw in those dark eyes a new world complete. And then his hand let slip his glass of water that banged and emptied its full contents onto the table and those around him laughed at him and she did too. And he wasn't laughing at all. Not at all.

"Hello," she laughed.

"Hi."

He knew right then like it had all been told to him by some authority on the topic. Just felt gut-level truth. They were even the same age.

She'd return next summer and the one after that but not the one after that because an economic hardship that didn't distinguish between states and provinces, between countries even continents forced the sale and that outfit changed hands again then lay dormant for a time with no hunters. Someone kicked over the first domino of a globally connected and highly leveraged banking world. Luxury trips got cut. Vacation destinations suffered. Mortgages were defaulted. The first businesses to start flooding the market were those that were least profitable to begin with. Operating costs for remote hunting outfits are high and profit margins can be thin and even in good economic times there aren't many buyers. A year after her parents sold the lodge a fire burned up nearly half that hunting land. The cabins were fine. That hunting outfit would lie vacant for a time. So she didn't come up that year—but it did not matter for when he asked her to come live with him in his cabin, she did. It was that year they started their life in a little cabin in the woods together where she would one day carry their child.

When her parents sold the lodge they didn't consult him about it. Not that they had to. And he understood they couldn't just give it to him as they'd paid over a half a million dollars for it and it wasn't like they even wanted to sell it in the first place. They had debt and bills to pay. He just would have preferred some type of consult given his family's long history with it. That would have been respectful. At least entertain the idea of somehow working something out. When their son was born she said she wanted the boy in coming years to spend some time with her parents at their home in the city. "The boy should know his grandparents," she said. The trapper tried not to hold a grudge and didn't like that he always did. Could be there were other things at play as well. Could be a part of him saw the grandparents as a connection to a world that might one day lure the boy from them. If that was the case, something was still working against that relationship at a deeper level. He could even ask himself if that's what was going on and still not get an honest answer because the workings of some biases aren't privy to the biased. After she'd passed, him alone in a dark time in a dark night, he'd said to himself maybe you're just a trapper of the boy. A trapper of the past.

There were four buildings on their plot, five if you count the outhouse. There was the cabin, shed, cellar and sauna all spread over the one acre that was never handed over a poker table where lay a bad beat four of a kind. Three sides of their land were bordered by Crown forest, the other belonging to the current lodge owners.

In time he came to know her eyes said things her voice didn't need to. He saw in them things beyond doubt. They looked at one another and there were basic truths in those eyes like simple sums that were obvious and foundational in the same way whole belief structures and systems of math and geometry are built from the base characteristics of parallel lines and properties of triangles and other such axioms. His boy too in later years would become that type of rock thing.

By the time she came to live with him his family had all passed on, some old and some young. Gran had died first and Granddad took that as his cue and followed shortly. Her parents after selling the lodge stayed mostly to their city. So with nobody around, the forest was their witness. That night they married in the woods wasn't secret, just private. She wore a white dress he hadn't seen before and they only had the one small set of shelves and hangers and he always wondered where she'd hidden it away. He'd slicked back his hair. The sky was clear and black and moonless and there

65

were stars. They both came by candlelight from their own path to the clearing and placed the candles down on a log stump, then held their hands between them, hers in his. She said keep her safe he said he would. She said she'll care for him and work for their family and do what things needed to be done but that she needs to be her own person too and he needs to respect her and always be kind to her and to let her be a woman even out here in the middle of the forest and he said he would. She said she might test his limits but wants his strength and she'll support him if he'll support her and they'll be more than two separate things added up together if he'll always be there and he said I will. She asked do you want me and no others. He said I do. And so did she. And old rings were slid on new fingers in a glade in the woods under the stars where the fireflies glowed and the foxfire glimmered, where maybe all forest light that night got lit from their union.

In the night they'd lie together, her spooned and tucked and pulled into him. Some nights he could barely believe it. Barely seemed real. Somehow she was his. Right there curled up in the middle of the woods. Somehow. He'd whisper to her while she slept. Things loving and also things that to other ears would be indecent but which to her ears were also loving. And she'd hear some in her dreaming mind and sometimes she'd wake up just enough to smile, once she even laughed, and then drift back to a sleep she hadn't entirely drifted out of, and his arm across one of her breasts and her other held in his hand while she slept and he sometimes did too. Then he'd wake and whisper to her again.

She was very smart and he'd say she was smarter than him. He had at times wondered if it kept their bond from being total. No bond is total. People are unique. Sometimes he held her tight trying to narrow a gap he felt he could never quite close. Like part of her could still be sitting on the other side of the room. He learned more from her than the other way around and it was mostly because of her that his ideas of the world filled out. If Gran and Mom had planted the seed then she kept up the watering. She wasn't slinging a rifle or checking the trapline but could have and would have had he asked her to. And she had dirt under her nails just the same and was more than capable of whatever tasks were at hand. Had he brought her a snowshoe hare at noon there'd be a wilderness gourmet that evening complete with wild herbs and what the season allowed from the cabin-side garden.

They buried fish and game carcasses deep enough in the soil that the scavengers couldn't pick up the scent but the soil was black-rich from it. They collected algae from the lakes and laid it down before the snow fell then dug more into the soil when the snow melted in the spring. Over-wintered crops of spinach, kale and garlic. That garden was something to see and its plot was the tilled land long-felled of trees from which their cabin had been built. An old family cabin with saddle-notched logs, chinked and daubed airtight walls. Even a low northern sun soaked the garden all summer, and it was elongated east to west to allow for as much sun travel as possible.

Buried deeper than frost-reach in that garden lay two generations of his blood, four adults: bones, clothes, and all. And maybe some would think that's not right but it's what they wanted. Maybe returning to the earth that way helped raise up what grew out of it. And having them lie close brought reverence for tradition and respect for their ways and an effort to honor it and so they're buried there right beside the cabin 'cause they'd asked to be.

When she wasn't seeing to the chores of cooking and cleaning and preserving food and gardening, chores that they both shared, or in later years caring for the boy, she'd often be reading. In prior winters after the hunting season at her parents' lodge and before coming to live in the cabin she had graduated with a teaching degree. She would never formally get to use it. When she first came to live at the cabin she brought a few books and then every year when they made the long trips into town, a few more. Mostly in the winter, snowshoeing over iced lakes with him pulling the sled of furs as there'd been no dogs for years. He told her that lining a log cabin with paperbacks is asking for trouble, and she smiled at him and said, "Babe, the fire's inside the pages." She'd say a thing like that and he knew he was beat like someone shot before he'd even had a chance to draw, like he was reaching for his then saw hers already smoking and back in her belt. The books stayed. And of those books it was science and philosophy as much as it was fiction, all having different and useful truths, she said. In the years since her death, years of long nights, summer nights and winter ones where he put the boy to bed early while he stayed up some, he didn't have those various books memorized, just almost.

They would put the boy to sleep in the evenings with the cabin warm and clean and even though they had a creek-side small turbine generator, they'd switch off the bulb and sit by the stove with candlelight and drink tea together. Most nights. No, every night. Just talking. Just simple things. On one occasion she stopped him and corrected his grammar and that cut the flow of his story in half. He said just never mind then, like a child. That was one of those little things he wanted back. That one didn't bother him as much as some others did. Mostly he tried not to recall those. And maybe she just wasn't as enthused about the specific behavioural tendencies of mature bucks in November. That almost made him laugh now. It wasn't all perfect but they made each other laugh and they cared. For something that was so good, it was that simple.

If it was the winter they talked of what they'd try to do differently in the summer, and if the summer they'd talk of things to make the next cold season a bit easier on them. She'd sometimes knit, he might touch up a blade, work on a hide. They'd plans to get a freezer to use for the summer months and shoulder seasons, and the generator could power it, but he didn't like asking her family for money and the boy needed some things. He hadn't guided in years. He said let's just see how the coming trapping season goes.

They'd read then talk about what they'd read. Talk about the garden and cooking, philosophy and litera-ture, biology, history, religion, family. Sometimes he'd challenge her opinions as they sat there by the fire, not so much that he disagreed, he just wanted to watch her mind at work, hear her defend an idea or flesh one out.

That tendency became a habit of mind hard to break as even after she left he'd sometimes debate opinions she hadn't given in years and converse with her in his own mind. She just seemed to have inscribed herself there. A couple times the kid heard him talking out loud to her. He said, "Who you talking to?" So the man tried not to do that.

The sun had crested and spilled a little colour outside the window and he heard the boy move upstairs. But he must have only been turning in his sleep as he did not make his way down.

She was raised Christian and her parents took her to church most Sundays when she was growing up, outside of seasons at the lodge. But from the ideas she'd read over the years and in observing how easily life can be taken and the scale at which the innocent suffered by acts outside of human control, her faith turned into short-lived agnosticism before settling into resolute disbelief. One night she said the world seemed to be generally indifferent to the well-being of the life within it. How can you account for all the suffering? She asked that and looked at him like she was waiting for an answer. She said a god could stand outside of the hard laws of logic and make impossible things possible. A god should be able to square circles or what's the point. Kindness for its own sake, she said. Love because it's love. That made more sense to her. To him too, he said.

He watched her as she changed from holding a strong belief in the afterlife, to losing that faith. That loss brought with it a kind of resentment to the teachings of her upbringing. It came with a cost. But it was a resentment without blame. She loved her parents. If anything she seemed more present, more committed knowing that it was all up to her, to them. When he watched her holding their boy it was like a fruit pit fitting to the hollow core, just two shapes made for each other. Once with the sleeping boy in her arms she looked up and said smiling warmly that she felt filled with gratitude to have life—just life, *just this*, knowing how quickly it can get taken away or made hard. Looking back that seemed sick prophesy or a bad joke by a cruel teller.

More than anything else that they talked of by the fire it was the boy. The months before his birth, the days leading up to it and every day after. How to raise him. Make him strong where he needed to be but still gentle in others. Don't make him false promises but show him you can live without certainty. Raise him honest. Show him beauty. "We can do it our way," she said. "We will," she promised. She had promised him that.

The sun now lifted free of its horizon and his mug empty.

She was perfect. She was perfect in his idealized image of her within the lush skin of cherrypicked memories. He was capable of memories that hurt, he just tried not to willfully recall them. Who would blame him? But by not often recalling them they contributed less to his image of the past. Every day their dead marriage becoming more faultless in his mind and she her own type of legend living within it. Sometimes in the night he did get a stab from out of the shadows. Like a painful memory he had tried to ignore somehow got dislodged after he'd bumped it in the night.

Mostly trivial things, stupid minor failings that must be common to every marriage. She asked for a shelf. *A shelf.* More than once. Wanted to put a pot of sprouts by the window. What made it even worse was that the favour wasn't even just for her own ends. He never got to it and was asked more than once. On another occasion, the fall before the winter she died, she had asked for help harvesting the garden. It was during a week of significant geese migration. Said he'd help her later but this matters more. Later he was tired. Later than that he forgot and she went from feeling ignored to feeling unimportant. Low on his priority list and told him so. *Geese.* It wasn't an isolated event. "For someone so in touch with the forest you could open your ears to me a little." She didn't say it trying to be unkind, just trying to speak in a language that might get through to him. It did sting.

She had heard they'd called him the trapper. Overheard it on a trip to town or someone mentioned it in a letter, or given that nickname had started earlier, could have been from when they worked at the lodge together. Either way she made a joke that she regretted for days and apologized several times. Sometimes words sound funny in your head and don't when they arrive to ears. He knew she didn't mean it and didn't hold it against her, but some nights he could still hear its old echo. And you might not think someone like him would be so sensitive. He gently put their baby down and quietly closed their cabin door. Didn't come back till morning. His own rage scared him sometimes so he took it outside.

Some nights memories reached out from the shadows and coiled around the handle and turned the blade. Memory itself like a sheriff travelling through time knocking on doors to imprison the accused for petty crimes of which a reasonable jury would absolve him for significant time past. Seems like one night while that sheriff slept someone heated a spoon hot then held him down and blinded out his eyes and now he's crawling around in the dark and if he finds a leg, any leg, he puts a shackle on it. Gets it wrong sometimes. But it was morning and the sunlight was pushing back the shadows and the trapper felt no pangs from those former bee stings. He was thinking of her breath in bed. Her holding the boy. Those were real things too and he just preferred to recall the sweet ones. So for one more minute before he woke the boy and they started their day he just sat there with his empty coffee drinking the snake oil of nostalgia and looking at the cartoon pictures in his mind with all their sharp edges buffed away and all that's left is just pretty lines and gentle curves. Sat with his faulty memory's glossed version of the past.

The dead lie perfectly still and they're so easy to love.

8

A coloured forest like quilt-work Gran used to stitch, reds yellows oranges vibrant nearly glowing from a fall sun that sets early in the North. The trapper and his son had hunted all day and it was another one deerless. They neared their cabin and the tired boy walked on ahead to check the snares they'd set earlier. The man watched him walk ahead like he was watching a memory. Every day with this boy was as if some tiny coppersmith, some artisan living inside his shriveled heart, was swinging a little hammer and tapping at those walls, slowly sizing them back out and ever larger. Tap tap tap. He could feel it.

Rabbit snares aren't sprung like leg or conibear or deadfall traps, nor do they lift off the ground what's been caught like in a movie. It's very simple. The rabbit hops through a loop big enough to allow its head but narrow enough to restrict its body. When the rabbit tries to run free the thin wire bends and gives no slack once taken. In the panic of it the rabbit struggles and from that it strangles. Like something fallen in quicksand sinks faster from the fight. It can be quick. The angled stick above which the brass wire is tied makes that more likely. When the rabbit moves under the higher end of the stick its forepaws may not touch the ground any longer. It's usually quick, occasionally not. Still, compare that to being eaten alive by a fox, or lifted away by talons piercing your gut and flown to a high nest to be picked and torn apart. Compare that to staring at the wall alone in an old-folks home where your family has kindly placed you. Occasionally and for whatever reason a rabbit caught in the snare doesn't run like this rabbit didn't run, and then it waits for what lurks the woods or for who hung the wire, when there is a difference.

In the day's fading light the young hunter approached the low pine branch. He crouched down with his red-mitted hands, ones Gran had knitted, on his knees and stared at it.

"Look. Dad. He's still alive."

He crouched down too behind the boy to see. Under the pine tree they watched the rabbit trembling, its wet nose flaring and shutting faster than its heart rate which beat like it would trying to lose a fox. It didn't run. Sometimes terror paralyzes.

The boy crouching there, his head tilted in observation, his mind having not yet travelled towards the inevitable. His dad kneeling behind him and before standing back up reached for a heavy rock.

He knew what the boy would ask before he asked it and he wondered what it would cost. What do you teach and at what expense? There is an expense. Maybe the boy does it one day when I'm no longer around and the winter storms come and the lake freezes too thick to chop and fish through, or he injures a leg with no food-stores or the deer come into a disease cycle and I taught him it's okay to let food go free in harsh woods. What's the price here for what the boy will ask? It's not nothing. Love the boy so do hard things for the boy. Teach him hard lessons at your expense if that's what it takes. Take that burden upon yourself. And if he doesn't speak to you for a while, take that upon yourself because you need to raise a thing harder than the hard lands that will try to grind him away when you're not here. And you will not be here.

The trapper held the heavy granite stone in his one hand while the boy watched the rabbit. Arrows can be reused but they sometimes snap or bend. That costs money and they had little and a rock is quicker anyways. He dropped the rock to the side of the boy, who felt it thump, who knew what it was, who did not look at it.

"Take the stone," he told him. The man took no pleasure in this lesson.

The boy looked at the rock. He did as he was told and slowly reached for it. Picked it up and held it in his two hands. It was heavy.

"This is food. You know that. There are lots of rabbits in the forest. We're lucky to have caught it."

Kneeling in the last rays at sunset a little boy watched a scared rabbit and said nothing back.

"What do we think of the animals?"

The boy hesitated, then said, "We respect them and love them."

"Who do we hunt like?"

Whispered the boy, "Like the owl."

"How does the owl hunt?"

Whispered the boy, "Swift and without remorse."

"How do we hunt?"

Whispered the boy, "Look, he's still alive."

Grey fur body strung from a brass wire loop shaking in terror spasms.

The man stood behind the boy behind the rabbit and the last evening light glittered up ice crystals so fine and light they hung shimmering where they studded the cold air, where it seemed the whole forest was watching this fabled scene. Even the trees towering above might've been leaning in right then. Two plumes of breath unstirred in the windless evening hung above the trapper and his boy like apparitions that might stir to life after these two walked away. Would it matter to those misted spirits if the words that birthed them were kind ones, were cruel ones?

The man watched the boy holding the heavy stone in his two hands and waited for it. It was coming.

Whispered the boy, "Dad?"

"Yes?"

Whispered the boy, "Can we let him go?"

Whispered the man: "Yes."

What did that cost?

9

It's been told before but that doesn't make it not worth telling now. Some things should be retold. She died and this is how.

He was allowed to stay with her by her bedside. He stayed. And when he was not allowed to stay, he stayed also. Tell him to leave, but then others might hear of that violence too. She wanted nothing more than to hold her boy. It likely would have done both of them good because good things happen when a mother holds her baby as their bodies are doing things not obvious like exchanging pheromones and biochemicals and warmth and love and that'd be a type of medicine for both of them. For all three of them in fact. But after the cold trip to the hospital the doctor said the child looked weak and they wanted to see that that weakness didn't worsen into pneumonia and he should be in his own bed and that's just across the hall and he'll be well cared for. After two days the child did stabilize. They brought him in and she held him. But by the evening they thought he should rest alone again and they might have got that wrong because it was pretty hard on both mother and son, on all three of them.

When she wasn't resting and had the energy they'd talk and when they weren't talking she'd write the boy. She had asked the trapper to get her some paper. From a clipboard by the door on which the first page had more question marks than you'd want to see in your loved one's diagnosis, the trapper tore off a sheet.

"More." He went and asked a nurse at the front desk and she handed him some paper from the printer. He returned and gave the paper to her saying just tell him those things yourself when we get home. She looked at him, then back down and kept writing. Sometimes she'd fall asleep pen in hand. At one point she had what looked like ten pages double-sided stacked up beside her, things crossed out and underlined, and he wasn't sure if she was trying to write out as much as she could for him or get just one thing said well. He hardly slept at her bedside but one time he did drift off and when he woke up he saw a big X drawn in shaky lines over the whole page. That front page and those behind it all a little crumpled. There on the nightstand he saw a single small piece of folded paper with the pen on top. It had a heart drawn on it. He didn't reach for that folded paper but he knew what it was. When she woke she pointed to it and said for him to give it to their boy later. He took it and would do so but didn't agree, because by agreeing he felt he'd be complicit in her giving up and he wouldn't do that. "Just say it to him yourself when we get back." He thought in some ways he knew her better than she knew herself, and as far as ignorances go that's one of the sweetest. He took it and kept it folded and though he never did read it, one day the boy would.

Disease tore through her body and the small hospital staff could hardly believe how quickly she deteriorated. Looking back, there had been signs of it at the cabin. Fatigue, stomach pains. Maybe they could have caught it earlier, but it happened so fast. After only a few days at the hospital she already had sunken eyes and a sallow face, limbs she could barely raise. He had to work to see what truths others kept telling him. Mostly he couldn't see it. He was more convinced by the light in her eyes than the waste of her body, and those eyes were slow to fade and so he the last to see it. To see it for what it was. He just thought her body would eventually stop fucking around. He said something like that to the doctor.

"You're fine. Come on, let's go home," he told her.

In days to come her eyes weakened too. In a scene that happens somewhere every day and is happening somewhere right now too, she told him to let her go, to let her pass. And like most men selfish or scared or lonely or disbelieving or delusional, he said no. *No.* Can't. Won't. Sorry, he said. "Come on, it's time to go home, little babe."

She looked at him and said in a strained voice she loved him. "I love you," those words the sweetest there are, "but I have to go now."

"No. Stop. Fight harder."

"He's got a good dad, raise him as you are. Talk to him about things that matter. Find someone to help raise him," she said. "Find someone for yourself too." She coughed.

He looked down and away from her eyes and said quietly that's okay I'd rather not. Said he didn't agree to that from the outset and had vowed sticking, never not sticking, and to not do so would be its own type of infidelity and he'd just hold her memory close if she didn't mind. He said he was sorry about it.

"He needs a mother. Don't raise him with a ghost," she said.

He shook his hanging head, not to say no, more like in communication with his own self, or a future one, maybe life in general. How could this happen? He wanted to smash the room apart, throw things and scream and he balled up one fist and looked for something to beat to death, but his other hand was holding her hand, so that bottled rage just boiled inside him.

She said that soon she wouldn't be able to ask him again. She could feel that. "I don't want to leave my boys but I am." Seeing him broken up made her suffer worse. His disbelief of the situation was as romantic as it was cruel and he was trying to be neither. Had he known he was contributing to her pain, who's to say if he'd have been strong enough to stone his face over with some kind of fortitude when she looked up from her bed. Every man has his limits, false legends and otherwise.

He knew in his heart she was strong enough to beat it and he held the veracity of that truth with the same conviction of what familiar colours looked like and how warm things feel. You could not convince him otherwise. They tried. Her existence was fundamental to him, like blue, like fire. "You'll beat it if you keep fighting. This life is for you." People hold beliefs like this. He did.

Things had been decided and as much as husband and wife felt they ought to be privy to the details the deal was closed and didn't require either of their consent. In the end, she had nothing left to give. One night late he was holding her limp hand like all the nights he held it and she faintly squeezed it. He raised his head and looked up at her and saw her mouth the word *please*. No sound, just, Please.

He whispered back as soundlessly, Alright. Then kissed her very gently and kept holding her hand.

She closed her eyes and her breathing relaxed. Over the course of that night, her breathing slowed. Then it stopped. Nobody else watching including the nurse behind the window would have seen it because the muscles she moved were too slight to register with common eyes, too faint except for the husband who'd first seen that smile on a young woman at the lodge and then got to see it every lucky day she was with him and also every day she was not, for he played that smile over in his mind's eye on repeat. He'd mapped that face countless hours and so when her life already beholden to death faintly pulsed and tingled up the contours of her angel's neck and came down from her closing eyelids to arrive together at her lips, she smiled just the slightest smile for him. And of course that shrivelled up his already tiny heart.

10

The trapper was a boy when he asked Gran what their homestead was called and she had said why name a wilderness that exists within us all. Occasionally it was hard to get a straight answer out of that coy lady. Gran who when he had taken his seat at the kitchen table on a summer midday and shown her his palms all blistered up from splitting logs at the woodshed all morning, had said if one day you find yourself suffering you got lucky because now you have a chance to bear it well. He said what and reached for the basket and she slapped his hand so he retracted that paw now sore on both sides and listened further.

"Now you have a chance to put it to use and transform it," she said. "Will you one day do what's hard? Will you hold onto your values with a bear hug? Because for certain a day will come when it will be asked of you."

He listened attentively, even though sometimes a boy just wants what's in the basket—bread not words— but she'd probably have something to say about that too.

"Could you forgive when nobody expects it, or offer up your last piece of bread?"

He said in all seriousness looking at her, "Well. I'd try."

She had smiled at that then unfolded the kitchen towel covering the wicker basket and passed him a steaming bun.

In the shed he pulled the cord-switch to the hanging bulb powered by a battery that trickle-charged from the creek generator not far away. When the wind blew from the east he and the boy fell asleep listening to the creek murmur. The shed had dozens of shelves and hundreds of wall hooks, many of them just nails, with gear hanging on most of them and more from the rafters, some equipment spanning across them. There wasn't a lot of empty space but it was organized and clean. Many common tools for general repairs and carpentry, and then more specific tools for archery and gunsmithing, hide tanning, gardening, food preservation. Built into one wall a long workbench that oddly enough someone had painted blue a long time ago and you could still see the colour where it wasn't hidden from grease stains or worn away from work. It was for general tinkering and repairs and had assorted metal parts and straps and coils at its edges. There were drawers to it with odds and ends and sometimes the boy would look through them. In one corner stood a small table specifically for reloading ammunition and had a press and various brass casings of different calibers. Half of one wall was entirely dedicated to archery with both old and new strings, replacement parts like cams and rests, arrowshafts and tools for measuring and cutting. There was a homemade bow press. Empty mason jars with a small box of lids for water-bath canning and stovetop pressure canning. Vinegar for pickling. Fishing gear. Some old clothing, heavier coats and one all white and that was Granddad's that didn't get used much. The boy once asked if he could try it on and was told a hard no. One wall hung dozens of steel traps boiled clean then wiped and polished in a lightweight oil, decades-old steel put to work over long winters. They had no rust. He hung his bow next to the boy's from a rafter hook and better there with the shed's consistent temperature than in the cabin with its heating and cooling that tightens and relaxes the limbs and the strings, altering accuracy.

They had come back in the evening from hunting and the boy dropped his pack at the front of the cabin then came into the shed where he withdrew a thin curved knife from the knife block by the workbench. The man still shouldered his own pack and he turned and stayed still while the boy went to the back of it and untied the bootstring from which dangled two gutted walleye strung through their gills. "Nice fish, Dad." Light fell from the shed window to the chopping block outside where the boy filleted their catch without needing be told. They'd either boil the carcasses to make stock for a soup, bury them to fertilize the garden soil, or if it was winter they'd have saved and chunked them up for marten traps. But the boy's favourite was to lay them on a fallen log off in the woods near wet mud, then in the morning, return to see who had visited in the night.

They walked the short distance to the cabin together, the boy with four fillets and the man with two arms full of split and dry pine. Several years had passed since she last walked out that door and him walking through it now was like she hadn't gone anywhere. Didn't matter if a fire burned or dinner cooked or if dirty clothes hung from nails on the smoke-scented walls and that these two now bathed a bit less often than she'd ever allow, he still smelled wildflowers she'd picked for vases, that now stood on the rafters empty and dusted, scented candles she'd burned on holiday evenings, though no wax pools remained, a softer soap she bathed with that scented her skin under the covers as she lay curved up against him, them two curled up against the night's cold, that particular soap long run out of. Walking in the cabin like he was right now watching her fill those vases light those candles lather that soap. Maybe he was. In the nights after she'd gone he'd still sometimes wake up and sense her lying there next to him. And he didn't try to reach out for her in the night because in not doing so he kept it possible all had been a bad dream and she had never left at all. Her curled up sleeping right next to him like some Schrödinger Cat and he'd rather not test it, not reach out and so neither confirm nor disconfirm, just let possibilities and potential worlds exist. He would let himself believe her there, and at those times in the sightless night with nobody to say it differently him least of all, she did lie there next to him and any who would disagree can prove it otherwise.

The boy was warming by the stove with its fire he'd started and the cast-iron pan that sat atop it was nearly smoking its cooking oil when the man laid the fish fillets in and away from him so the oil didn't spit his direction. Skin-side down and they don't curl up. The battered flour fogged the oil. The fillets popped and sizzled and browned and cooked in short time. He lifted the browned fish with tongs, holding each piece a few seconds over the pan to drip, then laid one resting against the other on a serving plate. Salt and pepper. They both never tired of fresh fish cooked simply.

On the wall farthest from the fire hung three rifles and two shotguns, all of them old all of them tack drivers in capable hands. Their barrels looked wet from the oil that tempered their metal but the blued steel was dry to the touch having pulled that thin protective oil down into the metal grain where it warded off rust. Dark walnut stocks were darker still where generations of hands had gripped them to squeeze triggers that fed families. Squeezed triggers, not pulled them. Tools all of them but sometimes tools are still pretty, and both he and the boy liked to look at them there. He was allowed to take them down and hold them and dryfire them too because it doesn't hurt anything and it's good practice and helps in training to shoot without a flinch. But he had to ask first and handle them respectfully while pointing them to the ground and prove them unloaded. When they practised shooting as they routinely did to keep that skill honed, they hiked a ways to a small valley so as not to spook any game that came near the cabin. There the valley walls blocked the wind. The kid could name all the parts of the rifle, which isn't saying too much as there aren't so many, but the trapper had taught him how to disassemble all those parts and service them and then when putting them back together to feel for the smoothness and listen for the crispness of the bolt being slid into the receiver and the sound of cycling through the action and chambering a round. You could hear if you'd been a touch heavy with the grease, he told him. So listen.

Mostly they hunted with bow and arrow. He was raising him to be an archer. He had gotten his own first bow fairly late in life, from one of the guests he guided years ago, a rich guy leaving him, at the end of a successful hunting trip, a top-of-the-line compound hunting bow as a tip. It was camo. He liked it. A lot. Liked hunting that way. Bowhunting demanded commitment and came with an intimacy with the forest an order of magnitude more intense than with a rifle. Get within thirty yards of your prey not three hundred. It wasn't a matter of pride or legacy. Even though his dad and his granddad had dabbled with homemade bows, they only shot lead. It wasn't about one thing being better than another. But bowhunting was like taking a well-honed blade off the whetstone and stropping it on raw leather to make a razor that pops hairs off your arm nearly by looking at them, like a magnet held in reverse spooks iron filings. He wanted to make the boy as good as he could get him at hunting, which might one day save his life. Try to cultivate mastery. And hunting with a glorified throwing stick helps that process along. The discipline of it, dedication, faculties sharpened all of them: eyes ears nose movement planning patience determination intelligence grit. They hunted among the animals in stealth like they two were just a couple more animals, which they were. And to kill soundlessly is to kill with less alarm is to make killing a bit more likely next time. Teach the boy all that. But the rifles were at the ready and they'd reach for them if things got tough. Where they hung level on the rack on the farthest wall there the polished triggers occasionally seemed to call a little, like a girl at the dance waiting for someone to ask her hand, the triggers glinting a little like a pretty lady winking in the candlelight.

They were eating dinner and talking about the day and at one point the boy asked if that rabbit they caught was always going to be caught. He said, "Was that rabbit always going to be caught?"

"How do you mean?"

"Like if I'm going to grow up to be a hunter like you and your dad was too and his dad too, was that rabbit that we let go always going to be snared by us one day? Or could it have been a different rabbit? We need to catch some to eat. Was he always going to be the one we caught?" He swallowed his fish. "Or no."

The trapper thought first. Then he said, "I don't know. I don't know that anyone knows that."

"But what do you think?"

"What do I think. Yeah. I think he was always going to be caught by us."

"Oh."

The kid had put his knife and fork together on the plate after he'd finished eating like he'd been taught. He sipped his mint tea thoughtfully. Sometimes his mannerisms made him look to be about Gran's age. He lowered his mug and he said, "So Mom was always going to leave." He said that, he didn't ask it.

The kid baffled him sometimes. The trapper was a grown man so he was smarter than the kid, but he was not always smarter than the kid. Right now he was not smarter than the kid. An older man mostly frames the world through past experiences, fits current shapes into prior forms and often that's helpful, but sometimes it's not when you're hamstrung by a memory, or ill-conditioned by an experience that causes you to default to some interpretation of the world that might not be relating so well to its true account. And this is why age alone does not necessarily confer wisdom, there's more to it than that. Like questioning one's own default interpretations, suspending initial reactions, shutting up even when you think you know it and listening to someone else's take. The boy with fewer experiences to use as reference must have looked out at the world with fresh eyes, saw things the trapper himself could not. And sometimes that's helpful and sometimes it's not.

He said to the boy, "I guess she was."

"Oh. Why didn't she say?"

"She didn't know. Not until she did."

He sipped his tea. They both did.

"So is it like a storybook? Like the rabbit was always on one of the pages? And Mom was always on one of the pages? And I'm there too somewhere, far enough ahead if you looked?"

The trapper set down the porcelain mug and propped his bent elbows on the table. Rested his chin on his hands. "Maybe. But maybe it's like a storybook that nobody wrote. That nobody is writing."

"Oh." He said that oh looking confused. "But—"

The man knew what was coming and he had no answer for it.

"How does it get written then?"

He shook his head and needed no time to answer and didn't take any. "I don't know. I wonder it too."

The boy tried to raise an eyebrow. "Sounds like you don't know much."

"Now you're paying attention."

"But what do you think?"

"What do I think. Magic. I guess."

"Magic." The kid nodded pensively. "Okay," he said in all seriousness, "magic makes sense." He looked down. "And when sad things happen? Like when we killed the fish. Nobody wrote that, it just happened and was always going to happen?"

"Yeah. No I don't think anyone wrote it. But it was always going to happen because things came before it and those things have to go somewhere. They have to play out."

"I see," said the kid.

He almost laughed when the kid said I see.

"So sad things are also magic?"

"Well. Like maybe that's black magic there I guess."

"Do we believe in that? In black magic?"

He thought about it. "No. We don't."

"Okay, ditto."

"Ditto? Where'd you get ditto?"

"You said it once."

"I don't think so."

"So why was it that rabbit and not another? One rabbit got caught, another rabbit didn't. Why?"

"I asked your mom something similar. I asked her if she thought things happened for a reason. That's what you and I are talking about here. She said to me yeah but not the way people mean it. The reason might just be something big exploded a long time ago and we're bouncing around like marbles now. Complex marbles that somehow feel things."

The boy liked that and he laughed at the thought of being a marble. "We're marbles," he said laughing.

"Some things I do know. Like for sure you're a squirrelly little marble. I'm certain about that. And I've seen your target practice and that makes me quite sure there is randomness and chaos in the world."

The kid had put both hands on the table beside his plate and was still laughing.

"But she thought the world was beautiful too, regardless if someone was writing it. Regardless of chaos and marbles. Not always. But in lucky places. That's what she believed."

"What do you believe?"

"That's what I believe too."

"Yeah, me too," said the kid. "Do you think she still believes that?"

"Maybe. Maybe we're all just characters in the dreaming mind of some sleeping king."

"Hey!" the boy said. "You stole that! That's from my book!"

"Do the dishes."

He helped the boy clean up and then the kid went to the loft and changed into clean long johns and a long-sleeved cotton shirt that served as his pajamas. He took his favourite book from the small table at his bedside and brought it downstairs and of the two empty chairs by the fire, both wooden, both with worn buckskin leather seats and both having been sat in by four generations of his own bloodline, he sat in the one that was slightly bigger and so made him look slightly smaller. The book open in his lap and him sounding the words pointing his finger underneath like that'd help pry up their meanings that he was still learning. The storybook had been read to him so often, when a new one was suggested he requested the same, and he had it just about memorized, so sometimes when he pretended to be reading he was mostly recalling, though he'd get sore and claim otherwise if you accused him of such impostery. And now he couldn't make out those words at all as his eyes were narrow slits and his head was very slowly bobbing, then still and laid back against the chair.

The trapper walked over and lifted the book out from under the sleeping hand and then picked up the noodleboy somehow gone limp in every muscle and cradled him with the crook of his own elbow supporting the boy's head and gently carried him up the stairs to the loft. He laid the ragdollboy to bed and put the book by his bedside and tucked up the covers under his chin. He didn't want to wake him and instead of saying the words he just thought them in his mind, but then hearing them there he did say them anyways, just quiet in a little hushed whisper. The kid didn't open his eyes but said softly back, "I love you too."

In the hospital of the small town when she gave birth and he saw for the first time this new little human they had made, crying eyes and flushed skin and fingers and toes and everything so tiny that they couldn't even be real at all, in this newborn boy he saw those same divine contours as his wife's, the artist's telltale style and signature apparent at this second unveiling of holy work. Though he'd mostly lost his belief by that time, seeing the child being born nearly returned it like a dam broke and that belief came flooding in. So what did that make him? Some keeper of godly artifacts. And that was his working definition of father, of husband. So carve him in stone and give him a sword and set him outside the walls.

He came back down the stairs from the loft and sat in the chair beside the one he'd lifted the boy from. Legs stretched out before him, hands folded on his stomach. It was Granddad who'd made those chairs, carpentered them out of pine, upholstered the seats with tanned, smoked and softened buckskin pulled over thin foam inserts salvaged from old lifejackets beyond repair. Could see that man sitting in his chair whenever he looked over at it, see him now in the one the boy had left. He himself didn't sit in that one, but he liked that the boy did. It wasn't exactly superstition, more a kind of respect. But, well, maybe you'd call that a type of superstition just the same. Long grey hair hung down to his shoulders that were broad even into his old age from old-world strength of chopping wood and carrying it and going for water and canoe paddling, muscles that took their shape from the years of it. Sculpted by the North such as he was. A Rodin of a Northern man. Mostly kept that strength up to his last days like he'd have use for it where he was going. His hearing was fading out near the end as most of those guys from that era never wore earplugs when shooting, like the trapper made the boy wear. That hearing loss seemed to bother others more than it did him though. And the dog helped. His wolf. She did some of the listening for him and he'd look to her if she was acting like she'd heard something he didn't that he should have. He wasn't much of a reader but he was a thinker in his own way and his philosophies were not abstract, more so practical—but then again any philosophy worth its printed weight or spoken one should be a practical thing, in one way or another. He'd just be content to sit there with coffee after dinner, *tend the fire*, as he called it. What are you going to do now, Granddad? Oh, tend the fire I suppose. That wolfdog tuckered out too, warming on the hide where it curled at his feet in front of the stove. That dog, those two.

Once when that old man wasn't an old man yet he was hiking in the spring near a rock wall with big fallen shards and crumbled boulders at its base like some Rockbiter had passed grazing in the night. Heard mewing from an abscess among the rocks. Little yaps, just soft mewing, could almost be baby birds. Right there he shouldered his rifle without loading it 'cause it was always loaded and he unsafetied it and scanned over the barrel's open iron sights at the bluffs overhead. Then down to the forest edge. Finger on the trigger. She wouldn't be far. Gave it a few minutes but didn't see her. So he lowered his rifle and dropped his pack. The little den was small and had only one entrance and with a bedrock shelf above it and all the rest rocked off to the world. He had to kneel down on all fours and bend sideways to look into it. Within that enshadowed little cavity he saw, among strands of balled fur and bits of bones from who-knows-what formerly living thing, seven wolf pups.

Crouched there he looked back over his shoulder. Then back to the den. Them huddled together not moving much, probably their eyes were still closed as he couldn't tell in the dusky light of that hollow. He reached in an arm and filled a hand with three pups, then did the same with the other. Six blind pups held dangling by their loose soft and folded neck-scruff kicking and yipping into the day, their first. Unlikely that she'd be far out of earshot and he scanned around him as he walked for the creek without his gun. Didn't feel so good about it. He looked on ahead, he didn't look at them. But someone had raised him and that's what he was taught and we are what came before us, so to anyone who would fault him, tell it next up the lineage also, guilty just the same. And he also knew that in doing so he'd save dozens of deer and moose—and that's per wolf.

He knelt at the creek and the cold water ached his hands sunk to his elbows, and he told himself he's saving lives not taking them. The cold spring water like an extension of someone else's misery. Sunken hands gone white in the water. Little kicks, soft ones. Small life twisting in the current spun in his hands and there were soft kicks in his hands and they moved about some while he held them submerged. Then there was nothing. Just rags gone limp in the wash. Any movement was just the current twisting them. He released his grip and they drifted away downcurrent, taken by the creek. Stayed crouched there a minute looking into the water in front of him. Then he spat at what he saw there. Looked up and around still kneeling among the murmur of the creek and the chirping of spring birds on a warm day in a beautiful land that paid little mind to whatever tragedies or joys took place therein. Sometimes itself their perpetrator, benefactor. Anyways, he felt rotten. Then he heard a solitary mew. One lonely yip from the forgotten seventh. He stood up resolute and to just not think and to just do and walked over and wasn't even looking for the mother and he bent down and reached back in the den and pulled that wild puppy out by its nape. He made the mistake of looking down at this one he held in his hand. Saw its eyes were open but squinting fiercely into their first sun. Tiny mouth opened like it was going to make its first attempt at some pathetic howl, or maybe just yawning with that pink tongue and everything else all fur. Aw shit, he said. He went to the cold creek. He stepped to its edge. Then into it. Then waded across it. Wolf pup sitting at the top of his pack with the draw-cord only loosely drawn. A solitary mew heard walking off into the forest.

He hiked on with the pup to his cabin and as they did he felt that by killing the others and not this one he had guaranteed himself a failure in one way or the other, hedged his bets as a bad man. Someone else might say maybe just a pretty good one with some flawed parts. He and that wolf did well together. Named her Seven. And most people thought it was from his fondness of cards or his luck in them. He let them think that.

Those older generations were strong people living in harder times and even just remembering them you could draw off their grit. The kid liked hearing stories about them and he'd ask him to tell him about Gran and Granddad, the fur trade, his great-great- (the kid couldn't remember how many greats) grandmother he just called Nôhkow. The trapper called her that too. He hadn't told him the story about the wolf yet, not in full.

Granddad'd finish his evening chores then come sit down and that old wolfdog, arthritic like she was getting, would slowly rise up on her front legs, then wait a second for the back half of her body to follow too, having to get up in stages in her final days. Then she'd shuffle those worn bones over to the old man, a waddle made more awkward from a low wagging tail that kinda bent her in half. Like the tail actually was wagging the dog in this case. She'd just come over and put her big head on Granddad's lap, every night the same just every night a little slower. Loyal, hell. A big male cougar one time came near camp which they rarely did. They'd often be around while they roamed their territory but if they were in the area they mostly stayed on the outskirts of the cabin's footprint. One came in. Prowled in on shoulders like a high-bar gymnast but thin in the waist. Stood about waist high. Long body. That's what stands out about those big cats, how drawn out their bodies are. Maybe he came in looking for a hanging deer or snared rabbit, maybe even for Gran herself as that does happen from time to time and she didn't look as spry as she once did. For sure that cougar got lucky not finding her. Never bet against that wiry little woman to whoop ass: her boy's, Granddad's, whoever's. They knew her in town. Seven saw that big cat and looked from it to Granddad on the porch like she was awaiting an order, a reluctant one. She wasn't charging off on her own to pick that fight but would have gone in like a soldier. Either not capable of weighing the cost of her loyalty, or capable but not caring. Had the old man simply nodded that cat's way she'd have done her duty and gone a few rounds at least. But he never sent her. He just reached inside the door for the lever action .30-30. Jacked a round. Wolf lay on a cougar hide by the fire after that.

Now all buried in the garden. Granddad, Gran, Mom, Dad, that wolf too. And *her* too.

He filled the big stove with two unsplit log rounds and closed its squeaking door, raising then lowering the iron latch. He turned down the damper halfway up the stovepipe then closed the lower vent. That stove turned down like that would burn wood through the night, smolder embers past sunrise and into midday. He sat forward in the chair leaning in towards the stove with his elbows on his knees and his head atop his fists. He was thinking about her 'cause he always thought about her, and about the boy and the rabbit too. But before he went to sleep it was the yellow floatplane on his mind.

11

When the moon was full the trapper's dreams were wild if he slept at all. He's dreaming of walking on a vast ice lake under a textured sky from wisps of cloud highlighted by a dreamed up quarter-moon he could not see, though he gave a turn looking for it. The distant dream-trees at the edge of the frozen lake stood silhouetted, like cutouts on a stage play, or tree shadows cast in his mind from some-one else's dreaming world—as this all did not seem real so why would the trees be? Had he approached where they bordered the shoreline he'd see their needles had found their details and their leaves and their cones would emerge but not as ones he'd recognize and the bark on their trunks would slither and peel and though this looked like the North and it may have been, it was not the one he'd known. Stars innumerable.

He was some distance to the lake's centre but could see that out there on the ice was a yellowed glow he knew glimmered for him and him only, for there was nothing and no one else out there, a Chekhov Gun of the dreaming world, and as his path to it seemed ordained, so there he went. Dream this scene a thou-sand nights he'd never turn away. In actual fact he had dreamed this same scene several times before but the memories were forgotten or misplaced and so he was returning to old lands he had never come to know.

Carefully treading what the blowing winds had polished smooth as temple marble, he walked towards the soft glow whose flat orb radiated from the ice, and even though he walked slowly he did slip often. He looked to the ice and it was clouded and it was also clear: it was clouded if he looked anywhere but directly into the ice underfoot, and looking straight into what he stood on, there alone it was clear. The night sky had frozen itself into the ice, or was being reflected back from the polished surface, or he thought he might have been walking on some thin suspended icesheet, some crystal plane, and below that and all around him was starry night just the same. He could not tell for certain and on his long walk he alternated between those three theories while believing with great conviction each one for a time to be true.

He approached the light. He stood over top of the light and looking down saw a fire burned within the ice. Its brilliance faded out all other starlight. He tried to see it better and so knelt to it and lowered his head, and now he looked like some worshipper of an ancient sect who'd pilgrimaged and finally arrived at the place of his deity. He could see that it burned, he could not tell what fuelled it. His dreaming mind, relaxed of normal frameworks, thought that maybe at the fire's core was a source of perpetual combustion, some eternal wellspring of energy. It could be possible, not only in a dream world, because things either always exist—and this may be some such eternal thing—or things didn't always exist, and so at some point they started from nothing and that means something out there could fashion itself up without prior inputs, like some baffled sorcerer who just conjured himself into existence out of a cauldron yet to be made. This could be one of those, he thought.

He looked down at the ice fire below him and he wanted to feel its heat as his hands were very cold, so he removed his winter mitts that Gran had knitted and they hung from his coat with yarn Mom must have strung through his coat sleeves. He realized he was only a boy again. He did not want to be a boy anymore. He raised one hand to touch the wetness he felt on his red cheeks pulled tight from the wind, and he thought what he found there must have melted from his frosted lashes, but that fire burned cold and what streaked his face was not melted ice but tears of a boy. And realizing he was crying only made him more of the boy he no longer wanted to be, and that made him cry more. His falling tears pebbled the ice.

Looking at the light he knew in his heart that beacon glow would burn forever and he felt that truth indubitable and strong within him and he reached one hand to the bright ice and that ice burned his skin cold like snakebite and he drew back sharply and the fire snuffed out like it never was. Just gone. Poof. So quick. It even took the starlight with it, drained the sky of it. But he could still hear it crackling in the dark and that gave him faith and so he listened. He was wrong there too because it was the ice on which he knelt cracking and it gave way under him and he felt himself falling in his dream, unsure if the waters awaiting him would be cold or hot. And in that weightless fall a question was posed to him once, and then again: Who? it asked. Who?

He woke up startled in bed thrusting out his arms to brace his fall gasping in sweat-soaked sheets. For just a brief moment he lay chilled and scared like a boy. An owl was calling outside in these dead hours of a dark night. Hoo, it called. He listened for the boy breathing from the loft above. Soft little slow pantings, just the exhales. They calmed his own and he started breathing to the boy's rhythm. The bedroom window showed a pale moonlight. He got up and walked to the window and looked out. Lands lit by a moon he couldn't see, though he dipped his head and scanned above. Something did not feel right. Not at all. He dressed in the night.

12

With the knob turned to quiet the latch, the cabin door easing shut made no sound closing. Trying not to wake the boy, not wake the forest, him between two worlds such as he was. The lodge was not that close and so he moved fast to reach it, travelling under moonglow so bright it seemed like some white-hot iron fire poker had seared a hole through a thin shroud and any second that burn hole could peel back its edges and the whole sky'd be torched-up white.

He moved to be back before morning and was swiftly running gametrails between sleeping trees whose shapes he knew 'cause he'd watched them grow. Even their shadows took recognizable forms in this land so familiar he could nearly run it blindfolded, feet over root stumps like fingers over braille bumps, skirting the sides of small hills, leaping the creek at its narrow spot.

Perched high on a tall tree an owl, warden of the night, bobbed its vigilant head in eerie circles. Then dropped on broad wings the colour of snow soon to fall but yet to come. Like the colourless bird was an omen of looming hardships, or itself its agent. Now swooping between the treetops flying silently on serrated feathers, its yellow eyes between the dark pines.

After some time he neared the clearing of the old lodge and the owl lifted away, silhouetted by the moon like jailhouse spotlight. The trapper inside the edge of the woods and concealed by night looked out across the open property to the lodge's chimney. No smoke ascended. Beside it was the manager's cabin. A thin curl rose up into the night sky as though a grey hairlock of a witch were hanging down from it. No light in the cabin windows. He moved from the forest low and fast across the hundred yards of open expanse then laid his body up against the cabin's log wall. He listened there several minutes and in hearing nothing raised up to look through the corner of the window. A dim living room in this cabin he had helped build years ago. He watched for four, maybe five minutes. Dark and still. He turned and looked up to the sky for any hints of dawn and saw none. From his pack he took a flashlight he rarely used. Taped across its lens was a piece of thin red fabric. He shined it through the window and low to the floor at first. Nothing stirred and nothing sounded and so he raised that light and scanned about. They'd be in the bedrooms anyways. Saw on the table a small amount of dried goods, two boxes of ammunition, hiking gear, maps, crushed cans, full cans. In the one corner he could see stood two rifles. On a mat by the door just two sets of men's hiking boots. He didn't see big cases of canned goods and there was only one two-four of Coors Light outside and the men weren't even staying in the lodge. Probably the owners inspecting the place, maybe on a personal hunt, he thought. Didn't look like preparations for a full-on commercial operation.

He switched the flashlight off.

Him like one more predator moving quietly through the forest heading back to its den.

13

Dawn was not far off when he finally laid down his head. He dreamed of her. In the world that bloomed with his sleep it was almost as if she hadn't left that day she did but rather just stepped from his woke world into his dreamt one. Like her spirit transitioned to accommodate her buried body. A place where other dimensions get glimpsed from the dreaming minds that build them. Where time runs by different measure in the sleeping minds that tick it and dream length can stretch minutes into hours and even years get lived in the span of a few nights. He had now spent more time with her in a sleeping state than their former fleshed one. Whereas some truths exist on their own and can be verified by others, such as abstract math of two plus two equals four and certain properties of light, there are also personal truths. Felt things. Convictions of love, feelings of pain. And regarding those types, the one experiencing them is the sole arbiter of their truth.

When she came to him in his dreams, she existed. She spoke words he did not know in his conscious mind before he heard them. He listened to those words and was changed by them. *Real.* Who would tell him otherwise and how to even argue the point? She laughed and he laughed. *Real.* He carried within him during his day, words she whispered during his night. Sometimes he touched her skin and felt no less sensation than before. She touched him back and he was affected by it, warmed by it and comforted by it and aroused by it too. If some neuroscientist in years to come could show that her words were holed up in a hidden pocket of his layered mind and could prove that some part of his brain was fabricating her, the point remains that his conscious self still had no access to it. As a matter of his subjective experience, she was not him—she was her. And their time together mattered to him and there was more of it. He woke with new memories. What else to call them? Experiences that colour his day and affect his next one. And does memory and subconscious discount feelings that were made while dreaming, if the person affected by them feels no difference to their intensity, to the significance of their felt truth? No it doesn't. Those new memories mixed with old ones all just as real or none at all.

14

The trapper turned the damper open on the stovepipe then spun the lower vent to fully port the draw, and the coals and charred log remains enlivened by the fresh draft glowed red. The iron door squeaked on its hinge. He laid quartered logs inside. From the kitchen shelf he took the large tin of coffee grounds down and scooped some into the steel percolator basket then replaced the basket lid, lowered that into the smaller kettle with its water already warm having sat on the stove overnight. He centred it over the hottest part of the stove. Set two mugs to warm. When its little glass bulb bubbled a few minutes he filled the one mug then sat by the window, his hands warming, feeling the stove radiate out to his back.

They kept about a week's worth of oats in the kitchen, the rest in a metal bin in the cellar they'd built inside a hollowed out hillside and sealed with a heavy door. Vegetables and grains and dried berries stayed cooler in the summer and free of frost in the winter, as well they stored sugar, salt, flour, some emergency canned goods, a dormant sourdough mother they fed once every week or two and she was older than the trapper.

He heard the boy moving from up in the loft and he got up and filled their bowls and when the boy came down he poured hot water in the kid's mug for tea then handed it to him saying morning, wildman. Got a groggy "Morning" back. The kid was rubbing one of his eyes. His long johns were starting to look kinda small. They ate steaming oats topped with cinnamon and raspberries and hazelnuts they'd foraged earlier in the fall then slow roasted outside in a heavy pan placed directly on the coals.

They left on a different route than yesterday's, hiking towards sandbanks and natural gravel hills where ruffed grouse pecked the pebbles and grit to aid their digestion. Today the boy led the way and he walked a little taller, the man seeing breaks of daylight under the kid's footsteps, because today he carried his own bow too. Almost walked with a little hop like a deer prance. His bow looked similar to his dad's, only its draw weight was turned down some. It still pulled heavy enough for even a large animal at close range, but it was better suited to rabbits and grouse and that's what they were after. Occasionally they would stop and listen for the drumming of feathers. A sound that started like half notes through to quarter, then picked up to eighth, and finally crescendoed to a near-uniform purr. Like someone was throwing down on an old plane propellor that sputtered a bit before it caught. They both liked to hear it.

It wasn't long before they saw one give itself away perched on a spruce branch when it turned its head backlit by morning sun. Grouse survive less on wit and more on camouflage and short breeding cycles. The boy had taken from his quiver a bludgeon-tipped arrow made to deliver blunt force to small game rather than pierce through them. He laid the arrow into his whisker-biscuit rest then nocked it to the string, all the while not taking his eyes off the dull bird. He stepped towards it, hanging his foot in the air a second before he placed it. The grouse blended in so well when still. It bobbed its head. It turned its head away gazing cock-eyed at the boy. He placed his last steps softly as he could on the frosted gravel. At ten yards he raised his bow then drew back while sighted on the target like he'd been taught. Like he'd practised till his shoulder ached. The arrow in the bristle-rest slid silently backwards and the little hunter's upper body wavered just a touch as he pulled through the heaviest section of draw before the cams rotated into their let-off and the final string-travel pulled easy until it hit its stoppers. He anchored the knuckle of his index finger against his earlobe exposed below his toque. Touched the string to the tip of his nose. Everything smooth. Relaxed his forward hand holding the bow, the blunt tip just beyond his fingers. His dad watching from behind. Sight-pin floating gently on the bird's chest. He exhaled half his breath then drew his release arm straight backwards until the shot surprised him like it should and the bow limbs transferred their pent-up energy to that braided string pushing an accelerating arrow on a flat trajectory over a short range to smoke a fat bird backwards off its branch. A few errant feathers tossed up above a dead bird falling below.

The kid fist pumped. It wasn't his first but he still smiled ear to ear.

The trapper smiled too, took pleasure in watching the boy. He looked good. "You looked good," he said.

"Did you see me?" Exuberant whisper.

The trapper held out a low fist and the kid rapped his knuckles.

They walked over to where it lay unmoving. The boy picked the grouse up by its tailfeathers, turning it slowly while they looked at it. Its short wings spread open. It was actually hard to tell it'd been shot, just broken up inside. It always felt special to be that close to a wild animal, even one no longer living, even one you had taken the life of, and there was a reverence for it. Though some would think those things are mutually exclusive, they're not. The boy said, "Thank you, grouse."

He laid it down on the ground and put his small hand sideways against the tailfeathers to measure. Pointed out the unbroken brown band. "I think it's male," he said. He laid his bow down carefully and unclipped his pocket knife hanging inside his pant pocket like his father's beside him and made a small incision to slit the belly. Then he lifted the bird and slid two fingers inside the cavity and eased out the small clump of entrails that fell in a steaming plop to the ground. Shook out some gutbits from the wild chicken. Then finding a patch of grass dragged it clean on the frost-grass before he held it up to Dad who turned around so the boy could tie it to the outside of his pack.

"I'm just your packer," he said facing away. "Nice shot Robin Hood."

"I *am* Robin Hood."

They walked on in the crisp fall morning and banks of gravel and sand began to merge with the edge of autumn woods. Another hidden grouse that could no longer be still flapped up beside them erupting the calmness of the morning and startling both of them. Some they saw first and the boy arrowed two more and the man was content to watch. The boy leading would occasionally point out some bit of nature that caught his eye. Sometimes he'd turn back just to smile, see his dad there following him. Once he crouched down examining the ground and when the trapper caught up, the boy pointed a small finger to the sand that he claimed was disturbed maybe by a fox print or some mink toes, he said.

The trapper saw nothing there other than some prior day's rain-dappled sand. The trapper nodded in agreement and covered his mouth then looked away observing something up in the sky. "Mink toes," he repeated back with his mouth still covered.

He was curious how exactly the kid saw the world. It was likely quite different than how he himself saw it. He wondered what it would be like to see the world through the eyes of another living thing. Not just the boy. For the boy he could ask him questions and he did, almost as many as the boy asked him. But he was curious about other points of view. The deer. What does life feel like for an eagle? Is there consciousness to a worm or a fly? How different is experience along the spectrum of various life forms and how keen are their feelings of pain and pleasure? Does being a plant or bacteria come with an experience? What about some thousand-year-old sprawling honey mushroom hundreds of acres in size touching every part of the forest glowing in the night? What was that like? In late spring they planted bush peas in the garden and come early summer he'd observe the peas' daily progress of reaching out their little tendrils to climb things in their vicinity. He'd read that plants shuttled nutrients to their own growing seedlings, even traded resources back and forth with other trees, communicated dangers by releasing phero-mones, smelling the air.

Wind rustled the poplars to the sounds of rushing water. Yellow leaves drifted about them listlessly like the lost broadheads of past millennia.

Years ago on one of the trapper's guided hunts while he and his client were sitting for lunch, the client chal-lenged him to go one minute without a thought. The same thing he'd tried with the boy the other day. It's where he got it from. It wasn't such a strange thing for the guy to say because people who could afford those fly-in hunting trips had all kinds of backgrounds and some of them were characters and when you spend five isolated days with anyone, all topics are on the table. That was far from the strangest thing he'd ever heard when guiding. They had stopped hunting and were eating by a midday fire and the client said he'd make him CEO of his company if he could go one minute without a thought.

The trapper tried like he'd had the boy try and of course he couldn't. And that was a strange thing to real-ize it can't be done. That something he assumed he had control over and was so close at hand actually required someone else pointing it out: that thoughts just arise on their own, that they seem to think themselves up. A realization that came with repercussions.

"If thoughts think themselves and they influence behaviour, then how could free will exist?" the client said.

"Well. I'm raising my hand. Look," he told him. "I chose that."

116

"But why did you pick that hand over the other? Why did the feeling itself that raising your hand would be a good counterexample arrive? Why didn't you hold your hand up a second longer or shorter?" The hunter looking at him by the fire. "Did you choose all those subtle things? Did you will them?"

They went on that day and the next talking back and forth about it. The client kinda drilled him on it. He said if you just paid close enough attention even things that feel like deliberate and conscious choices actually aren't. And it becomes pretty easy to see if you pay attention. There's no trick, you don't need to go sit in a cave for a year. No gurus, pilgrimages, or holy texts required. Just watch your mind for a minute. To bring the point home he had said, "I said you don't have free will and you sat there a second in disbelief. You felt disbelief. Did you will that feeling of incredulity? No," he said, "you didn't. But it went on and determined your subsequent behaviour. Behaviour that cascaded for the rest of your life."

The trapper just thought about that quietly, the days that followed too. In the evening by the campfire of their final day out hunting and backpacking together before their return to the lodge when that client would catch his floatplane to town, the man said, "We know we are conscious so we know we exist. To even doubt it proves it true. But if you aren't exactly thinking your thoughts, who are you?" The client grinned. "What are you?"

That was over two decades ago and he still thought about it. Had talked about it with her some too. He was looking forward to exploring it more with the boy—not even teaching it, he didn't understand it well enough to teach it, just looking into it together.

Where they walked now opened up into old forest with big wide-trunked pines. Trees likely several hundred years old, a hundred feet in height straight up and towering to the open sky like they commanded something, in the least, respect. Father and son in the tall company of those with a history that you wanted to ask a few questions. The temperature was slightly cooler from the increased air flow and even the acoustics of their breath and steps were different here, the forest auditorium-like from the harder trunks and open spaces. He knew the boy was feeling it too 'cause he had slowed his walk and his eyes on his turning head were wide open. The man placed a hand to the deeply channelled auburn bark next to him. This elder.

The kid had taken his pack off and had his knife out cutting the stems of the fruiting body of a mycelium. He was collecting Golden Chanterelle mushrooms, a fungi that grew symbiotically with these trees, sharing nutrients and water. They were easy to identify and after he had a couple handfuls collected he placed them gently in his own pack.

On a small cedar tree that the boy had already walked past the man saw the bark stripped up and so gave a short bird-whistle. The boy turned around and came over. The trapper pointed to the animal sign to say look, and to also say with a minor scolding: look at what you missed. They both knelt.

"See how the upturned bark strands are green. See how the sap is fresh." He pointed without touching it so as not to leave behind his own scent. "Still sticky in the grooves." He waited a second for the boy to take it in, then pointed to the ground where hooves had displaced the topsoil. "Big bucks can rub little trees so you never know. If it had been higher up and wider and the cuts deeper it could be claws from a bear or cougar. It could be elk but there's no elk in this part of the country. Low like this is a deer rubbing his antlers and his forehead gland on the sapling to communicate his health to the does in heat. We can figure things out we never saw."

The kid wanted to hunt not talk. He looked fidgety.

"Look." The man nodded ahead towards another rubbed tree. The boy followed the man's gaze. Saw it. Looked back. Upheld a closed fist with a pinky and pointer raised and mouthed the word *buck*. "Big buck," he mouthed smiling. The small hunter led on, each with a bow in hand following the rub-line into the light wind.

There are many ways to hunt deer. Spot-and-stalk or still-hunt, set up in ground blinds and tree stands, ambush at funnel and pinch points, hunt the bedding areas and staging zones and rut corridors. Deer can also be called in. A doe bleat in the rut communicates that she's ready. A buck grunt is a low bass note vibrating through the ribbed barrel of a deer's windpipe. Rattling a set of old antlers ranges from sounds of play spar all the way up to mock battle, start lightly in the early season just tickling the bone to replicate bucks testing their new headgear at the start of fall. Ramp up that rattling intensity as the days get shorter to mimic the increasing aggression as the peak of the rut nears. In November smash those antler racks together to imitate sounds of dominant males with mean intentions willing to fight to the death over a hot doe.

He had been teaching the boy how to bleat and grunt. They'd practise in the cabin, the boy trying to match his pitch, tone and tenor. Then they'd head out to the forest and put it in action, test it, watch how the deer respond and observe their body language. That's the best way to learn but it takes a long time. The boy's doe bleat was pretty good and he'd turned a buck around with it before. When he tried making a grunt it sounded note-for-note spot on exactly like a prepubescent boy trying to be a man-deer. It was charmingly pathetic. He never liked to laugh at the boy's effort for anything but this couldn't be helped. Just a joke that never got old even though he knew the punchline. He'd not once asked the kid to make that sound during a hunt and had no plans to because they both preferred to eat. But he apologized for laughing and told him that's how he once sounded too and to keep working on it. The kid didn't laugh about it. A fawn bleat signifies a young deer in distress and both doe and buck will occasionally come to check it out. There may have never been a fawn bleat coming from a human mouth that sounded more real than the boy's. If such a thing makes sense to say, he sounded even more convincing than some of the actual fawn bleats they'd heard coming from actual young deer they'd watched making them.

No frog croaked no squirrel barked no crow cawed.

He motioned for the boy to separate some, sit down on the one side of the gametrail, he'd take the other about thirty yards apart to widen their shooting

120

range. "If you have a clear and close shot and feel good about it, you can take it," he whispered to him. They lowered camouflaged among the ferns mostly breaking up their shapes. After they'd settled and sat listening awhile he looked over at the boy. Raised a hand like a duck puppet, then opened its beak. The boy nodded and laid down his bow. He pulled his neck-warmer down from his chin. He brought his hands together in front of his face as if he was going to pray, then parted where his thumbs met and hollowed out the middle. Brought his mouth to the opening like a conch shell.

On a fall's late morning a fawn cried in distress, a high-pitched and wavering plaint.

Then the forest in stark silence.

Another deer-cry for help.

The forest was mute as all life thereabouts registered an uncommon sound. The boy looked to him, watched him for instruction. They listened a minute longer and hearing nothing the trapper gave a slight upnod for a final third cry.

The boy made that sad sound.

The man circled a thumb and index with three fingers peacocked to signal okay. Then they sat as the forest sat, still for a long time.

Sometimes what's listening is what you'd prefer wasn't. A flare shot in distress but your pursuers are watching the sky too. This little fawn had cried and this little fawn had been heard.

The forest tight like the skin of a snare drum and the man suddenly realized it. Could be his subconscious identified sounds or the lack thereof before that insight registered, maybe smelt the fur musk in the breeze or felt the footfalls. Something. 'Cause his stomach dropped and adrenaline spiked and pupils dilated looking into the forest past the boy for what he hadn't yet seen coming. Then he saw it: coal black. A colour strangely uncommon in the forest. Time slowed and in his tunnel vision he saw only two things: *the boy, the bear.*

He didn't need to think and had already halfway pulled sixty pounds of bending aluminum bow limbs to send a razorblade-tipped killing-stick straight through bear chest. It wasn't hatred, it wasn't fear, it was pure resolve—this thing needed to be done now so do it: shoot a moving target head on at close range coming to kill your boy. The totality of his thoughts were distance and shot placement—that's it. Forty yards. Put it on its fucking chest. The arrow sliding back almost fully drawn now, the cams just about to come into full let-off as he pulled through peak draw-weight, and then the string snapped with the sound of whipcrack beside his face. Twenty-four twisted strands snapped loud then lashed at his cheek like burning serpent tongues from a raging Medusa, but he didn't feel that nor the blood trickling down his broken flesh.

He dropped the bow without looking away from the bear. A mature boar can outrun a horse over short distances. He sprang up from where he was crouched and sprinted towards the boy and he was closer and had a head start and he'd need it. The bear's eyes were locked on the kid but it hadn't charged, it was coming in prowling. The trapper tore through the ferns and pumped his arms to jack his sprint and he yelled loudly both to distract the bear and warn the boy. But the bear started its charge and the boy seeing the animal for the first time was frozen in place. Now full sprint fifteen yards to the boy, eyes locked on a coal-black face, and that charging bear outpacing him. The trapper's right hand swept past his pocket and he drew his clipped knife—didn't even thumb-button the blade it just swung open from the momentum—and steel shaving-edge sharp locked into place. The bear's beaded eyes hadn't left the boy who was frozen like the fawn he'd pretended to be. The boar was close with a half-open jaw showing yellowed teeth and its big chest muscles alternating in power strokes under that thick and shimmering hide. The trapper got to the boy first but didn't stop his sprint he kept on past the kid then threw his full weight at that oncoming bear. The blow stopped its charge and it was the first time it had seen the man it already had pinned below itself. The bear moving fox-quick raised up a big paw on its shaggy arm to swipe for the man's head, to beat it in. Lying on his back watching it load that heavy swipe, the trapper reached up and gripped its chest fur with his left hand and quickly tucked up towards it right close so it couldn't bat at him. With his head buried and blinded by its chest fur, his right hand held the knife not in a slicing grip but like an ice pick and he stabbed that blade behind its foreleg and drove it handle-deep into bear. The big animal twisted at that jab, but a four-inch blade doesn't stop an attacking bear nor does it kill quick if it even kills at all. The trapper didn't fight like his life was at risk, he fought like the boy's was. Total focus in some primal flow state with every muscle engorged and acting together trying to end what was trying to end him. His hand was white-knuckle gripped on the knife and he withdrew that weapon now slick with blood then stabbed it home again. The bear flinched away from that side and half groaned, half roared. It rose up higher on its hindlegs and swatted and clawed at the clinging man and was able to tear him free from its chest and press him to the earth. The trapper's hand slipped from the handle still sticking out sideways from the animal's torso. The bear brought its paws together hung overtop the pinned man. It arched up higher on its haunches, those big shaggy forelegs in the air, then it lowered a heavy stomp directly onto his chest like it was trying to smash open a frozen ant hill. His chest compressed. He heard bone snap. He blew out all his air and none came back in and he choked airlessly while trying to gasp with those paws spanned across his chest pressing down onto him. He couldn't reach the knife so he got a hand up above those weighty legs and searched for its face trying to sink a thumb and gouge one of those beady eyes from its socket. Now it was hatred now it was fear now it was anger and malice along with the boy. He wanted to rip one of those fucking eyes out and take it home. He groped blindly and felt its panting breath hot on his wrist and its nose dripping wet down his arm and he was able to get his fingers above its snout, but the bear drew up again. The forelegs now off of him he gasped. Caught a glimpse of the knife there in its side but too far to reach. Its hindlegs and total weight were fully over his lower body and once again it arched up higher to suspend those big paws above his chest with its massive head looking down at him. For a moment their eyes met and something was exchanged there. There was a strange small part of him right then that liked the fight, liked even the feeling of pain: this felt raw and that felt good. The bear swayed its hanging paws like it was taking aim to finish him off. He knew from his laboured breaths and aching chest that next stomp would cave in his lungs under his ribs it'd already cracked. He saw the knife too far to reach, those mean eyes too far to gouge. He tried to tuck up towards the bear again, then tried to roll, but its heavy weight kept him pinned. He didn't like that he was losing. He didn't like that he'd lost. He looked up at the boar and knew that was it. Some see a bright light and some see the ceiling of a hospital room and some the back of their own eyelids. His was the soulless little eyes of a northern predator. This crippled guardian with a lost sword warded off no dangers at all. He some crumbled version of his own lie, a failed mass of fallen stone and a broken myth dying under a real bear and the death of a self-proclaimed safe-guarder of stars and keeper of holy artifacts. The only thought in his head, *Would the boy be okay?* The bear's paws suspended and centred above his chest, and nothing he could do but cross his arms to soften the blow and he knew that would do nothing at all. He waited for it and knew it was coming.

Then he watched the killing tip of an arrow slowed from the hide and tissue and life valves it had just torn apart, exit through bear hide and stick out the other side. Not a bludgeon tip. A pretty broadhead. It didn't pass fully through the bear given that bow's lower draw-weight but it did spray into the late morning air pink-bubbled heart-froth from the hole it had just cut through it. He saw three gory blades dripping red life-juice, and nothing looked sweeter. The bear's heart muscle was ripped through its centre. It moaned loud in a pained roar and flinched hard away from where the arrow had entered. It batted a paw towards its side like it'd been stung by some vicious bee, then looked up high and clawed once at its own chest. It swayed there, still sitting up high on its haunches. The trapper watched it, teetering like a drunk above him, its eyes even half closed. Then its jaw lowered like it was going to say something. But no sound came out and it toppled forward and came down heavy and dead on the hurt man.

Man and bear lying in some kind of embrace. Him with the wind knocked out of him and immobilized under its weight. Things awfully quiet. Then he gasped and sucked in breath and his eyes were very wide looking up through the branches into the heights of the sky above. Those old trees now with one more story to tell spectating above him. His head beside the bear's. He breathed in a hornet's nest and they stung at his insides. He just lay there a moment in utter shock, feeling the calmness of the breeze entirely out of place cooling his sweaty face. Drew in a laboured breath under heavy weight, then drew in another.

He looked to the side, the only side he could turn his head to, and a few paces away he saw some wild little cherub frozen in perfect archer form. The boy's release hand still up and trailing away behind him. Like he'd been taught. The kid standing statued there looking something mythical. To the man's eyes, something holy. The boy was still staring at the side of the bear where the buried arrow had gone in seeking out a heart to stop. Still his release hand that had loosed that fated dart hadn't come down. So the man just watched him a second, he couldn't move anyways. Holy hell. The boy's eyes were unblinking and his eyebrows were bent over them as if they were funnelling a stare so intense it might have just bored through that bear and blown a hole out the far side and the trailing arrow just happened to come along for the ride. Holy hell. Somehow he had made this thing. Or at least half of him he had. This boy was his own making, his own blood. And that blood beat damn hot right then.

"I see you elected for the heart shot," he wheezed up to his little guardian.

For the first time the boy took his eyes off the bear. He turned his gaze to his dad. His eyebrows softened. "Did you see me?" he said.

If the trapper's chest would have allowed him to laugh he might have. "I missed that one," he said hoarsely. He said to the boy, "Thanks."

With the kid grabbing a heavy foreleg and him pushing up from below they rolled the bear off him. He got up to his feet, slowly. Stayed bent a second. The kid with two hands withdrew the knife stuck in the bear and wiped its blade on the grass then closed it and handed it to him. He clipped it inside his pocket. He felt at his cheek bleeding from the string lash, and that was the least of his problems. The trapper ached but he could walk. Wheezed though he could breathe. Standing there he lifted up his tattered shirt to look at his chest and the boy said oh wow and the trapper let the shirt back down. He took a step and bent and grabbed the protruding arrowshaft and pulled it through its original course and handed it, bloody shaft and all, to the marksman who'd sent it. "We'll put that above your bed," he said. "Or mine."

He hobbled over to where his pack lay and found his canteen. Sat down with his back against a tree. Drank water. Put his wrists over his bent upright knees. Took it in a minute. A hulking black mound of fur a little ways off. A boy picking up a broken bow that lay among ferns. Birds, some of them chirping. The trapper just listened and watched and breathed while feeling the feeling of almost dying, of leaving the boy alone. As well the relief of not. Shook his head. Guilt and joy and fear mixed with the ache from his wounds all throbbing within him at about equal magnitude. The woods so radiant like the place had just been polished. He held up his hand to see if it shook. It did not. His heart was pounding though, not rapidly but deeply, like some sacred big drum only struck at ceremony.

The boy walked over carrying two bows. He sat down beside him and they shared the wide trunk and that little cherub brought him back to reality.

"Why'd your string break?" the boy asked him. "Was it from when I kicked the arrow on it?" He had the broken string that hung from the bow in his fingers and was turning its frayed end. Raised it up so the man could see. "Do you think?"

He looked at the frayed string. Then the boy. Then broke from that shared gaze and off into the woods. "Nah," he said. "Probably a mouse chewed at the wax in the night."

The kid was squinting up at him like he was looking for a tell at a poker table, looking for a sign of soft untruth in those eyes that were looking away. His dad reached out stiffly then pulled the kid's toque down to cover those squinting eyes.

They each had their own first aid kit and he took his out and disinfected the cuts on his chest and arms. There was a tensor bandage better suited to an injured wrist or knee but he got two wraps of it around his chest and thought that the dressing plus the backpack straps would keep it from swelling up until they got home. His ribs were very sore but he thought maybe just one got fractured with a few more bruised.

They went back over to the dead bear. "He's huge!" the kid said and used two hands to lift up a paw with its rubbery pad nearly three times his own hand size. "Thank you, bear," the boy said. The trapper just looked at the bear.

They went to work skinning it out for hide and meat. Two knives surgically placed. The furred belly opening up like a zipper. The boy reached in and cut the windpipe while the trapper cut around the anus, then they eased out a hot load of organs, a gut pile with a busted heart rolled onto the earth. Liver excised. The trapper pointed out two small punctures in the bear's left lung. "See, I had him."

"Yeah right," said the kid. They made long cuts following the direction of the hairline down the four legs and one under the jaw then pulled and sliced the hide from the fatty sublayer, and the animal was shed of its hide with the ease of a hostess helping you out of your coat. It didn't take long and they were both bloody to their elbows and nowhere else.

"Do you think the wolves will be here tonight?" The boy wiped his arms and hands on the newly frostless grass.

"Probably. If a wolverine or another bear or coyotes haven't gotten to it. First the birds though." And he pointed with the knife to two black and silent figures in a leafless ash tree. "Already here," he said.

They popped the hindquarters from their hip sockets while leaving the hamstring tendons intact allowing them to hang those heavy quarters off the ground by a tree branch they'd delimbed. Draped the hide over those meaty quarters to protect them from flies and birds while they were gone. Maybe they could have packed it all out at one go if his ribs weren't smashed up. But the cabin wasn't so far away and the afternoon not so late and if his body felt up to it after the first trip they could do two before dark. "See how it goes," he told the kid. With their field processing finished and their heavy packs waiting on the ground loaded with meat, he took in the sight of the bear once more. Big furry head attached to its naked body. Looked over at what so recently was an imposing presence. He left his pack on the ground and walked over to the carcass.

Of course it wasn't personal: it had been attracted to the sound of food, it hunted, it then fought what fought against it. That wasn't personal or evil, just nature being nature. Good and evil, love and hate, compassion and vengeance—those dueling forces, where if it could be said such abstractions do have essence in the world, they're only the manifestations of the wild and stormy places within us all. He bent down. A pink tongue lolled out its closed mouth. A wet nose and half closed glassy eyes staring at nothing at all. He reached out and jabbed his thumb into one of those lifeless sockets and dug into that wet recess until his nail hit the curved skull behind it. And from that squirmy hole he wrenched out an eyeball that came away with a sucking sound. The bear now making some kind of sordid and prolonged wink. He stood back up and walked to his pack, ocular goo and pink strands hanging from his fist. Then he put the eye in his open pack and pulled the drawstring shut and sat back into the shoulder straps and pulled at a low branch hand over hand to winch and pivot himself up. Groaned doing it. He led and the kid followed and neither looked back. The load was heavy and his ribs hurt and his legs felt weak and it took him a little while before he stopped grinning.

15

They were walking a gametrail homeward. Unseen ravens cawed from a tree nearby and the boy noticed some matted ferns to their right and some hanging askew where the stems had been snapped. A pungency in the air. Their path was intersected by another path, faint but fresh. They could just make it out winding away into the forest. They stepped off their trail and towards a section of flattened undergrowth.

The kid went to crouch at what he saw but in lowering himself he was tipped off balance by his heavy load and fell on his behind. He leaned forward and touched the dead bear cub with his bow. "What happened to it?"

The blood seeping from its caved-in head was not dry and there were yet no flies. "A sow without her cub is going to breed again sooner," he said. "Some big boars hunt their own. I'd bet what's hanging on your back happened to that cub."

The kid didn't say anything, he just looked at that misshapen skull.

"Come on." He put his hand on the kid's shoulder below him, but the kid didn't look away from the cub, so the man held out his other hand blocking the view and the kid took it and the man pulled the boy up to standing and they hiked on.

When they reached the edge of their cleared land the trapper stopped and kicked a divot in the earth.

He dropped the eye with its pupil facing to the forest and covered it over. They were tired after that first trip. They were nearly sleepwalking in the dusk when they finished the second. At the shed he first helped the boy out of his pack then backed himself against a waist-high table to rest his own load while he unclipped its belt. Slowly eased his shoulders out from under the straps and his ribs panged from that twisting motion and his shirt was soaked through in sweat and spotted blood. Now out from under that dropped weight he felt like he was nearly floating. They'd age the meat a week at these cool temperatures, allow the muscle fibres to break down, age it for both tenderness and flavour. But tonight just get the meat separated and hanging to allow the air to cool it. That's all he had to do and he told himself that. He was wasted, the long day with two heavy hikes on its own was tiring enough, never mind getting in a fight with a bear and losing. At the top of his pack was the liver. He gave it to the boy and started telling him how to cook it but the kid cut him off saying I know how and took the liver to the cabin. He began hanging the meat by hooks from the rafters. The backstraps and tenderloins he placed in old cotton pillowcases they washed clean at the creek and reused. He tied their tops and hung them from above. Untied the game birds hanging off his pack then strung them each up from a single foot, like some macabre dance step.

After an unsuccessful hunt there's lots of work to do so now there was more. Eventually he'd cut the meat into steaks, grind and sausage some of it, then smoke it or wrap it fresh if it was cold enough to freeze. That can be a day's work on its own. Then detail all the gear clean of any blood, grass, and soil. Boots waxed with mink oil to keep them waterproof. Look for any knicks or tears from the terrain or a misplaced blade, for any buckles and straps stressed under a load. Keep things pristine so they don't fail out in the field. It's easier to touch up an edge than to start over from a dull one, so sharpen the blades, the broadheads. From where he was in the shed he could hear the cabin's stove door opening. He'd never seen it but he had actually heard a mouse could snap a bowstring chewing at the wax in the night, so it wasn't exactly a lie, he reasoned. I should have caught it though. Coulda been that nick was on a part of the string under the cam, someplace hidden. Even just a small one coulda been enough to weaken it under the pulling load. His arguing mind. Still though. I should have caught it. Sometimes you just get unlucky. He looked over at the bloody arrow. Or lucky.

When he came into the cabin the boy was serving dinner. The liver is the most nutrient-dense food on an animal and he had oiled it and seasoned it with salt and pepper then laid it in the cast iron's hot oil to sear. He had cubed potatoes boiling. The mushrooms he picked were sautéing. The man sat at the table and watched as he cut the bloody liver down the middle then halved one of those pieces and put the quartered servings on their plates. He wanted to say something to the kid but he didn't he just said, "Thank you chef."

He ate. Slowly. He chewed very slowly. Then sorta tilted his head in a wordless question and towards his shoulder like he was going to cough. Or like the swallowing of that bite made the shortlist of hardest things he'd done that day. He cut a large piece of raw onion and ate that, then another, then drank some water. "Pass them taters, please." He was watching the boy chew his first piece.

They didn't have lemons and he'd never seen Gran eat a lemon. But if she did, the trapper thought the boy's wrinkled-up face about approximated it. The kid spat that ragged grey morsel to his plate. The trapper hardly ever swore and he'd never heard the boy yet, but if the kid was going to right then he'd have allowed it this once. Grave times call for serious language. But the kid just said *eww* then stared at it. Looked over at his dad. "That's disgusting," the boy said.

The trapper laughed at him and when the boy finished drinking all his water the boy laughed too.

"I just figured that's how you liked your liver cooked, a purist for that strong and wild flavour." He spooned potatoes and mushrooms from the bowl to the boy's plate. "It's not like muscle meat, is it. You have to purge it in water a few times, season it. Flour it heavily. And then even still it's more a meal of fried onions with a side of liver."

"Do we have to eat it?"

"I was hoping you'd ask." He forked the liver from the kid's plate to his own then back to the serving dish in the kitchen reuniting that liver as a nearly intact but wholly unpalatable organ. "We'll try something different with it tomorrow." He left the cabin then shortly returned with two grouse breasts that he seasoned, and after wiping the pan of its remnant liver stain, laid the wild chicken to fry in fresh oil. Minced garlic from dried bulbs that hung overhead next to the hanging pans. When the grouse breasts had cooked through he sliced each in half and put them on wholewheat sourdough buns with more raw onion. Layered on the last of the season's lettuce leaves. It was one of the kid's favourites. His too.

After dinner he cleaned and took water warmed from the stove and filled the stoppered kitchen sink and washed the dishes. The boy asked him if *woulda* was a proper contraction and the man said if you woulda just got the dictionary from the bookshelf like I'd told you to last time you woulda known the answer on your own. When he was done rinsing the last of the dishes, the remaining blood he hadn't washed off his wrists the first go had coloured the dishwater red. The boy had been quiet, and when the trapper finished and turned he saw the boy's head lying on his folded arms over his grammar workbook. He looked at him sleeping there and almost begrudged the fact that he was going to make him carry him up to bed with his chest aching as it was. But he didn't begrudge him. "I'm just your packer," he said quietly. He carried him up the stairs, and when he wasn't grimacing he was smiling. Ducked the rafter and laid him down to bed. Above the bed, hanging from nails driven in at imperfect angles, were crude trinkets and crafts only of any worth to a child. A couple small animal bones attached together by a piece of string. A small branch with illegible markings scrolled into the bark and split down its middle to hold a stone. You'd think it some manner of voodoo, witchcraft—nope, just the artifacts of a funny kid. He sat with the funny kid, watched him, mirrored the kid's easy and rhythmic breaths and that helped calm his own shallow and sore ones. What would have happened if it brought that last thrust down? Cave me in, crush my lungs? Would you have gotten away, little boy? Would you have been alright? He thought that actually he might have been. The kid was smart he could see that. Even before his eyes he could see the changes, him getting better at everything sometimes daily. It was actually incredible. And he knew a lot already. Probably he'd be okay. Would you? He almost asked him that out loud. Just wondering it made his stomach pit up as he sat there. How could I have let that happen?

He got up a bit laboured and went back down the stairs and out to the shed then returned to the cabin. At the stove he dipped half a rag into the warmed water. Carefully wetted and wiped clean what he held in his hands. Spun it and it shined and he dried it with the part of the rag he hadn't dipped. On the highest book-shelf at the far right was a book he told the kid not to touch. He didn't actually care if the kid touched it or not and he knew in saying that to him he likely would touch it when he wasn't around. It was a decoy. Because at the far left on the highest shelf was a partic-ular book he didn't want the kid to touch. That's the one he reached up for now and when he opened it, its pages naturally parted. He took out that folded paper with the heart on it he'd kept safe to give to the boy. The man didn't unfold it and he never had. Sometimes he'd try to imagine what she had written. The reason he didn't read it was that she wrote it for the boy and he respected that. It was between them. He wanted to sleep very much but that could wait. He carried her note and took a candle and paper and a pencil and the other item he still held in his hands then went back up to the loft.

16

earing the stove's muffled burn coming from downstairs, feeling its risen warmth where he sat in the loft's bedside chair, the trapper put the candle on the small table. Lit it. The boy looked deep asleep. He laid the cleaned arrow with its shiny broadhead level across two nails on the wall above his sleeping head. This little archer. You *are* Robin Hood. He watched him while the candle flame wavered in unseen drafts and with it the boy's face moved from light to shadow, light to shadow. He leaned to the table beside him and began to write. Some things are easier to write than say.

There were ideas they'd talked about before she died and he'd promised to bring them up one day with their boy. He planned to do that slowly over the years but after what happened today who knows about later—there's always a bear coming. Later is a bad gamble for things that matter now. Some ideas he'd lived or they'd been passed down or he'd read of them and though he hadn't lived it all so well himself he still wanted the boy to hear it. He was doing this as a father who after today was afraid he'd one day leave his son on his own too early, as his own father had. There were things he wanted to say.

He drew a breath through his beaten ribs like a barbwire vest.

He wrote:

Little boy. I'm going to take some things from you with this. But I'll try to give something back. I don't want some of these things to be true but I think they are and I didn't want to tell you them and even as I walked up here I wasn't sure that I would or how this would end.

The boy slept.

There are lies in the world told often. They aren't even bad lies. They're nice lies. So nice I want them to be true. I mean that. They sound like this: Things are happening for a reason. The world cares about you. All hard things are there for growth. People that hurt you are there to teach you. When you have loss it's to make space for something else to take its place. Things will work out in the end.

He wrote:

I wanted to tell you them too because they're nice things. But she said pretty lies are still lies and better hard truth. Alright. And I'm sorry they're not true because I want them to be. I want to believe them and maybe they'd make you feel good and maybe you'd tell someone too one day. She said some pretty words are still empty and there's not always solace in the truth but there is a type of strength in knowing it. If we wanted to raise you strong we'd need to raise you honest.

He felt like he was rambling already. He looked at the boy. She would've talked a lot with you about this and would've said it better. He spoke that in his mind, he didn't write it.

He wrote:

She said start with the innocent, it has to work for them if it's going to work at all. What do you tell the fawn being eaten alive by wolves? What do you tell the child born into a house of abuse? The people digging mass graves when droughts caused famine and a whole community starved? The hurting and the ruined, tell them everyone you meet has something to teach you, that they were a bad person in a past life and whatever other lies. No. Start with the innocent, she said.

The blanket was already at the boy's chin but he touched it up anyways.

I'm sorry. Life can be hard and not for a reason. Sometimes it's hard because it's hard. Sometimes it's hard a person's whole life and that life is short and then they die just like plants die and maybe that's it. Nobody knows for sure but I think that's how it is.

He stopped and looked about in the semidarkness like he was waiting for someone to dispute his irreverence or what more was to come. Only heard the boy's soft breaths and the stove's muffled burn. He looked back to the page.

And mostly fairy tales don't exist. Believe them and you think that's how it's fated to be and if one day you find out it's not exactly the case that comes at a cost. Relationships break down and many people live their days alone and for a lot of unions that do last not all the people are always so happy. Love is not guaranteed. He underlined that sentence. *You are not entitled to it nor anything else except some air for a time if you're lucky. Love is loyalty and determination and compromise as much as it's laughter and candlelight. But if you're lucky it can be those things too and you're more likely to get that with effort. I hope you find what I once had. You'll need some luck so I wish it for you.*

He stopped writing and for a minute maybe more he thought about her. Then he wrote on:

143

Sometimes when life gets really hard some people don't keep going. It got hard and they gave up and it's not because they're weak, they just hit their own limits. That's what they had. I think it's hardcoded and if you found a bit of strength to go further and think you pushed yourself beyond what others could have—that's what was hardcoded. Nobody pulls themselves up from their own bootstraps. Not really. But you can't know your limits beforehand. She died and my heart too. Maybe things get better but maybe they don't. Some will say brighter days ahead and maybe there are and maybe there are not. Nobody knows. But for certain you won't know if it gets better without trying to keep on. Turned out my heart regrew. You did that. It doesn't happen for everyone and some people will run out of time and die broken. But you never know what's over the next hill and things can change quickly. That is true. In that meantime I hope you find the strength to defend love. Defend it from yourself.

He looked up at the boy then the candle then back down to the page and aimed to finish:

If you ever get really low, lost, hungry or hurt you just try to call forth whatever it takes. And whatever it takes is alright by me. I know you're capable of incredible things when tested because it's in your bloodline. Not me, not Granddad. The human bloodline, the whole thing. So you find some place to push off from. Call forth whatever makes you feel something. Wake it up in you.

He had to stop to rest his cramping hand and he put down the pen. He bent to the kid's sleeping ear and just whispered so very silently: "If you're hurting bad one day, bad enough you feel you can't go any further, think of me. I'll be listening. Just point your back to

the north winds. I'll breeze you forward, little man."
He picked the pen up and wrote beside the dreaming
child:

I want to instill in you how short life is. If you remind
yourself this is all just temporary, things start to shine. For
me they do.

The arrow above the boy was glinting in the candlelight and he reached out and spun the shaft slowly
where it lay across the two nails and the shining broadhead moved coloured shards of cut light over the boy's
face.

Little cherub. If you believe these things then I've
taken away some of your compass points. But truth can't
make you more lost it just shows you've been navigating
with a bent needle and I hope I'm straightening you out
not making it worse. She said a false compass is worse
than none at all. So what have you got left? Choose your
own way. I hope you have the courage to do that. Keep
what matters close at hand. Be tolerant of others that see
it differently but defend your values from those that would
compromise them. Mostly that'll be your own self. Here's
what I think: Life matters and there is beauty. Laughing
children are better than crying ones. And most things pale
in comparison to love. And you can love for love's sake. Not
to get it back, not to take you somewhere. It can be some-
thing that stands on its own. I mean that. So be worthy
of it.

The man writing there was wrapped up as a scared
father who'd so recently seen that life could be taken
too soon and many things were coming to mind and he
wanted to write them all, wanted to write a thousand
things and everything even trivial things in case they

might help in any way, how to seed the garden and how to fix the roof and what to read and silly things and just tell the boy every single idea he could think of like he was putting armor on his little knight and sharpening his blades before he went off for whatever battles awaited. And also the opposite, just wanting to tell him it's good to be kind and open and gentle too sometimes. But he knew he could never say it all. So lastly he wrote:

Remember this: you're going to die. Then remember this too: you're going to die. Ask yourself what matters. Then struggle and take risks for that. There's worse things than failure. If there's a chance to be in the service of others, do so. Keep your word, both to others and yourself, and it's that second one that will be harder. Lastly, he wrote, *Get out of the cabin in the woods, at least for a while. Boy, we got lucky to have even gotten a shot is how I see it. Try to make it count. The world of storms and famines and cold and hard things spinning in space doesn't care about you, owes you nothing, you're not special to it.*

He breathed in and he loved hornets and he loved barbwire.

Just to me you are. To me you are. You are loved, little boy. Even if one day by nothing other than your memory of me.

He leaned forward in the candlelight in the warm cabin and gently kissed the boy on his forehead and that'd be the last time he did that.

His hand was sore 'cause he hardly ever wrote but he was finished anyways and he read it over. He folded the pages down the middle. Then he took her small and folded note with the heart on it and put that on top of a book on the boy's night table, and he took what he'd just written down the stairs and opened the stove and put the papers in the stove and watched them burn. Telling the boy to find his own way then telling him all the ways to do it didn't make all that much sense to him and if he'd done any good raising him so far he'd figure it out on his own and most of what he'd written down he'd not lived all that true himself and that made him feel like something of a fraud and hopefully he'd shown the boy a few things already and with any luck maybe the rest they could both work on together.

And he knew she'd have said it better anyways and whatever she'd written to him would be all he needed anyways.

17

The stove's door hinge squeaked and the trapper heard, from his bedroom on the main floor, the kid blowing up a little flame, then logs laid and the fire sparking as it caught. "Morning," the man called to him through the open door. His breathing was still rough but he hadn't swelled up anymore during the night.

"Morning," the boy said dully.

"How'd you sleep?"

The kid didn't answer.

"Did you see the arrow?"

"Yeah," he said quietly.

The trapper didn't ask him about the note. "Not a good sleep?"

"I dreamed of the bear."

"Of the bear?"

"Yeah."

"What about the bear?"

"He was chasing me. He was smart." The kid was talking from near the stove so he could barely hear him.

The man eased his back up the wall at the head of the bed. "Sounds scary," he said. "Did he get you?"

"He almost got me. It was really scary." The boy had come to the bedroom door. "Do you think it's because I killed him?"

The man thought. "I dunno. Would that have changed your decision?"

The kid was looking at the bandage over the man's ribs. He shook his head no. "But do you think he'll be there every night?"

"No. I'm sure he won't. He'll move on."

"How do you know?"

"I know. Watch. He'll go away. Don't worry I get scary dreams too. But they don't last."

"He was really fast. I tried to run."

The warming stove was popping the wood of the cabin.

"Maybe you could try talking to him."

"What should I say?"

"Well. Is there anything you want to say?"

The boy was looking down and didn't answer.

"You could ask him what he wants."

"Could I say I'm sorry?"

"I guess that's up to you. You can say it if you are. Are you?"

The kid took a second. "I don't know. We don't like killing the animals but we do it when we need to. He was going to kill you. And we even took his meat too. Do we apologize for things we'd do again?"

The man sitting up looked at the pine-board ceiling. "I don't know if we do. That's a good question. But I'm glad you sent that arrow. I know that."

"Me too."

"I guess you could apologize if you are sorry you had to take his life. If that's true then you can be sorry about it and wish it hadn't happened the way it did but still know you'd do it again. If you had to. And if you mean it maybe it'll make you feel better. Maybe that's what he wants to hear and he'll move on."

"What if he doesn't listen and keeps coming?"

"His reaction is out of your hands, isn't it. You just do you."

The boy said he'd think about it. Said maybe he wasn't sorry, he wasn't sure.

"Alright. You think about it. While you're churning that over, brew your ol' achin' dad a coffee."

The kid got their hot beverages going and their oats too. The midmorning light swathing the fireside table like it had been laid with a bronze tablecloth. He asked the boy through the smoke of his coffee, "What's seventeen plus twenty-nine?"

The boy said forty-six.

"Four multiplied by seven?"

He said twenty-eight.

"What's forty-four divided by seven?"

In general the kid wasn't a big fan of their home-schooling and seemed even less so of this morning's pop quiz. "I don't know," he said.

"Yeah, me too. Was hoping you did. I genuinely wanted to know that one."

The boy didn't look up from eating his oats.

"How would you feel about skipping school today?"

The boy stopped midchew. Squirreled his oats to the side of his mouth to conform with the table manners an older generation he never actually met had set in place, so as not to risk having this rare offer rescinded. He swallowed. "All I had to do was save your life, huh?"

"That's good for a four-day school week every time. Every single time. Do you want to fish and hunt grouse?" he asked the boy.

"Yes."

151

"Hunt rabbit?"

"Yes I do."

"Alright then. I'll make your lunch while you get your gear ready. You be back here an hour before dark."

The boy didn't squirrel the oats this time. "By myself?"

"Don't talk with your mouth full."

"By myself?"

"Are you okay with that?"

"I dunno."

He waited for the kid to expand on his insecurities. He didn't.

"You'll be fine," said the trapper.

"Hmm," he said. "I dunno. Maybe not. No I don't think I want to." The boy asked him what he was going to do.

"Just take it easy around here and let my chest heal up some. Clean up a bit. Maybe work on that bear hide and the meat."

"Yeah, maybe I'll just help with that and wait for you and we'll go together when you're ready. Maybe I actually should do some grammar, I probably need it you know." The kid tilted his head trying to sell it.

"Cute. You'll be okay out there. You know what you're doing. I've seen it. You're ready. Let's ask that bear if you're ready."

"I'm scared," he said.

The kid just killed him sometimes. "That's okay," he told him. "Good. That means you're human. I was scared too the first time I went alone. I'd be concerned if you weren't scared. Some things still scare me."

"No they don't," the kid said.

"Some things do. Promise. But we do it anyway. We suck it up and do it. That's what makes us men."

"Girls can't do that?"

"Well. Yeah. That's what makes us humans, I mean. Strong ones. We do hard things sometimes."

He was looking down and turning his spoon in his empty bowl. He kept turning the spoon. "Can I take her note?"

"Her note?"

"Yeah. I found it this morning. You put it there."

"Yeah, okay. Sure."

The kid was thinking. "Alright. I guess so then."

"Alright. Good. Just go slow and watch where you put your feet and watch the forest and listen. Use your compass even if you don't need it."

"Alright."

"You'll be fine."

"But what if I get lost?"

"You won't, you know these woods and the land-marks. Watch the sun. Start heading back before it's even close to dark. In fact, I want you back here an hour before the sun sets. Just go slow and stay on the gametrails and everything will be fine. Do like as if I was with you."

The kid looked unsteady.

"You're good," he told him.

The boy was looking off through the window.

18

While the boy was putting on his hunting gear and lacing his boots his dad packed his lunch and water and first aid kit into his pack. He said, "Hey, if you have a problem you just start wailing on this sucker." And then dropped a whistle into the open pack. "But you won't have a problem." The man held up the pack and turned it away from himself with the shoulder straps open and the boy came over and put an arm through one then the other. The trapper went to buckle the waistbelt for him but the kid said I got it so he just kinda stared blankly with his hands half outstretched while he watched him buckle it himself. Then he went and got his bow for him that was hanging in the shed.

In the fall morning and on the cabin porch all geared up with his bow in hand and knife on his pants and pack on his back, the boy smiled nervously. They both did.

"You'll be fine." The man said that like he was telling his own self that. He nodded at him. "Good luck. Have fun."

"Okay. Thanks." The kid looked around. "Which way should I go?"

"Your call."

"Okay." He squinted then turned and looked straight ahead. Nodded upwards. "I'll go that way."

"Good call."

The small hunter looked at him, then stuck out his fist at his side for a bump, and his dad bumped it back. Then the man just pulled him in and hugged him.

The boy set off and walked alone into that northern forest for the first time. As he did he looked back several times and waved to the man on the porch who was waving back. And when the kid had walked across the clearing and into the woods and could no longer be seen, the cabin door still had not closed.

***

In the late morning sun the boy breathed deeply of the forest smells. Light shined in angled shafts between trunks of paper birch and black ash, between jack pine and white pine. Small birds played and twittered in the low and leafless brush and others larger flew overhead. Where he could see the sky through the trees it was blue. He looked to the forest as if seeing it for the first time. You can be prepared to go it alone and know what to do but you won't know what it feels like or what it even looks like until you're finally out there alone. He'd stop and just listen sometimes and not so much for animals. It was remarkable to him just how immediate the sounds were. How sharp and immense it all seemed. There was an acuteness to it like someone had struck a tuning fork beside his head. For the first time it felt as if he was wired up to the woods he'd lived in his whole life. He now the sole decider of when to wait or move on, turn or go straight, shoot or not shoot. He rolled that idea over in his head, felt both its thrill and its weight.

Thin glass sheets iced over the puddles in the shadows of trees. He stopped at the first frozen puddle he saw, lightly tapped it with the toe of his boot. It spider-web-cracked. Then he stepped heavier on it and caved it in, its centre pooling. After walking a ways farther he took out his knife and picked up a stick and tested the knife's edge he already knew was sharp. Then walked with his unfolded knife in his hand even though he knew he wasn't supposed to.

He stalked under the tall trees alone in the forest as a wildman trapper from one of his stories, bearded and buck-skinned with a raccoon toque. He was an old Indigenous hunter before even the fur trading days and the bow in his hand was made of ash wood and the arrows of birch and the string was braided sinew of an animal he'd slain earlier that day. Ask him about it. Arrowhead of flint he'd knapped to shape before he set out. When he came across a cedar tree that had grown out of a lying cedar tree, he stopped and looked at it for a minute as it was the first time he'd noticed a nurse tree before. He also realized he'd been singing to himself.

When he was not lost in his imagination he remembered to put the wind in his face, but not so long after he'd find it at his back and he'd get frustrated and correct his course, then once again notice the wind trailing him and wondered how long his scent had been blowing to whatever was ahead. Whatever was no longer ahead, he thought. Sometimes the wind just veers and backs and swirls on thermals from temperature variations caused from different terrain features and it can't always be helped, but he didn't know that.

He hadn't seen any animals. It was well past midday and the wind was cold and so was he.

His hands were always the first things that got cold. Even in gloves they easily turned white. His dad said that happened to him too, but he said that to everything so who knows. Once when they were hunting last year in the snow his hands felt frozen to the bone— but he didn't tell him 'cause he thought that next time he might not bring him back out, and cold or not he wanted to hunt too. When his dad wasn't watching he took his gloves off and saw they were white at their tips and so he blew on them. His dad heard. Came over and kneeled down and took one of his hands in his own and looked at their colour, their lack of it. So his dad unzipped his own coat. Then holding the boy's wrists he put those skinny little iced hands under his sweater up into his own armpits. Little frigid digits in his hairy pits made the man gasp then shiver and them both laugh. Crouched there looking at one another smiling as their breaths plumed up together, one set of hands in the other's armpits. Like the smaller was just about to lift the larger up, or had just finished doing so and was setting him down. Made the kid smile now remembering that.

He switched the bow back and forth between his hands and whatever one was free he balled up in his coat pocket and hunted on. Let my eyes do the walking. He slowed his travel and tried to focus his mind and he moved deliberately and sometimes not at all. Sometimes his only motion was raising the binoculars up from around his neck. He glassed branch limbs and bases of trees, patches of open forest, and then even up to the open sky where he glassed the edges of clouds, eyes wandering where his young mind couldn't help but take him. He'd take a step and wonder if he was going too fast and then he'd slow down but then wonder how to get anywhere at all, so he'd speed back up. The forest was still because this erratic little hunter was not. The forest quiet like an audience at a hack performance.

Then the first heckler. A few sharp chirps and a pause, then a barking chitter. Then another joined too. He spent a couple hours zigzagging in the variable winds listening to relentless barking while seeing no sizable life. Then on a low tree limb at a comically short range perched one of his nemeses. It sat upright on its back legs, its small arms held to its chest with its paws actually clasped together. Their eyes locked. The boy slowly shook his head no at it. Give me a break you little bastard. The squirrel took that as its cue and barked once, looking him in the eye. Understood the boy's glaring silence as signal to continue and it began pulsing endlessly while its tail flinched. Then so too did its jerk-off brother somewhere unseen. Then the forest echoed with them in a chorus of jackasses. The boy brought his bow up and put that spasming furry chest under a sight-pin. At that distance it's about ninety-nine out of a hundred. But he didn't draw back and wasn't even all that serious about it when he'd raised it up in the first place. He lowered the bow, though didn't dislike them any less, and walked on under furred chatter.

Into the afternoon the wind picked up and swirled about playing with the forest. What he saw ahead of him stopped him in his tracks and he just stood watching.

Huge falling maple leaves all yellow and curled at their edges fell in twisting columns from an old tree. It didn't look real and he thought it might not be. There were other trees around it and some older maples too, but not like this one. Giant tree broadly branched and the sun lighting it up made it almost look like it glowed or was on fire. He still hadn't moved. The gold leaves fell turning and already a pile mounded around its trunk. He walked to it. Under its canopy the leaves came to his knees and the pile was dry and light and crinkled loudly as he moved his legs through it. He knew he was making noise, yet he swished on. This discovery was as good as finding a mature buck and he'd give it its due. He put his bow down on the pile and looked straight up into the dizzying leaves that softly clattered against bare branches and each other. He turned slowly, and in turning almost fell over. He stopped and held his arms out in front of him and some drifted down beside him and eventually one did fall to lie in his open arms, he didn't even have to move. Looking down at it cradled there. He took it by its edges and held it up to face the sun. A leaf wider than his own chest. The sun behind it showed its dark veins and inky blotches. As if he was looking at a map. A map not where to get to but where he was. *You are here.* The veins and blotches and the light behind. He took his backpack off laying it beside his bow on the leaf pile while the leaves drifted down around him and he sat down cross-legged and just sat still. Listening to the gentle clatter of falling leaves. Looking at this one he held. Smelling for them in the air. And feeling such a feeling, what to say other than thanks, and he did say that. But you'd have to ask him to whom.

In the sun his mind moved to other places, to the dream-bear, to his dad by himself at the cabin healing, to how he had never killed a buck yet and how much he so wanted to his first time out alone. Could you imagine, he thought to himself. He looked down at the big yellow leaf in his lap. Where to go next. Then with his pointer finger he traced upwards along the leaf's midrib.

He left the timber for a small glade and was taking high steps through sagebrush when he flushed out a cottontail. It bolted like it'd been kicked in the ass to start it on its way, white ball of a tail bouncing as it ran fast then darted sharp right only to hairpin back left without losing any speed in zigzag turns trying to shake whatever it thought chased it. Except for the kid's head snapping back and forth trying to follow those crazed vectors, he stood frozen. Then lost it in a sight-trail of moving low bushes. Finally only heard it far away and faintly rustling. Then neither seen nor heard nor rabbit at all. Just gone. He hadn't even raised the bow.

"Huh," he said. He raised the bow.

He stalked over quietly to where he'd last seen the brush shaking, trying to creep up on a rabbit that knew it was being hunted. A strategy about as bountiful as walking with an open pack and hoping a goose might just fill it from the fallen sky.

Later in the rabbitless afternoon he took off his pack and sat at the edge of a meadow to regroup. Took out the leaf and though he had tried to be careful it had cracked some. He laid it in front of him. He had no particular use for his knife but he drew it and unfolded it and laid that down beside the leaf. Drank water and ate a bun with grouse meat for a late lunch. He pulled a wide-bladed grass and put it between his thumbs then brought his cupped hands to his mouth and blew out a reedy noise a few times. Wasn't trying to call anything, just wanted to do it. He looked around at the meadow. Some sedge or wood reed grasses bowed as the light wind warmer now drifted through them. He pulled a longer one and pinched off its dirty root then put the grass in his mouth and chewed on the stem. Deliberated. Not sure if there were grouse in that area of the forest. Didn't have much luck with the rabbit. Even me and Dad together so far haven't seen a buck this season, he thought. Sitting there looking around knowing evening wasn't so far away and this wasn't exactly how he thought the day would play out. Took the stem from his mouth and threw it. And then he remembered. He took from his pant pocket her small note that wasn't even smudged yet. Unfolded it.

***

The trapper had been watching the recessed shadows of the forest's edge for nearly two hours and when finally the boy did emerge he could see his head was down, not even looking at the cabin. Saw him barely raising his shuffling feet to walk. His first thought was to scold the boy for pushing the light, as it was already getting hard enough to see. But when he saw if it wasn't for the boy's waistbelt his backpack might've just fallen off his shoulders for all that they slumped, he knew what had happened. The same thing that happened to him his first time too.

"How many moose did you shoot us, little man?"

The kid just shook his head.

"Big ol' stag bucks you get us three I'll follow you to where you got 'em strung up out there and already gutted?"

"No," he said with his head still hanging. He unbuckled and dropped his pack that thudded to the porch then he set his bow on it carefully. "I didn't see anything." His voice cracked. His eyes wet. "One rabbit."

"You got a rabbit?" The man said kinda stoked.

"No I mean I didn't get him." The kid rarely raised his voice. "Only saw one rabbit. And he ran away before I could shoot."

The kid told him about everything that had gone wrong over the course of the day. "I mostly didn't know what to do." The kid wiped his eyes.

The trapper wanted to laugh as it was all pretty endearing how much it mattered to the boy. Couldn't hold back smiling though. He put his hand on the kid's back and pulled him in to where he stood.

"Hey. Look. Do we always get something when we go out together?"

The kid shook his head.

"Are you hurt?"

"No."

"Did you get lost?"

"No," he said.

"Did you quit out there?"

"Uh-uh."

"Did you learn anything?"

He thought about it. "I don't know."

"C'mon in, we'll talk about it. You just didn't feel like ruining anyone's day out there. You were just giving them fair warning you'd be coming back so git yerselves ready 'cause it's game on next time." He wiped the boy's nose on his sleeve. "You did just fine. Let's eat."

The hanging yellow bulb inside the warm cabin gave a soft lighting and the table was set with candles. Take something from the cold and the damp and the dark and warm it and light it up and feed it and see how it feels. The boy washed his hands and face in the kitchen sink then sat at the table where on their plates with the late-season greens, the man was serving them each a thick bear steak cut from the tenderloin. Red juices from the meat pooling out encircling the halved and sautéed brussels sprouts. Sourdough garlic bread. The boy said, "Wow."

The kid was at work with the pepper, the steak now about total granular black and his dad said, "Looks like you take a touch of bear with your pepper. I respect a man that knows what he likes." The kid smiled but didn't break from his focus of peppering. Thought lines between his eyebrows told the table that his mind was hashing something out.

"Dad," he said. "They knew where I was the whole time. I tried to hunt like we always do but I was not good out there. I sucked." He looked at him. "Why do you think?"

The man was cutting into his own steak. "It's different going alone. Go easy on yourself, you're just learning."

"So you're done learning?"

"No. But when you're young there's some big first things to figure out. We all suck when we start. Nobody does anything well day one. Not even the owls. I was no different, same for my dad same for my granddad too. You want to get good, you just do the work. The talents of the great is a story of their work ethic. That's it. Every day get a little better and stack those days together." He nodded the boy's way and the boy passed him the pepper saying don't use it all.

"Natural ability exists but raw and untrained it's not worth much. A six-foot arm span doesn't make an Olympian, the years in the swimming pool do. Someone might hear or see better than almost anyone. Like my dad saw like an eagle sees. But that's not what made him good. Days and more days practising how to stalk and when to move and when not to. Getting it wrong a lot but always trying to do it better. Not just to see well but what to look for. And discipline. Discipline is huge. It's almost everything. Do it when it's hard. Especially then. Just trust the process and show up and sometimes improvements can be lumpy." He chewed and swallowed and said, "There's no secret." He drank water and set it back down. "Here's the secret: Work. Talent comes after work, not before. Like Granddad would have said—"

"—Got it."

He looked at the kid blankly. "What?" His mouth was full.

"I get it. Practise."

He just stared a second and then went back to chewing. "Alright then," he said.

"I'll take the pepper back if you're done with it," the kid said.

19

The sauna was small and square with cedar log walls and a slightly pitched roof and a small potbelly stove whose chimney vented out the back wall. Benches built in to the walls. That night he went out back and loaded the stove and started the fire. Even later in the year in the middle of winter, fifteen minutes was all it took to raise its temperature hot enough you could slow-cook brisket in it if you wanted to. One afternoon wrapped in a towel he walked out to the sauna with tinfoiled deer ribs under his arm that he set on the bench beside him. After a half-hour when he had finished his sweat, he left the meat four more hours to cook until dinner.

The forced stillness and structured quietude of the sauna made it a simple pleasure and a contemplative place. Nothing but heat and sweat and a calm head and calm thoughts to think through ideas. Things he'd seen in the wilderness or ideas he'd read. And when the boy joined him, there was pleasant talk too. It'd be hard to disentangle any health benefits of the open pores and sweat-purge of toxins and increased heart rate, from the simple grounding effect of time in stimulant-free contemplation with nothing to clean or cook or fix or sharpen. It was a special place and that was why old cultures around the world had their versions too: steam rooms, saunas, sweat lodges. He only had to build it once and it would last a long time and that kind of asymmetrical payoff is not that common but they feel like treasures when they're found.

He had a candle and a book with him but hadn't yet opened it. In the early days of her passing he got some respite from the heartache by reading her favourite books, his eyes moving over the same words hers once had, being moved by what she'd been moved by. There was something to that, like they were travelling some road together. Though not one that took him to a place where the past was left behind.

He believed in words. Some words, not all words. Sometimes words could do great things, or undo bad ones, if said honestly and at the right time. Even just one word if it got where it needed to get could return a person out there lost in the woods. Words brought us the moon. The right combination would tell us how to live forever.

Some of the textbooks in their cabin were old enough that their theories had been overturned by others on the cabin's shelves. It made him a skeptical man. Made him question what can be trusted in navigating a world of uncertainty, what truths will last, and whether certain areas of knowledge were just self-contained puzzles. Maybe there were other ways of arranging the pieces that showed a different picture, told a different story, and one was not more true than the other—compasses among compasses each charged to their own metals. And where proofs told of some certainty, maybe they were constrained to their own abstract puzzle and we could never be certain of that truth's application to the world at large. But shining through the small sauna vent and lying on the floor was a patch of moonlight. White square patch. Science put a human on that distant rock and brought that human back safely. At least some theories must correspond truthfully to the world or people get blown up. Couldn't it be that simple? Science is not always right but surely it gets some things right, transplanting organs, such as it was. That seemed to make it categorically different and more trustworthy than other systems claiming knowledge, alleged truths arrived at through intuition or authority, divination or dogma.

His mother had made him medicine from hemlock and stinging nettle when he was a boy with breathing issues, coughs and allergies. She used beth root and bearberry and ginseng, among other wild plants too. She said it had been in their family for a long time and a lot of it came from Nôhkow. She called her that too. Those plants healed and that knowledge was credible—it was willing to put itself at risk, to die by its own sword. If those plants didn't work they'd have no effect or make things worse and so be rejected. All that process was of a relation to science if not one and the same. And how could you not respect all the sampling of various fungi it took to figure out which ones healed your ailments and which ones buried your delirious ass. Trial and error and coming up with good reasons for beliefs. And that's different than palm reading and telling the future in tea leaves, and he remembered bringing back newspapers from town in the wintertime when his mother herself would start the evening fire with the horoscope section.

The sauna door opened and a naked boy carrying his own book with his own candle walked in. Buck naked. The boy was also a type of truth. One beyond doubt. There in the dimly lit sauna the man was just grinnin'. "Evenin'," he said to the boy closing the door.

"Hi Dad."

After their sweat the boy said he was tired and took his book to read in bed in the loft where it was warmest anyways.

"Why don't you take the short rod tomorrow for casting."

"I want to take my bow." His voice coming down from the loft sounding like it was half asleep and half grumpy.

"You can still take your bow just strap the rod to your pack. Get us a dang fish for dinner."

The kid didn't respond. Then, "Okay," dreamily.

"Did you hear any planes out there today?"

"No." A sound more like a sigh than a word.

"Alright. Goodnight wildman," he said up to the boy.

The boy was asleep.

The trapper pulled the chain-switch turning off the overhead bulb and then brought the candles from the dinner table to a smaller table by the stove. He put a tin can on the warm flat of the stovetop then opened its cast-iron door, its warmth radiating out, firelight brightening the chairs in front. A butcher's apron hung in the kitchen and he lifted its neckband over his head then tied the waistband behind him and went to the shed and returned with the bear hide. He sat down with the long apron draped over his knee, the furred side of the hide overtop it. With a thin blade he sliced under the fat of the black bear and lifted the translucent chunks away to drop in the tin can. Warm pooling grease within. As he worked the hide he came to the first ragged little hole with three symmetrical blade cuts. Paused a second. Stuck the tip of his finger through the hole. Could still see those heavy forelegs hanging above him, shaggy fur with the long dark claws curling at the ends of those black pads ready to stomp out his life. Shook his head. He cut the fat away from the flaps of the arrow-hole then he looked to the other fireside chair out of an old habit that didn't die hard 'cause it didn't die at all. "Our strong boy, you should have seen him." He looked to her photograph on the bookshelf. Her brown picture eyes in the dusky light billowing up memories into his tired mind like swept dust. He was fading at his work and drifting off in the chair and his last sight below heavy eyelids were her eyes looking back at him. He watched them a second like they might blink.

20

They were eating breakfast and the boy was talking about his dream while feeling at his dad's ribs. They were still blue all over but the man said they looked worse than they felt. The trapper said, "You just hang in there, he'll leave you alone. He's just a dream-bear and you're a real boy and dream-bears can't hurt real boys. That's fact, it's in one of the books on the shelf. Look it up."

He asked the boy if he was okay going out alone again.

"I guess so."

"Why don't you come back and have lunch with me."

"Yeah, I'll come back at lunch."

"Alright, good. I waxed your string last night."

After breakfast he watched the boy walk out to the forest again and this time he only turned back once to wave. He cleaned up then finished skinning out the bear cape. He'd later salt the hide and in days to come would massage a tanning oil into it and he had a bottle of that in the shed. The last step would be working it over a wooden sawhorse to make it supple. He wasn't telling the boy his plans for it.

Come midday the boy came back to the cabin empty-handed but he seemed alright about it, seemed something had clicked with him hearing that his great-granddaddy just showed up and did the work and his granddad and his own dad too and so he would too and he'd get better every day a little bit at a time by doing the work. He'd been smiling since about the edge of the forest where he'd smelled the fresh baked bread wafting out to him. He hung his bow up outside and took off his boots on the porch and of those boots there wasn't much visible leather or laces to them, covered up to their tops in mud both dried and wet and with protruding sticks that weren't all that small. They looked about twice their normal size and sounded three times as heavy when he stomped them on the porch before taking them off. He came inside saying I'm hungry then sat fireside where he outstretched his legs towards the stove to warm up his feet in socks that dripped to the floor, his pants wet to his knees. In seeing all this the trapper didn't even ask 'cause the kid didn't mention it and he seemed fine about it anyways. So he just handed him his tea. They talked about hunting and the kid asked questions and they spread wild strawberry jam on the bread and drank black tea kept warm on the stove.

"Listen, we're doing a day's class in this one lesson so pay attention 'cause it's straight from my own daddy, your granddad. He said it worked in life like it worked in cards."

The kid drank from his mug patiently and he looked thoughtful because he was thinking about the forest and strategizing his hunt.

"Okay, in Granddad's words. Suppose you got a feeling," said the trapper, "that the river card is gonna come up a queen, like you just know it, and that'd make your two pair a full house. On the turn you push your chips in and get called by both players and so all three of you are all in."

The kid knew poker as they played heads-up together some nights.

"Everyone flips their cards over and you're losing to a better two pair and the other guy's boat. It's a big pot and so you're all nervously watching the dealer. He burns and turns. And there she is: that sweet and royal lady got laid down and you made your better full-house and get shipped the pot busting them both. Gut feeling—you knew it was coming."

The kid was paying attention now.

"Okay good story," the man said. "Go ahead and tell it. It's a romantic story and people like to hear them. But my dad said you operate that way over time boy against players using reason to back their judgments, in the end and over the long term you'll go bust every time. He said life is no different. You gotta use your head not just your belly. Do you get me?"

"No," said the boy.

"No, I mean that's what Granddad said to me, he asked me when I was a boy if I understood."

"Oh. What'd you say?"

"Well, I also said no. Okay my dad went on to say it's not just how often you'll make it on the river, it's how often but it's also its impact. It's those two things considered together, not just one or the other. The chances of it happening and then the payoff or the punishment." Now he looked at the kid. "Okay. What do you think of that?"

The boy wasn't even looking at him anymore he was staring beyond his outstretched feet into the fire.

"I have no idea what you're talking about. No, I don't get it."

"Alright, think of it this way. It's December and you want to jig for walleye but you're not sure if the ice is thick enough. But you think it's really likely the ice is thick enough. That's not where you stop thinking. *Hey.*" He snapped his fingers in front of the boy.

The kid looked at him.

"It's not just the likelihood of the ice holding your weight, it's that considered against the outcome too." He waited for the kid to nod or shrug or something. He didn't.

"What's the outcome here?" the trapper asked him.

"I dunno."

"No, think."

"A fish."

"Yeah a fish. And what if the ice doesn't hold?"

"Swimming."

"More like drowning if it's cold and you have your clothes on. So even if you think it's unlikely to crack, if you do bust through it, you drown."

The kid's tip of his sock was hanging off his foot and he reached out and wrung it and water sprinkled the floor.

"So it's still early winter and you're not sure. What do you do?"

"I dunno." The kid was over it. He just wanted to get back out hunting.

"No. Think. Answer. This is school. What do you do?"

He thought. "Well," he said. "Eat rabbit I guess."

"Okay. Eat rabbit. Correct." The trapper smiled to that answer.

"So how do you ever know when the ice is thick enough?" asked the boy.

"Good question. You just wait for someone dumber to go first then. Watch for big deer tracks. A bear. Even you just send your old dad out there to test it. I'll toss a big rock ahead." He drank the last of his tea. "The point is, unlikely events still matter if their impact is large. It works for both good or bad things. Keep it in mind."

He lifted the kettle warm on the stove with the tea bags still steeping and it poured out night-black and he drank and almost coughed and did wince, astringent something fierce. "Jesus," he said. "Anyways, your granddad suffered sometimes from not always practising what he preached. But I do think his general formula there was right. Must've got one of the inputs wrong. Up against a rigged deck. Something. On that note, lesson two: Don't bet your house on a card game."

"Got it. We done?"

"Alright, that's it. As you were." He got up first and went to the kitchen.

"I heard a wolf today. Only once, one howl," the boy said.

"Close?"

"Not that close."

"Which direction?"

The kid pointed north. Then he closed the stove and walked to the kitchen leaving wet tracks. "Was Great-granddad's dog really a wolf?"

"She was."

"How'd he get it? Just find it? Man. Imagine finding a little wolf pup. Can I have a wolf too? If we find one?"

"You have to find them in the spring when they're young. That's how he got his."

"Can I have one if we find one?"

"Maybe. Go get us our dinner first, we'll talk."

The kid liked that answer. He was at the cabin door about to head into the afternoon of his hunt when he got hit in the back with something. He turned and looked at the fresh pair of folded socks that lay on the floor behind him.

"Put 'em on."

The kid smiled. Put them on. Then backpack, bow, feet to forest.

A couple hours later he was following a gametrail towards a small lake. As the forest gave way to shoreline he could see a bit more of the water's edge with every step, so he slowed and scanned the closer he got. He was about to skirt right inside the tree line when he caught a bit of motion. A doe mostly hidden by the tall grasses separating them lapped the water. Small ripples moving over the glassy pond. She raised her head looking out across it. Then turned and stared his way. Blinked. He likely wasn't the most threatening looking thing she'd ever seen, maybe not even that same day. She hadn't spooked. If a deer sees you, you have two options. You can freeze bone still, and with its poor eyesight it might not decipher your shape from your surroundings, it might go on about its day. The second option is to act unthreatening and slowly look down and then away, like an uninterested animal, not a predator. The boy angled his head away from her and relaxed his posture, then watched with cornered eyes until his vision reddened. Relaxed them a second and returned to watch more. Maybe she'd have a buck with her. He lowered into the tall grasses. Unalarmed she returned to browsing some of the lush vegetation of the shallows, her jaw chewing side to side. She looked his way, but also turned and gazed other directions too in her general state of calm alertness. The boy watched enthralled. This was a first. She flicked her tail at a fly occasionally. Twitched an ear. The boy didn't even blink. She never stamped her foot nor snorted but she did gradually feed away from him. Eventually she stepped those slender legs gracefully up the pebbled foreshore making only a minor clatter and walked away into the forest.

He kept on looking to where she'd entered the forest and even as the minutes passed his heart was still racing. He couldn't wait to tell him. She didn't return and no animals arrived and the boy eventually took out the stubby rod and tied on a silver spoon. Shucked off his boots and rolled up his pant legs and waded into the cold water and cast a shiny lure for the fish to chase.

***

With some chores done the trapper picked out a book then set a chair out on the porch. He looked up often from the page. When he was reading he sometimes had the feeling that he'd arrive somewhere complete after he finished whatever it was that held his interest. Like he'd internalize some new way of looking at the world and everything would snap into place. But when he finished whatever book he was on, even if he had some new concept understood or skill attained, that feeling of completion still remained one step further out.

His eyes were on the forest's edge about as much as the book in his hands. What was the boy up to in that exact moment? Right then. Was he lost or in trouble? Was this too soon? Was this maybe a mistake? Sat there listening for a whistle he knew he wouldn't be able to hear all that far away anyways. Last fall the boy had asked about a rocket ship. He'd read about one in a story. That's easy. No, he had told the boy. Boys don't get rocket ships. Rocket ships didn't scare the trapper. This past spring the boy had been reading and he looked up and said it would be kinda fun to be on a soccer team. The trapper had almost dropped the dish he was drying. He smiled and said to the boy, I'm your team. The boy looked at him. Then just back to the book. The trapper glanced over to see what he was reading. It was about a fisherman. Next day early the trapper balled up an old sheet and roped it into a tight ball and when the kid got up they kicked it around outside. He did seem enthused for a while.

Wasn't it inevitable? He'd one day want what a tree didn't grow and the lake didn't hold and a book couldn't offer, and he'd ask for something I couldn't make him from the shed. The trapper looked up at the clear sky, storm clouds in his chest. Trapping furs is a dying trade anyways, he thought. The trapper watched the forest.

***

Early that evening the boy returned with a bony pike. He had gutted it but he hadn't strung it to his pack, he just carried it out in front of him like a trophy. You'd think he'd swum in there and wrestled it up off the bottom, proud as he looked walking up to the porch. Marched up the two steps and across the wood planks then held out his catch presenting it like he'd just fed the tribe, the clan. He had. "There you go," he said and nodded at his filleter. "Tell you about the doe I saw later when you're done." He said that all nonchalant-ly-like.

His filleter took the fish. Said, "Thank you. Mind the daylight next time."

The boy went and checked the cables of his bow then waxed the string and hung it up in the shed. Gave his gear a once-over. Cleaned his boots then set them close enough to the fire that they'd dry by morning, but not so close it'd crack the leather.

For several days their routine was unchanged. The kid was often bothered by his bear dreams, but dreams meant he was sleeping and he always woke recharged. Every day he would try to decipher the subtle rabbit prints in the soil and find better spots to hang his snares. The snows were very close now his dad said. With the kid out during the day the trapper was preparing for winter. Burying carrots in pails of sand to increase their shelf life, spreading out onions and potatoes to cure before hanging them in burlap sacks in the dugout cellar. He cold-smoked some of the bear meat and every other day would bake bread and when his ribs had mostly healed he split and stacked wood. A couple times he went out and picked wild mushrooms.

During most of his tasks his thoughts were looped: the kid, the coming winter, the woman, the kid. They hadn't seen another floatplane and that eased his mind some. It'd be even better though if those two pairs of boots he'd seen in that cabin that day had walked back onto the Beaver plane that brought them. They had not heard any shots from the direction of the lodge.

One night the trapper laid bear-caul fat over a skinned rabbit set in a heavy Dutch oven on the stove, layered in potatoes and halved mushrooms and onions. When the rabbit was cooked he removed it and added a bit of water and flour to the juices and caramelized bits in the pot and made a gravy. Served it with steamed quartered beets drizzled with olive oil, sweet rolls keeping warm on the stove. He said *lapin au jus* while serving it, but he didn't speak French or whatever that was and the boy just shook his head and reached for the pepper. A wild-raspberry crumble for dessert. They talked and candles shortened.

21

When the little pot-belly stove warmed, a cedar aroma infused the sauna. The trapper wasn't sure if it helped him heal, but it didn't seem to hurt and it did help him sleep and sleep helped him heal. Last night the kid wanted to try if they could get a pine scent going so he took some sap from a tree using a small stick and dabbed it on the hot stovetop and it did give some amount of fragrance. Mostly just smoked. The kid said he liked it. Tonight the man was alone and he turned the vent of the stove half-shut with his toe as he was now sweating profusely. Blew out the single candle and the sauna glowed a faint red hue from what little light escaped the stove.

A few years ago he was sitting fireside in the evening reading a book of hers on physics. Read that a cosmologist by observing the warped path of sunlight hypothesized the existence of a yet-to-be-seen small planet whose gravity was bending that light. No telescope powerful enough existed to search for that planet. That story stuck with him. Putting your uncommon beliefs on the line with a claim so specific that would allow them to one day be confirmed or rejected. And you'd either have to own up and acknowledge you got it wrong, as well all your life's work that led you to having that conviction, or if the planet was confirmed, it'd be hard to argue you hadn't established something utterly true. And in a world where ideas worthy of belief were not so obvious, adding to that list seemed like a worthwhile pursuit. Basically that guy had walked up to the plate and pointed out to the far bleachers then waited for the pitch. One day a telescope sufficiently strong enough to reach out into those farther heavens was built and did confirm that small planet. That maverick hit it out of the park.

When the trapper first read that he had wondered if a powerful and kind god could be inferred from the fortunate acts among us—and a devil from the cruel ones. But no, now he saw that as flawed. Could be the world is just a wild place with potentials for both joy and sorrow on extreme levels: no kind gods and no cruel ones required. Could be the world is just a spectacular place rather than a supernatural one.

A small pool of sweat now lay on the sauna floor. He toed the vent fully closed and was almost cooked and ready to call it. If he didn't make a conscious effort to turn off his mind he'd think the sleepless night away. Sometimes meditation helped and the sauna was a nice place for it. He'd just sit there and observe his mind, how it churned up thoughts and feelings on its own and how that flow didn't stop. He had read of Buddhism and they had two books on it but he was not a Buddhist. That *the self is an illusion* because thoughts think themselves is a testable claim, and in testing it, it seemed to be true. But they lost him at karma and rebirth and spirit beings. That seemed lacking credible reasons for belief. Seemed like more doubtful claims and superstitions in a world not lacking them. When he occasionally meditated it was not a religious thing. Just being aware at a very basic level. It seemed that which was aware, wasn't entirely coloured by the things it was aware *of.* In the least, it allowed a break from noisy thoughts, a certain amount of clarity and peace accessible at hand.

The heat was making his heart rate rapid and pounding and every pore was pushing up a sweat bead and he sat there wetly studded with them. With the sauna being a practice for health, its discomfort from the intense heat near the end of a session didn't exactly feel so bad. It was peculiar how that worked. Had he been captured by some ancient Greek tyrant who put him in a brazen bull to bake until he died, the very same physiological sensations from those same high temperatures would feel unbearable. And the difference between those two experiences would be from the thoughts that accompanied the sensations—from the story he would tell himself. The stories, *discomfort for health* versus *discomfort for death*, imposing at times more suffering than the raw physical sensations. For the first while anyways, one was manageable while the other was torturous. The sauna, just like jumping into a nearly frozen lake, which they occasionally did, or hiking while strained from a heavy load, which they often did, was where he could test while under greater duress his ability to not be entirely identified with what stories got told in his head. With what feelings arose. Sometimes when he felt his mind being pulled towards its obsession with triumphs and failures of former times or uncertainties of the boy's well-being, he was able to head it off before it got away from him. Right then he was feeling that pull. He closed his eyes and opened his mind and sat a few more minutes bejeweled in the sweat of his concerns in that sober dark.

22

He woke after sunup and the cabin was already warmed and fragrant of food and coffee and the boy didn't drink it. He pulled on sweatpants and a wool shirt and arriving to the living room saw atop the stove the percolator full of coffee, its brewing basket removed to the sink. At the table the man's mug was set and on his breakfast plate there was a bun. On top of the bun were two nuts and a carrot, like a smiling bun, a crazy one. Crazy in that the smile looked insane, and crazy because only the mentally perturbed would suggest a carrot for breakfast. The boy's bowl lay empty in the sink. He hadn't even heard him.

The fall sun cold and risen threaded its gold through frosted branches and a boy moving in the forest had never walked quieter, never breathed lighter or observed sharper. He wasn't a wild fur-trader and he wasn't an old chief and he wasn't the man who had raised him either. He wasn't thinking about being anything. He was scrutinizing shapes and colours between the limbs and the leaves, looking for deer brown, antler curve, black bear, eye blink, ear flick. Listening for sounds between sounds within sounds. He was a deer and a tree and the wind and the sun and the moss on the rocks and the space between those things. An owl doesn't focus, it just is. He just was. The beauty of nature around him did not hold his marvel because he was not separate from it, wasn't observing it from a place by which to admire it. He was of it—he was the thing worthy of marvel. And in that state he barely registered time passing.

The forest's undergrowth thinned out. He came to a mature stand of mixed trees. At the base of a fir he noticed a circular patch of matted grasses free of frost. He knelt on one knee, lowered his hand to test it for heat but felt no warmth. Brought his nose close and got a faint musk smell. A couple piles of droppings, not steaming but wet looking. He stayed kneeled and moved his head on a slow swivel.

He'd rested his back against that fir tree and watched the forest, but the only thing moving was the sunlight slowly rising on his chest. The light gradually coloured up to his neck, then his face. When the rays shone to his eyes it was blinding and so he closed them. Warm orange light through closed eyes. He was listening for rustling leaves or snapped branches. Then in his mind he spoke to the forest and the animals and the sun and the skies above. He told of his respect for not just what he was pursuing for food but for the trees and the birds. For even the squirrels too, the moon and the stars at that. He said they didn't take more than they could eat and they never would. He had not been taught to pray but he'd known of it, overheard from Dad or read in some storybook—but that wasn't exactly what he was doing anyways. More like expressing an idea, putting out a wish to the world and making clear an intention. And so in that regard he was both offering and asking. But a request not addressed to anyone or anything in particular, just in a type of communion with his world. The one he knew. Some of these things he just made up as he went along, as is the pleasure of being a child discovering the world and sometimes creating it. With his eyes still closed he moved to his knees and ungloved his one hand and unpocketed his other. Clasped them together. Bowed his head. Said finally he'd be really grateful for an animal, and so made his request for one. Then he did say amen 'cause prayer or otherwise he knew that's how these things ended.

This boy kneeling beside tall trees like unhewed walls, lit by sunlight shining through coloured maple leaves like stained-glass lighting, under canopy branches arched high overhead like vaulted ceiling, making his request none more humble in a communion none more reverent on grounds none more sacred, lacking neither birdsong choir nor even holy commandments—though unscribed to tablets he knew theirs nonetheless. This boy praying in his church for that's what it was.

And with eyes still closed and hands still clasped he drew a full breath. And exhaling, opened them. He looked around in the midday light for life in the forest. He listened with ears so strained he heard his own blood pumping.

Right then a bird thumped up flapping noisily from a juneberry shrub not far away and roosted a low branch. Ptarmigan. The boy's heart pounded. He unclasped his hands slowly and nocked a shaft then raised his bow. Drew both breath and arrow. The bird looked off into the woods. He sighted centre chest like he'd been taught. Then with his dad nowhere around, he slowly floated that sight-pin higher up that forest-chicken and loosed a fletched dart with a bludgeon tip for its awkward head and the shot was good and that head half crushed before it was driven separate from its body, which fell stone-dead to the forest floor.

The boy exhaled. He walked over to it. The body of the bird twitched on the ground and partially outstretched one wing. Then slowly, slowly it retracted that wing and never moved it again. He watched it be still.

He stepped on its wings and pulled from its legs to cleanly remove the breast meat from the carcass while also concealing the headshot from his dad, shooting with his ego such as he had. That night they cooked the gamebird. Floured breasts seasoned in salt and pepper and a Cajun spice they kept on hand plus a baked potato. Little tangle of broccoli sprouts grown in a window-side pot. Over dinner the kid told the story, twice. Both times he told it he acted it out with an imaginary bow. The second time the bird was farther away and he squinted his eye at the table making the shot, which also came with the sound of whistled arrow-flight. He told of his wish and had called it that.

Both times the man listened he held off on something he wanted to say to him and that was easy because he was captivated by the teller. It was a good story and it was the hunter's evening.

"I'm proud of you," the trapper told him.

The kid was about levitating off his seat.

23

Outside the cabin it was quiet, black, starless and cold. The boy was asleep upstairs in the loft and the trapper sat alone by the stove where two small squares of light escaping the vent flickered together on the floor. He had cut the pliable bear hide in two halves and one draped fur-side down over his knee where he was sewing a felt backing onto the skin. From a coil of small-diameter cotton rope at his feet he unwound a foot-long length and cut it. Then again. Held the ropes up to confirm their lengths were the same then cauterized the ends by sticking them in the stove vent for a second. He stitched one end of each rope onto the narrowest part of the hide and just over a foot apart. Holding the hide in the air by those two drawstrings he looked at it, turned it around in the air slowly. He got up and climbed the stairs to the loft then he came back down.

The cabin's smoke wisp so still it looked to be some grey fissure cracked in the obsidian wall of night. The first snowflake of the early-winter season fluttered down alone like it was lost. Just one ice-leaf falling languidly as if someone had shaved it from one of the hidden stars above. It landed on the cabin roof. Then from the heights of the dark sky an endless sea of falling white. White speckled firmament in the vaulted black. What fell weightless individually was heavy together and over the night branches began bending like heads bowing to a presence worthy of respect. That could either continue the current order or cause wild disarray. The snow like something imposing you hope only for apathy from, as even its fondness puts you within its scope, and that current favour could be subject to change with something as variable as the cosmic winds that somewhere out there were stirring things up, and for all you know were headed back around.

When the trapper's granddad died the lodge owners heard of it and one of them must have called a priest because one actually flew in by floatplane. It was the only time the trapper ever met one. And with the old man laid in the ground the priest read to the few people there, *For what is it to die but to stand naked in the wind and to melt into the sun?* And even today the trapper remembered those pretty lines and remembering them now he thought, precious emptiness. And the priest that day had continued. *And what is it to cease breathing, but to free the breath from its restless tides, that it may rise and expand and seek God unencumbered?* And remembering those pretty lines now he thought, empty words. The priest had said, *Death the sister of sleep.* No. He'd seen death. He'd caused a lot of it. So had his granddad for that matter. It looked like suffering and degradation and then a mind switched off, energy spent and so too with it life like a broken machine.

He walked over to the shelf and pulled out a book from its spine and opened it to a dog-eared page and read words he had long memorized. *The gods envy us. They envy us because we're mortal, because any moment may be our last.* And he thought to himself, romantic nonsense. I'd rather be immortal. He read on.

Everything is more beautiful because we're doomed. And he thought, perhaps.

The snow fell on the forest, now tightening, now tense, now taut.

24

Stomps from the loft, then heavy steps on every second stair, then pounding on the cabin floor, then for a brief moment in the semidarkness of dawn no sounds at all while a boy hardly more than a furry shadow flew into the man's bed wearing long johns and a black bear cape. The weight of the kid landing on him and the fur against the man's skin with the smell of the bear all in the haze of the morning almost had the trapper reliving that trauma and fighting off for real this fake attack. Then he saw the kid in the cape with his wild bed-head hair looking some version of crazy entire. The boy went for the man's neck and growled and mauled his neck with a burrowing head and bites and clawing hands and a black hide stuck up in the air. The man's ribs had healed and if they weren't they'd have ached both from laughing and fighting off a monkey in a bear suit. The boy postured up. The trapper said looking up to him, "You found your coat."

"This is amazing."

"You look like a crazy person."

"This is the best thing ever."

"Is it too heavy?"

"No, it's perfect." The boy had even tied the drawstrings around his neck up there in the loft. "Can I wear it outside?"

"What'll the deer think?"

"They won't see me. I'll be stealth."

"It might weigh as much as you if it rains."

"I'm wearing it."

"Alright. Glad you like it."

"I really like it, Dad. Thanks."

He lifted the covers for the little bear to crawl in.

"I was older than you but not much and had the canoe out in the spring. There was still snow in places on the riverbanks. I was a ways from home up the river and scouting for moose. I'm standing in the canoe which was stupid and have my binos up trying to see over a section of brush by the riverside. I thought I was being careful and it'd be okay. The bow of the canoe got pulled into an eddy and the stern kicked and I lost my balance and fell in. The water so cold, just shocking. I tried to grab the canoe but I was heavy and it wasn't and it got swept on ahead. My clothes felt like lead and my boots were filling with water and they're pulling me down and I try to front stroke as hard as I can and the water's up to my mouth and ears. And at first my thoughts were I just didn't want to lose the family canoe, I didn't even realize at first how dire it was all getting."

The boy listened holding onto one drawstring.

"I watch that canoe go around a bend. And now I can just barely tread. I try for the shore and that's what I should have done the second I fell in, but I'm stuck in the current and with my clothes it feels like I'm swimming in cement. I'm yelling. Just yelling help. Help over and over. Nobody's gonna be out there. The current's moving fast with all the creeks feeding into it from the snow melting and I'm getting turned about. Then when I try to yell again, I can't. Nothing comes out. The cold's taken my voice. I could hardly breathe,

I can barely gasp even. I'm up to my ears and then I'm swallowing ice water and choking on it. I can still remember how that feels in my throat and my lungs, that ache. Sometimes I can taste it even, like metal. Up until that point in my life it was the most scared I'd been. I'm coughing with the water in my lungs. Not sure if it was the cold or what but my vision starts going red. For a second with just my face above water I can see some of the sky. I close my eyes and I pray to God 'cause I was raised that way and I pray just help. Just God please help me this one time. No help me and I'll do this or I won't do that. Just help. I open my eyes and I cough and draw a bit of air and try again. I don't yell, I *scream*. Loudest, highest pitch I can make.

"Your Great-granddad was near deaf in his later years but his wolf wasn't. And Granddad'd listen to that dog just lookin' at her. And she's barking. Wolves actually do bark too sometimes. I could hear it faintly. I can hear it right now too. And I'm bobbing there swallowing lake water and I'm done." He looked at the boy beside him and the boy's eyes were wide as he was listening to this one. "Done. That's it. I die as a drowning boy. That's me. And then I see that old man come running out of the woods one strap of his overalls unbuttoned and sailing out behind him. I'd never seen him run once in his life—not before, not after. Both of them come running like fury itself tearing out of the forest. It was something to see. One of the single best things I've ever seen. One of 'em." He sorta pushed the boy under the covers and the boy knew what that meant and smiled and said keep going.

"He doesn't kick off his boots on the shore or anything, just charges into that cold river and water is spraying up everywhere as he goes. What narrow vision I still had he was in the centre of it. I could see his eyes. His beard. I could see he was yelling but I couldn't hear what he was saying. Things were hazy but I see that old man and his wolf kicking up spray running side by side straight across that current past his knees then to his waist then he strides one time and dives forward. Hat goes off. Huge splash. He was not a small man. I go under. If I hadn't even seen him I'd have sunk before that. Seeing him somehow gave me a couple more kicks, but still not enough to keep my head from going under. My eyes can't see anything in the turbulence and I think they were mostly closed anyways.

"Well you know he got there. First I feel his hand on my head and then he's pulling me up by my hair then an arm under mine and I'm back above the surface gasping, and he's kicking me across that river and talking to me. Telling me to hang on, which is kinda funny 'cause I'm not holding on to him he's the one that's got me. My head's on his chest and I'm coughing and his one arm under my arm and across my chest, his other kinda backcrawl paddling us, and the wolf with just her head above water right there beside us dog-paddling. He gets us to the shallows then pulls me up to the pebbled shore and we're both on all fours on our knees and hands and I'm coughing and spitting up river water, but I'm okay. I look over at him doing the same. Long wet grey hair hanging down, water coming off his beard, a strand of spit hanging down from it. And as he's hacking away he looks over at me and he's smiling doing it. He's smiling. Reaches over and gently starts slapping my back to comfort me or help me purge water or to say don't do that again. Probably all three."

The boy only said wow. Then he looked up. "You're crying."

"One tear doesn't count, everyone knows that," the trapper said. Then he said, "Loved that old man.

"So what do you think of that? I called at my last breath, truly my last breath and was answered. God. Right? Something. It felt like it. Still feels like it today decades later." He looked at the bear-boy. "What do you think of that?"

"It's amazing," said the boy with a kind of wonder in his voice.

"Yeah. I think so too. Does it remind you of anything?"

The boy was still, then shrugged under the covers.

"Like the ptarmigan?" the trapper asked him.

"Yeah. Kinda like me asking for the bird and the bird showing up. We were both heard." The kid looked up at him.

"I carried that feeling with me for a long time." The bear hide laid up against the trapper was like a furnace and he folded the covers down. "But look, the idea that something out there was listening to me, watching out for me. It's a really nice feeling. But I'm telling you this 'cause you're a strong boy. Looking back I don't think anybody heard me that day. Nobody other than the old man I mean. And the wolf. Some people would see it differently. The reason is because right now little kids, even a little boy like you is calling for help. A little boy like you is hurting right now somewhere else. Many places else. Kids hurting for reasons not their fault and not anyone else's either. That don't get saved like I did. If I think someone heard me I have to answer why not them. It doesn't hold up. If you try to square it you become some self-centred ego monster. Or you have to make up other stories like past lives or future ones to try to make it all fit and I just don't think those stories are true. We can say we aren't sure and that's okay and still go on. The dark's not so scary. I wasn't special, I was lucky. It's nice to get lucky and a lot of people don't. We're fish in the creek and sometimes that creek runs dry and not because the creek is mean. Some things that end up happening aren't caused by what you think even if you feel sure, even if one thing happened right after the other. Like the prayer and the answer, I mean. Sometimes those things just happen to line up."

The trapper looked down at the boy and his face was blank and who knows what was going on in there. Might've lost him. There was also a real chance that he'd moved on to thinking about squirrels. He doubted whether he'd actually convinced the boy that those gut feelings were not always the best guide because he hadn't entirely convinced himself about it either. They lie deep like bedrock and it's like you're wired to believe them and some of them you do need to navigate anyways.

"You still with me?"

The boy nodded.

"Look. It's not always happily-ever-after, but it's rabbits-in-hats. That's what you do get. You get magic." He pointed to the doorstop which was an old-fashioned iron that he'd never seen anyone use and wasn't exactly sure who brought it up there originally. Maybe Gran. The boy looked.

"That iron," the trapper said. "Go back far enough and somehow you and me grew out of that. Out of rocks and light and heat."

The boy in breathless disbelief said no.

"I'm serious. And change one little thing in the past and we might never be here. This universe is too big to even say, and we don't know how it all works and there are forces out there that could fold our world into a thin little story never heard again. But somehow we're here. You and me," the trapper pushed him under the covers, "somehow we're suspended among stars spinning through seasons. That's magic to me. And last thing. Here's what you get," he said to the boy. "You get to love something you can't understand."

The kid looked up at him quick. He had pulled his own section of covers up to his face and just his eyes were showing, and those eyes shifted back and forth above a collar of fur. Just eyes and fur. Then he nodded slowly. "Okay," the boy said.

"Okay," the man echoed. The sun had now well lit the bedroom. "Should we get up?" he asked the boy.

"Yes. I'm hungry."

"Wait. Did you dream about the bear again? Tell me."

"Yep. Every night."

"Did he come at you?"

"Yep."

"Did he get you?"

"Nope."

"Speak with more than one word and tell me what happened already."

"Well, I saw him far off like every night. He was coming my direction 'cause he always knows where I am. I could see him moving through the forest. He turned then came towards me like the other nights. Big body. Every night I run and every night he catches up.

"I started to run like always and then I stopped. Turned around. I just let him come this time. I watched him slow down, staring at me. Stalking in close. His head low. I just waited. I was still scared but I waited this time. Mean eyes. He's a bear but his teeth look like a wolf. His snout too. Like he's a few things put together. He stared at me and his mouth was open as he came slow." The boy paused. He was telling the dream-story with fixed eyes and he was looking at what he saw.

"And then?"

"And then. Then he walked that big head, those shoulders towards me and showed those big teeth and mean eyes. I drew back. I put the pin on his chest. I drew and loosed and nocked again and emptied my quiver."

The man squinted at him. He hadn't seen that coming.

"But the arrows passed through him. Like he was made of air, or the arrows were. He was still there. I felt like running 'cause I had no more arrows but I always run and he chases. So I just watched him. This was the closest he's been. He came right to me. I looked in his black eyes and I was shaking. I said what do you want bear? He didn't answer. But his eyes kinda grew really big and then all I could see was his eyes and the forest became black like them too and everything around too and I was just looking at the night. He was gone."

The man didn't say anything and the boy looked like he was still in his own mind.

"Were you still scared? After the bear had gone?"

The boy shook his head no. "I knew I was dreaming."

The trapper lay there listening and had no words for the dream-teller. He flatly wasn't sure what to say. What do you say to that? That's good. That's bad. It will be okay. It will not be okay. You did well. You did not do well. He had no advice, no words of comfort, no reflections either. They just lay there. His arm was around him.

The kid said, "I don't even care if he comes again."

The man cleared his throat. "Well. Sounds like you're done apologizing."

"Yeah."

"You know for nine you're kind of a badass. Like I'm glad you're on my side."

"I'm ten. Don't say ass."

"You just did."

"Because you did."

"If you don't tell anyone I'll make you tea."

"Who am I going to tell?" the boy said.

The man shrugged.

"You'd make me tea anyways," he said.

"I know."

"Okay. Deal."

"Okay. Can we go deer hunting already?" he asked the kid.

25

Like a new world everything changed and the snow so bright they squinted walking out into the day. For a moment the boy just stopped dumbfounded there on the porch and took it all in. Then he ran on the deck in his bear cape past the trapper and threw himself into a drift. Got up smiling and brushed himself off. Then did it again. The snow crystals in the hide glinted in the sunshine and made him look like some weird little glitter-bear.

The bare woods had a stillness about them and the air was dry and cold. The boy had stopped then crouched to check out a set of prints and when the man caught up they looked at them together. "Wolf," the boy said first while his dad was about to.

"If there's a gloss sheen to the imprint it's not so fresh," the trapper said. "If it looks like the track walls could crumble with a wind, if just looking at them seems like they could slough some snow-grains into the paw shape, look up. These ones are somewhere in between." They saw rabbit and marten and fox prints, then they saw the actual red fox that had made them looking back their way over its tail bushed up as big as its torso and of the same colour, which was more of a burnt orange than red. Thin black legs stepping away in the snow like some stocking-clad ballerina off to her winter performance.

The boy led. The trapper could hardly recognize this new hunter: quiet, deliberate, smooth. His steps slowed a split second before he placed them. His head moving slowly scanning for motion. His pacing like an animal, three or four steps and stopping, then a few more. Not constant like human travel. Mid-step the boy had unquivered an arrow then nocked it and drew back. The trapper watching from behind still hadn't seen what the boy was tracking with his loaded body turning measuredly as a turret right to left. Then a dull thud sounded with his release arm coming back smooth and the spent bow pivoting forward in his left hand while his breath rolled out smoking, first away then above. Watched him like watching some trades-man at his craft. The deftness and economy of motion where the only things that moved were things required, a synthesis of mind and body, bow and sight, inten-tion and muscle memory and wind and distance all linked up together and the shot even made between the forked branch of a tree gave the whole thing a precision that was a damn pleasure to watch. Artistry is boundless and shows up in places one might not think would exhibit it. For some trades it even takes a certain level of proficiency oneself to recognize mastery in another. The days the boy had been hunting on his own had clearly been some kind of accelerant. Had all those days that the man spent healing he'd have instead hunted with the boy, his instruction even his very pres-ence could have stymied the kid's progress. This little hunter here was starting to look wicked sharp. Most of the kid's technique was the same as his own, but he could see unique elements. How his fingers on his release hand pointed downwards. How the mist told he hadn't exhaled till after the shot. How he still held the release arm up a second after he'd sent the arrow. Just little things. Maybe even better things. The kid walked over to the dead animal and on his way he was still quiet, still hunting. And maybe that impressed the trapper most of all. Then he thanked the dead rabbit and gutted it in short time and bringing it to his dad gave him a cocksure smile and didn't ask him if he saw him. This boy here changing before the man's eyes into something at once gritty and sweet. Starting to develop a little hardness to him while still pure at his core, like veins of gold running through black quartz. The man turned around so his backpack was within the boy's reach and smiling while facing away said, "Guess I'm still your packer."

Sap in the air made it sweet to breathe as they moved through a tall maple stand. It didn't flow much now in early wintertime and they wouldn't tap the trunks till spring, but still the sugared aroma stickied the air like they were walking through a cotton candy cloud. You could see a dark-golden bubble where it welled in the bark then oozed from a notch in the trunk. You could see a wild little hunter in a black bear cloak lick a dirty sap bubble in these northern woods.

When they'd left in the morning the sky was clear and now it was grey and thick. Such is the North. It looked broody like it had been offended, or could be its tall reach into the heavens allowed it to see something ugly out there on the horizon and it was colouring itself, as well the lying world below, with shades of discontent. Between two trees a spiderweb hung frozen and ornamental with frosted webbing like a cut paper snowflake a child had crafted then lost to where the winds had taken it. Somewhere a child is crying. This child here looked up to the web, but the man was looking over it. He was watching what was watching him from a long and narrow treeless corridor just outside of a rifle's range. A lone black wolf the colour of a dead coal, the colour of night, the colour that was no colour at all. A timber wolf sized like two stacked huskies. He watched for its breath-mist to rise, to tell whether it'd been running or walking by the interval between its pantings. He watched and didn't see it and watched longer while breathing slow himself and saw nothing and thought maybe it just blended in too well with the snow because no plumes rose from that dark wolf. How long had it been watching? Could there be others? Though these thoughts were the man's they could have just as easily been the wolf's. He looked at it and was looked back, and two predators exchanged eyes over a distance neither was eager to shorten.

"Look," he whispered to the boy.

The kid took his bearing from the man's. "He's hunting too," he said.

Midday they stopped in a forest clearing and dropped their packs and the trapper said he'd make a fire and the boy walked the surrounding area looking for sign. The man snapped alder branches from standing deadwood then dragged a match on the metal riser of his bow and lit a small fire.

When the boy came back he asked him how he did. "See anything?"

"Yeah. Heavy sign, fresh droppings. A splayed toe print with a dew claw and dragging hindleg."

"Which way was he moving?"

"East. But not fast, not direct—the steps were close together. Sometimes circling," the boy said.

"What do you figure?" the trapper asked him.

The boy had a piece of jerky clenched hard in his molars and he pulled both his head and his arm away in opposite directions to tear off a piece, as if the animal it had come from still had some disagreement about the whole process. "We could track him that way. Wind's good. We could set up and try to rattle him back in." He looked over at his dad and with the jerky in his mouth said, "See if we can call him in?"

"That sounds good to me. We might be hiking back in snow," he said without raising his head to the hanging grey sky.

The boy looked up.

They sat and warmed and ate and the fire sounded like someone threw snakes on the fire.

26

Father and son stalking in slow tandem looking nearly mirror opposites separated by the shooting distance of a bow. Light flurries had just begun falling, and like the last moments before the curtain rises, the air seemed both hushed and electrified. It seemed both a delicate thing and a portentous one. There is some gravity here. They were each observing without conferring between them how very fresh the deer sign was. The animal was close. At the boy's side farthest from the man a small and partly treed knoll rose up from the forest. Looking to his dad he saw him nod him upwards to it and so he crept up its side and sat just shy of its top, allowing a full advantageous view of the surrounding woods without himself being skylined to anything incoming. The hill acted as a funnel point that channelled the movement of animals and made their passing more likely. The trapper stayed down low in the forest to the other side of the gametrail where with any luck a deer would pass between them.

They unshouldered their packs and lowered down concealed amongst the brushes and snow. The forest so still that the light flurries sounded like tinkling stardust from stars long crushed in a god-palm now opened to scatter seeds falling on a land too cold to receive them. Just tiny sounds, tink tink tink.

The boy watched him take out two old antlers from his pack. The trapper held them chest-width apart and paused a second, then drove them together to rattle a mock battle. The indelicate smashing of antlers bone on bone echoing off tree trunks cold enough they absorbed little sound and so that rattle roamed about the territory like the animal itself that once sported that rack. A sound that would scare some does even some young bucks, but a sound to make curious or enrage a mature one.

Toque tops dusted with snow-caps, two hunters looking and listening for prey.

Two hunters finding it.

The boy heard it moving before he saw it. Then a buck stepped out of the forest onto the gametrail and looked down the path. Flared its wet black nostrils inhaling, but found no scent, neither of bucks battling or a hunter rattling. It pawed the ground then sniffed again then stamped. Snorted a big mist-cloud, then stepped on through that manufactured aura. Four-point rack elegant and stately atop its head.

It does not look upwards to the knoll to see a kneeling boy mostly hidden pulling string. It does not hear flexing bow-limbs. It does not feel the distant sight-pin floating over its chest.

The boy is gently squeezing his index finger on the arrow release. Union of mind and muscle. Let the shot surprise you, his mind whispers.

At that moment a rifle's crosshairs sighted on a bear back.

Five hundred yards away a piece of conical lead sheathed in a copper jacket rests at the end of a brass casing filled with gunpowder explosive pointed at the back of a bear. The finger curled against the trigger is pulling steady pressure. Everything about everything here is delicate. Better if this moment was frozen forever and all parties were painted onto the side of a porcelain tea cup. But something is moving. The trigger is gently creeping. The firing mechanism now only a few atom grains away from breaking and letting go its firing pin.

"It's a bear for sure," Jacob whispered with an eye unblinking behind the crosshairs.

"Looks like it," Dave said, looking through binocular glass.

"It's not moving much but it's a bear for sure."

"Looks a little small. No?"

"That's just the top of its back."

Dave was rolling the focus knob of his binoculars. "Hard to even tell what with the snow and all."

"I can tell you it's a bear. For sure. You doubt it?"

"And if it's a sow? You can't even tell this far."

"A sow's legal and I got two tags and we're eatin' good tonight." Jacob said that with his cheek pressed softly against the checkered-wood stock of the rifle.

Dave lowered his eight-power binoculars better suited to hunting inside the forest than glassing open ranges. He took his eyes from the black-furred body now mostly a blurry speck outside of the magnification. He looked at Jacob. "I dunno. Doesn't feel right. Something. We could get closer."

"Dave. How far did I ring that iron pig at the range last week?"

"It wasn't snowing."

"Doesn't matter. Go on say it, how far."

"Six hundred."

"Six hundred yards. After four Lucky Lagers, mind you. What's this?"

"Range finder says five-twenty."

"That's right, five-twenty. And I haven't had a drop on the day. Sober as the falling snow here." Jacob hadn't looked away from the back of the bear in his scope and he was speaking quietly. "This is why we go to the range. This is why we practise. And this here wood-laminate stock, stainless steel and fluted heavy barrel mounted with the best German glass money can buy is purpose-built for shots like these. Why spend the damn money otherwise. I'm set, braced, steady." He was lying out prone with his backpack as a shooting rest sighted on the distant knoll. "I'm taking the shot," Jacob said.

"I don't like it."

Taped to the stock beside Jacob's cheek was a ballistics chart for his particular rifle calibre. He whispered: "Daveyboy, I do appreciate your hesitancy in this most pivotal moment and we here at Sportsman's Lodge North Country do respect your conscientious objections, especially at a time this critical with my finger already well curled around this finely machined and well-oiled .300 Winchester Magnum." He took a breath. "And furthermore I will personally be recommending you be promoted from hunting guide to reception. I'll even see to it someone gets you wildflowers for your desk each morning." He further whispered as he further squinted down his unscoped eye, "I'll even pick 'em myself. I'm shooting."

"Shoot then, jackass." Dave plugged his own ears.

And that curled finger squeezed softly until he touched the shot off.

Then from nothing to everything and this thin porcelain moment is shattered. The trigger breaks causing its chain reaction. A spring pulls the firing pin to strike the primer and ignite the low explosive which flash-burns in an instant. Copper-jacketed lead accelerates rocket-fast through a hardened steel barrel and the rifling scores spiral channels into the soft bullet's dizzying rotation. Fire-blast licks out the muzzle like dragon breath and the bullet is propelled so fast it compresses sound waves in the direction of its travel until they stack together and it overtakes them with a sonic boom of whipcrack-deafshot. The bullet so fast it even compresses time in its little bullet-world which ticks slow to its own bullet-pace. This magic lead with the power to outrun sound, to alter time, to change worlds. To even end them.

The destined bullet parts a few thin bear-hairs on a kneeling boy's back then passes through the hide and into his body. The shot would have been imperceptible, silent before the sound caught up, had his down vest not burst forth feathers like the stuffing of a doll and a puff of red speckles not spattered the feathers swirling in the tail drafts of that exiting bullet. The bullet carries onwards, barely slowed by what the boy was made of. The shot boy releases his arrow on a wayward path that thuds in an alder tree beside the deer. The startled buck braces frozen, watching the blurred fletching so close to its head. Then it bounds away.

The man watched wide-eyed as the boy dropped his hunting bow. Then his mind snapped together sick puzzle pieces. And he said: "No." Then again before he ran to him: "No. God no." He whispered that.

The bullet's lagging sound caught up to its impact and the shot rang out like a struck clocktower. It rang like first cannon-fire across lands soon to be embattled. The kneeling boy's body relaxed its muscles and he fell forwards to the snow. Under his fallen chest snowflakes mixed with down feathers, both of them once white now turning red in a widening circle. His eyes staring into the dark of the snow. His eyes already glassing over. Already gone when the trapper knelt to his side and rolled him over and held his face then looked to those eyes. A face already whitening. Air expelling. He held the boy's wrist and felt a pulse there so faint, so faint, so faint. He looked into his eyes but they did not look back.

"No. No. Oh no. Don't. Oh please don't." Whispers.

He tore at the boy's vest to see the wound and seeing it he stopped. Just stared at that violence. Looked back up to his face. He'd seen it a hundred times, been its agent nearly as many. And deer or rabbit or boy, turned out it all looked the same. Such vacancy. He didn't even run for the first aid kit in his dropped pack. The man's brain flooded with adrenaline and neurotransmitters slowed time. He was outside his body on a space-ring watching a planet implode. He was watching what he most loved and even what he loved in himself, the guardian of a star, fade out. Eyebrows bent in confusion and disbelief as he witnessed a circle becoming a square. When right there a star died as a dead son, what orbited it was sent wayward. Released into a vacuum, lifted into a void, fallen into a hole that permitted falling forever. Just empty, cold, vast, and already he felt some terrible void inside him, in his chest, coming up his neck, he even held his breath as it finished its rise. He could feel his own heart shrinking. Where once a little coppersmith was tapping out his heart walls with soft hammer-beats to size it ever larger, now that little heart-artisan had his swings constrained by those shrinking walls, now could swing no longer, now those walls like sheet plastic were wrapping him up immobilized and his gaping mouth opened to scream was sheathed over, both to silence his horror and eternalize it, like a Munch painting: forever screaming, never heard.

The gun's tremor-wave rolled out into that northern country. From the caverns it rattled out bats. From old-growth trees it spooked roosted birds off their branches. And out there its sound twisted and contorted and reformed itself and was returning as a warped echo, like the lone belly laugh of a ghoul or some single rumble of demented thunder. A noise so misshapen from its original, and this evil crescendo was coming back louder like it was amplified by what it found out there, having sourced some fright or charged itself from misery in a land that had it to spare. As if above those lands the dark folds of the sky were the cloth of a sorceress's cloak, and from out of that fabled sky two immense and gnarled arms, their veiny skin like deep ridges of channelled bark from ancient trees, reached down and outstretched to the evening horizons. Then that sorceress swept her huge hands together like pushing waves of water beneath a thin liquid-skin, rolling up a sound wave from all the torment of living things that had died under her long watch. And right above the trapper those swift hands came together in one single deafening clap, and that sound tunnelled into his ears and its queer sound split what it found there like lightning striking cedar like a lake splitting across in the night like frozen water cracking granite. Cold smoking ruined bedrock inside his head, and whole feelings and memories and words and worlds got fractured, got cordoned off.

He died.

He was born.

Above him a raven black as a rotted soul perched in a dead tree. Its eyes were darker still of polished charcoal that though they glimmered, somehow still seemed devoid of life. As if the black bird was only an extension of something, acting on another's behalf. A messenger, or one sent to return with a message. Its dead eyes looked to the boy. Had he a stone. And then a second raven floated down from out of the sky like a piece of black ash that a fire had risen up some long ago. Fluttering in from that wasted and flurried sky. And it perched, and it cawed, and its dead eyes looked to him.

27

"It's down."

"I don't see it," said Dave.

"I smoked it. Dropped it. Slid down from its hill there out of sight. That's a dead bear. Count on it."

"Let's just watch a second, see if it gets up."

Jacob ejected the spent shell and chambered a fresh round. ".300 Win Mag doesn't wound much. It's not getting up. C'mon, let's get down and go see. And in my generous mood as a participation award I'm gonna let you hold my rifle." Jacob passed off the firearm and started moving down lower to the forest floor.

Dave watched him make the short few zigzags down the hill. Then he turned back to look at that distant knoll. Just saw an empty hill. He'd left his own gun in the cabin that day and he raised Jacob's rifle and looked through the magnification of the scope on its max ninth power. Nothing. He could not see that just out of sight lower on that hill there was a man kneeling at the side of his boy. Who was now gathering him up in his arms. Who was now holding the boy, cradling him. Whispering to him. Dave couldn't see that just out of sight a bit lower on the hill a world had been destroyed. Two of them.

Then the father did stand up. Dave saw him appear in the rifle glass. Just his head in view over the side of the hill. The man was looking down to his little world greying away. The trapper wasn't crying he wasn't angry he wasn't sad he wasn't anything but in the middle of some total ontological shock. Then he slowly raised his gaze and scanned for what hunted them. *What hunted them.* And seen between scattered trees and on another hill similar to where he stood was a man holding a rifle. Pointing it at him. Maybe the trapper was still in shock or maybe in that moment he would have followed the boy if given the option as he didn't even duck. He stared and watched that far-off man lower his rifle. The distance prevented the details in their eyes from being fully shared, but for a second that shared gaze was locked. The face of the man holding the gun seared into the trapper like an iron brand across his eyes.

The trapper broke from that stare and looked down to the boy in his arms. Then back to his enemy, then back to the boy. He turned for the cabin. Then he ran for the cabin cradling a boy that dangled a limp arm.

Things will be different now.

28

"Holy shit."

"What?"

"Holy Christ."

Jacob turned and looked at Dave back up the hill. "Well, what?"

"I just saw someone."

"You did what?"

"On the hill. I saw a face."

Jacob turned in the direction of the far hill he could no longer see given his lower position. Then back to Dave. "No you didn't."

"Man, I swear I did."

Jacob eyed his face looking for a muffled grin from a weak joke. "Who'd be out here? Hey? You saw the bear lift its head or something."

"Oh man. No. Something's wrong."

"Dave. Who knows what state your mind's in 'cause I've seen schoolgirls hold their lemon gin better than you held your beers last night. You just saw whatever your hungover and clouded mind just conjured up. Come on, let's go have a look. We'll go find your face."

Dave turned once more to the hill, the now empty hill. He raised the rifle again and looked through the scope but couldn't see tracks at that distance and the blood was a bit lower anyways. His heart pounding in his chest made the glass of the scope pulse along with it. He lowered the rifle then himself off the rise and followed Jacob.

They had not hiked far before hearing the sounds of flowing water.

"Well shit," Jacob said seeing the river.

"Wonder if it narrows."

"I think that's Artery River." Jacob picked up a long branch from the bank and stood on a rock at the edge of the water. Stuck it out as far towards the middle of the river as he could. "That's over shoulder high, and that's not even the deepest. Will be damn cold and we might have to swim partways."

"And it's almost sunset," said Dave.

"And it's almost sunset. We'll be wet skinning it out and wet coming back. In the dark, mind you." Jacob threw the branch into the water and they both watched the river carry it away. "My vote's we head back to the cabin. Hip-waders tomorrow. See if we can find a narrower spot. The meat won't spoil any in this weather."

"What about the wolves?" Dave said.

"Worst-case scenario they get the meat. The wolves are happy the deer are happy we hunt another bear another day. Sounds like everyone's happy and it's good all the way around." He looked at Dave. "How do you feel about that?"

Dave stepped to the edge of the river and was looking north. South. Neither showed signs of narrowing. "Yeah. Seems fine."

"Alright. Till tomorrow then."

The darkening folds of sky told of an early demise to the day and dawn the longer in coming. The men turned westwards for their hike back to their cabin beside the lodge and travelled through a forest of stretching shadows and pulled silhouettes, last light shining through flurries that was chased then winked out altogether by the darkness behind it. Those two hills and the land around them returned to their prior stillness as any disquiet was swallowed up by the woods. And the snow so lightly falling in the cold forest almost tinkled if you listened. Like the sweepings of angel-grit falling on the land.

29

eadlamps lit their way through the forest. Dave was thinking about the face he'd seen. A part of him wanted to believe that maybe his mind had just played a trick on him—just some weird imaginative slip, some one-off hallucination and those things are probably more common than you think, that part told himself. About midway on their return the trees were sparse and above them the canopy of branches receded showing the winter night sky. Jacob was leading and Dave called out to him saying hold up a minute. He had switched off his headlamp and stopped trekking and stood there in the snow. Jacob turned and saw that he was shielding his eyes from the light beam he was casting so he switched his off too.

Dave said, "Look." Jacob followed his upward gaze. Above them a patch of star-pocked sky. The flurries must have been carried on high currents because they floated down from that cloudless circle and so looked less like snow and more like thin shards of chipped stars, some kind of astral dust, and the light that shined in the prisms of the whirling flakes dazzled the air around them with no less brilliance than what shone from above—the essence of one a particle of the other—and it seemed they were now floating among stars falling about you.

"Let's just take it in a minute." Dave was staring up into it, nearly swept away by it.

Starlight travelling from so far away that the stars themselves that shined it may have already burned up and left a world without its sun. It's a strange place where things can be both brilliant and devastating. As they were gazing, a meteor shot hot and fast trailing its burning tail across that open patch of sky. Hard to fault someone who feels they can divine meaning in the world by the awe they feel when looking up into it. Hard to fault someone not realizing those stars were their own little burning worlds, but rather just seeing them as shiny things made to twinkle on your behalf. As if someone made you something beautiful.

Dave, caught up in that wild sky, was feeling a little better about it all, about the face. He said to Jacob beside him, "Do you feel it sometimes? You know, just something? Like you can't not know it. Something bigger than yourself. Or whatever to call it."

Jacob was looking up.

Dave said quietly, "I do."

Jacob turned to him. He didn't answer.

"Come on," Jacob said. "Let's go. In case the snow picks up."

They hiked silently the rest of the way home while their headlamps could barely make out their earlier tracks.

As both parties neared their cabins snowflakes larger in size close together falling fast were blown about by a northern wind. An impartial fury to rage in the night that would cover tracks, cover packs, cover blood and trails too. As the snow fell it stacked weight. In some places that could bear it, it caused no immediate effect: the open lands, the unfrozen lake water. Other places where it caused a limb to bend or muffled a creek, its effects in the world were contained in a closed loop—not every flapping butterfly churns up windstorms. But in some places the snow fell like sand grains weighting up to break a camel's back. Myriad little flakes accumulating. Until one tiny flake tips something not to be righted. A branch snaps and an animal spooks and some predator on the brink of starvation gets its prey and another doesn't and one mother returns with food and one does not and some future hunter has game to hunt or lacks it. Families eat or starve. Big things change from small things, rippling outwards to far-away lands.

30

The boy he carried in his arms felt weightless. He entered the familiar cabin and pulled the cord-switch to the light with one hand while carefully supporting the boy with the other. He swept the table clear with the backside of his arm. Condiments and books clattered to the ground. A mug smashed on a stove leg into sharp porcelain bits while the handle remained intact, now attached to nothing. He gently laid the boy on the table. Looked his boy over head to toe. He untied the bear cape's drawstrings from around his neck then eased it out from under the boy. Held it up with two hands to the bulb. The light passed through a small hole near the centre, the second time this hide had a hole torn through it. He let go one hand from it then drove that fist hard against his chest. Looked back to his boy: This root structure, foundation, religion, simple math truth, this light that lit dark things, something that stood on its own, something that shored him up, saw himself there too and her too and saw something beautiful and unique and embodied love and God too and both his pupil and his teacher. Saw it all lying there and contained within itself and ready to be buried. To be buried.

Taking from the chairback a folded afghan that Gran had knitted he covered the boy's sad chest. He touched the boy's face then drew his hand along it and though it was cold it was still soft and smooth like always. That didn't seem fair. He smoothed his hair like he'd done a thousand times, like he'd even done last night. How could things change so much in so little time, he wondered. This type of shift ought to require the passing of centuries, the drifting of continents. He smoothed the boy's hair and in doing so he accidentally smiled because he'd never not smiled doing that to the sleeping boy's face and he was conditioned to smile upon it. With the afghan over him the boy did in fact look like he was only sleeping. The trapper's smile didn't last long and the corners of his mouth gave it up. He closed his eyes and brought his forehead to his son's. "I'm sorry." Whether he said that to her or to him. "I'm sorry." Words incapable of ferrying that lament to the depths they needed to go and in his own ears they sounded so inadequate, so feeble and stupid that he said nothing further. Didn't apologize anymore, didn't speak of love or memory or regret. This was too far beyond words. He brought his cheek flush with the boy's own. Breathed in his scent. He let go one tear and that doesn't count as crying and everyone knows that. He let one more go and that fell from his other eye and maybe that one was for her, whether from wanting her with him or failing to fulfill his duty to her. He slowly lowered himself to one knee, then the other. Hung his head in the sombre light there. Then his face streamed with them.

Eventually he rose up and looked at his son for the last time. From his wet face a tear ran down his chin then dropped and landed on the boy's cheek. The trapper watched it roll to the corner of his son's closed eye. As if all this sorrow was too much for even *time* itself and it was trying to undo things and uncry the boy and take it all back.

Little boy. Little bear. Little man. Glitter bear. Cherub. Wildman.

The trapper unfolded the afghan that Gran had knitted over the sleeping face.

The snow had kept the grounds from freezing. He left the cabin and went to the shed and emerged with a long-handled shovel. Next to the boy's mother in the garden he swung the shovel down through the snow to the soil and stomped the kickplate and drove the shovelhead in deeper. Pitched it. Repeated. His stomach was empty even before he stopped to vomit and his mind was chaotically broken. Out there now muttering to himself in some kind of tumultuous unwell with troubled thoughts joining troubled thoughts in a chorus of agony. He hadn't drunk any water since midday either. He grew up not feeling separate nor distinct from that land, and so each shovel swing was like a cat-o'-nine-tails lashing against both the earth and himself. For hours in the dark of a hard night he lifted dirt and fallen snow from out of a slowly deepening hole. He went farther down into the hole.

His shoveling pace in the night didn't slow—it quickened like fever-stroke—and if the flying dirt invisible against the black backdrop of the night could be seen it'd show it travelled in a high arc. The hole now so deep only his head was above ground. His bloodshot and bleary eyes couldn't see more than the distance to the shovel and didn't need to. Just followed those lengthening grave walls down deeper with his sweat-soaked wild digging.

When he was nearly at a depth sized to his height and shoveling through a final layer of stiff clay, the wooden handle broke. That made him pause. Like a finger-snap trying to return someone from a trance. He looked down at the broken handle in his hands. Then he flung that out of the pit and reached down for the shovelhead stuck in the clay and pulled it out with a sucking sound and flung it out of the pit also and it made a sound of broken glass. He dropped to his knees and dug at the final scoops by hand then lifted out dirt and clay in clumps and lowered back down to sink his nails into the earth and rake and claw through the soil with its little rounded stones embedded in pockets of clay. His fingertips went raw then they bled then he tore a nail clean off. Again for a moment that arrested his agitated mind and gave him pause, as pain is capable of calling attention like little else can. It throbbed. He touched the bleeding finger with another. The warmth there seemed misplaced. For a brief duration, that focused pain gave him respite from a hurt more total. But the stinging finger was soon numbed over with the cold and he got back to digging.

When the grave height fully matched his own he stopped and looked around in the near dark. Took some care and hewed and shaved the walls square and geometric in any places they were not. Then he patted the floor and pit walls smooth. For a second some ridiculous human part of him felt satisfaction in his labours. He took care when lifting himself up from a corner of the tomb so as not to crumble the walls and sully his efforts.

Dehydrated. Filthy. Sweat soaked. Bleeding. His bent shape stiff and hunched from hours of digging looked like it was made of mud and sorrow. He walked crookedly to the cabin.

He stood beside his boy lying there covered in the old afghan Gran had knitted. The small shape of him. Took him up in his arms just like many nights and no less tenderly. Only this time he went out through the door rather than up to the loft. He was walking very slowly. Then so carefully, so as not to wake the boy, he climbed down into the grave. Very softly laid him to rest. "One last night putting you to bed."

And the gentle earth as if all this time she had been waiting received the boy with a mother's embrace: she asked no questions and she judged not and she received unconditionally. That which was returned to her, inevitable. Like something lost she'd always known would find its way back, in time. *It's all right. It's all right. Quiet now.* And with his arms crossed on his chest under the afghan, the boy was held close by the earth while the gently falling soil covered them up.

The snow sifted down over the final layer of soil that showed a thousand pats from the trapper's hands.

31

The trapper closed the cabin door behind him, softly by habit as always, the night without, though the darkness within. Looked around at a cabin lit by the warm and offensive lighting of the hanging yellow bulb. Books. Pictures. The boy's things. What he saw in the cabin had the valence of an antique world and he looked around and he moved about like someone who didn't belong. Someone who'd been banished. Standing there dazed in the structure of a house that no longer felt like his home.

He drifted around the cabin like a drunk. Now what? All his possessions looked like artifacts from old stories, relics belonging to someone else. Him with a loosening grip on the past and little that felt like his own. Had he tried to recall particular events he'd find their details fuzzy and unbeknownst to him some memories were gone entirely.

In the yellow light he saw the bookshelf. Those empty stories from failed teachers as no words could redeem this. This: *All dead. Bloodline dead. Everything gone.* He touched one finger to the top of a book, slowly pivoted it out on its end-spine until it fell from the shelf to the floor. He pulled out its neighbor. Then several more until he stood in a pile of open pages and broken spines.

He wandered the cabin and in his amblings he stumbled on the shovelhead. Only just saw now that it had broken one of the cabin's front windows. He bent for it. He held it with both hands and saw the hard clay still stuck to its tip and the bit of splintered wood where it slotted for the handle. He turned and in turning threw it like a discus across the room and it rang off the pans hanging overhead the kitchen with an enormous rattle of some lurid windchime, so loud, bing bang bong. He looked to the shelf and selected an empty vase, a chalice of dust and dead memories. Chased the shovel's target, and the vase's shattering timbre played higher up the octave scale. Then he was less partial. Whatever closest. Threw chairs. He punched the stovepipe denting in the shape of his fist, then lowered for a swing that would be a body blow on a man and that pinched it in too. He stumbled around mumbling, mostly unintelligible sounds, but he did say make the boy strong. Then he laughed.

He had backed against the woodpile beside the stove and so turned to see who was flanking him. Grabbed quartered logs in each hand and threw them up to the loft and they landed heavy and broke things and shook things free and some of them fell to the floor. A trinket of the boy's lay at his feet, a small and scrolled stick wrapped with string. He raged on in mad sorrow, this troubled man crazed and fevered. The cabin disarrayed so looked an extension of his disordered mind and he smashed and threw and furied about. When he saw the warm yellow light above him he swiped an open hand at the bulb that popped like a champagne cork and shattered like a broken idea. Tiny glass rained. Now in the dark he screams loud and long and if those surrounding woods were not quiet yet, they are now.

And he's panting through bared teeth and his eyes are narrow for violent acts and he kicks the cabin walls and pounds on them with elbow blows and lastly he swings his throbbing and rabid head against the hard pine logs of a wall intolerant of abuse, and that lays him out stone cold to the plank floor.

And so there he lies.

And then come days of black.

And the northern storm rages on.

32

"**W**ell. Whadya figure. It's about four p.m. somewheres I'd say."

"I think the expression is five," said Dave.

"What expression. You want one?"

"Why not." Dave was sitting at the living room table and Jacob got up from it and opened the cabin door to heavy snowfall obscuring the afternoon light, making it look closer to dusk. He reached into the big snowdrift and grabbed two chilled beers. Passed one, opened the other.

"We should have brought Scrabble," said Jacob. "Freakin' Trivial Pursuit or something. Learned to knit or crochet. Could have had my taxes done using only long division by now. Day three snowed in we really could have put this cabin time to some pro-duc-tivity."

Dave was looking out the window. "Got to imagine the wolves will have gotten to it by now. Right?"

"I think all this snow just made it a lot more likely they didn't. It'll cover the scent some."

"Maybe it lifts tomorrow and we can go see."

"Maybe it does that," said Jacob drinking his beer.

Dave was looking off to the woods in the distance being blurred away. "It could have been *him*," he said.

Jacob had a map of the area unfolded on the table. "What?" He looked up. "Who?"

Dave gestured his head sideways in the direction of the lodge. "Him."

"Oh. Him. The trapper. The wildman legend." Jacob shook his head and looked back down to the map. He said without looking up, "You know his name, don't you?"

"No. What, you do?"

Jacob looked up at him then back to the map. "Yeah."

"Well. What is it?"

He was snaking his finger along a river contour. "It's Jack."

"Jack? Really, hey. I wondered. Jack."

"Yup. Jack." Jacob said and looked at Dave. "Short for jacking off all day alone in the woods." He smiled to himself and looked back to the map.

Dave shook his head and looked away. "I did see something. Someone."

"I bet you did, Dave. Bet you saw whatever your cagey-ass hungover mind coursed with adrenaline from shooting a bear scared up to you in that snowfall." He raised his beer in a toast. "Drink and forget about it."

Dave didn't raise his own. "If I said I saw a face, I saw a face."

"Nah. Bullshit. Maybe another bear." He drank. "Maybe a wandering beaver or something."

"You heard that story about him trekking in with her, hey?"

"Everyone's heard it," said Jacob.

"Three days nonstop."

"More bullshit."

"Brought her back too, after she'd passed. With him too—with the kid."

"See to me, that just seems sick. A little deranged. Hiking back in with her body dead in the sleigh. What the hell. Probably a law against that. Should be."

"Wanted to bury her at her home. In the garden is what I heard. Heard the whole family is buried there."

Jacob burped. "That's backwater shit if you ask me. Surprised that was even allowed. Does that seem normal to you?"

"I don't think he was going to be told what was or wasn't allowed."

Jacob gave a short laugh. "All that just gets exaggerated. What's allowed. Like he's some one-man army. People like to talk, is all. If he's still up here he's just some bushed-out hillbilly. Likely a hairy and squirrely one. Probably smells, too." He raised his eyebrows at Dave. "Tell me I'm wrong." He got up and got them two more beers and threw one to Dave then sat back down.

Dave caught it, tapped its top a couple times, opened it and drank at the foam. "Why wouldn't he be around?"

"Well, that family seems rather poorly fated if you ask me."

"I heard his grandparents lived to be old. It was the old guy that started the lodge. They seemed to do fine. Yeah his parents died young but that was weather." Dave drank. "Or the pilot. Both, maybe. And his wife got sick like anyone can. Anyways, he's around. Why wouldn't he be. Traded in furs last winter and came in with the boy too."

"Well, good for him. Hope he remembers who owns the land and there won't be any problems if he stays on whatever scrap parcel he hasn't gambled away yet. Maybe we'll get that too." Jacob winked.

Dave didn't say anything at first and normally he wouldn't have. But it'd been three days now. Three days cooped up in a small cabin. Three days a little restless. The wind blowing the snow outside and a few beers inside. He said: "I don't know why you always gotta talk like that." And as soon as the words left his mouth he wanted them back.

Jacob smiled. "Oh David. Aww."

He'd started it so he continued it and said, "Just negative macho shit. It's constant. Why shoot him down and that family? And it was his dad that lost the lodge gambling, not him. I think it's impressive to make it work up here. What's wrong with that? Why belittle that? Wouldn't be easy to make a go of it up here. And those stories about him don't just come out of nowhere." Dave drank. "Where there's smoke there's fire, kind of deal."

"And their life up here. How'd that work out for them?"

"Like I said, some of it is just bad luck like anyone can have bad luck."

"Nah. I don't think so. It's ill-fated backwater hillbilly shit if you're askin' me, and we're talkin' about it so it sounds like you're askin' me."

"Either way I just don't see why a person wants to talk like that." Dave looked out the window but it was dark and there wasn't anything to see. "I mean this was even their home. Literally their cabin. Why not be a bit respectful."

"Of what? Former home. Respectful to who?"

Dave was looking around the cabin, the darker corners. "I think you put that much time in a place, generations in a place, there might be an attachment to it." He turned the sweating beer can where it stood on the table in its wet ring. "Even if you don't live there anymore."

"Here we go," Jacob said. "Ghost stories. Give us a ghost story, Davey." And he put his elbows on the table and wove his fingers together and rested his chin on them smiling at Dave.

"I'm not saying that. Just." He shrugged his shoulders mildly. "Well there are those. Stories from people who've stayed at the lodge that didn't know about the stories before they came up."

"The lady in white," said Jacob.

"That's just one. The lady in white is one, but there's others. How do you explain so many people seeing it when they didn't know the story beforehand? Before they came up?"

"Tales from the soft of mind. People like to talk and word gets around. None of that shit is fact-checked. That's it." Jacob burped. "Someone half drunk or low on sleep in the middle of the night heard something or saw some mist or whatever the hell and let their mind run away with them 'cause it's fun to tell stories. Sit around and talk and bullshit and pretend. There. That's ten thousand years of ghost stories told by ten thousand different cultures summed up for you. It's all bullshit."

"Well, regardless. I'm just saying there's better language to talk about other people, living or dead."

"My little sweet Daveybaby. I like this side of you. Who knew it only took a couple days cabined up together and you'd be flashing me all your tender parts. I like it." He opened the door and reached to the snow-bank and closed it. "It's cute really. Who knew." He passed him one. "I got it all wrong, Daveyboy. You are fit for up here. These northern lands, you're made for them. You're like one of those precious little snowflakes falling outside, Davey. Davey, I could see you on top of one of these hills reaching for the sun like the tender little wildflower you are." He drank. "A daffodil blow-ing in the spring breeze." He smiled saying it. "A sweet little daffodil soaking up the sun. Just so cute, really."

"They don't grow up here," said Dave.

"The fact that you know that. Don't ever change, Dave."

"This is what I'm talking about. Why talk that way? Why not just be a little kinder. What's the world you want to live in?"

"Alright. You're cut off before you break into song. Or a poem. Jesus. Like I'm concerned you're going to break out into interpretive dance right here on the cabin floor." Jacob leaned back rocking on two chair legs and reached behind him where a travel-sized pack-age of Kleenex lay on a shelf. He threw it at Dave and it bounced off his chest. "Let it all out son, we don't judge up here." He raised and lowered his beer and said, "But if you start touching toes under the table or come crawl in with me in the night, that cold sleeping bear's getting some company, good buddy." He winked.

Dave shook his head and looked away. "I'm just saying a little kinder wouldn't hurt anybody. Kindness to others more likely it gets returned." He got up and didn't go far out the cabin door and peed in the snowbank. Closed the door and switched on the head-lamp they'd hung from a central rafter for cabin lighting and sat back down.

"Dave. You're so innocent it hurts my teeth. Open a history book man. The only person who could say something like that is someone who hasn't ever. Kindness so kindness returned. Dave. You're sappier than a sugar maple and you say shit like that you sound about as bright as one. Pay into it and get it back later, hey, like some kind of pension program? Only the sheltered most blind could say that." Jacob drank then lowered the can and held back a burp, saying, "Only precious little wildflowers can say that. Karma." He burped. "Karma's a joke. Grow up. Who could believe that? Think Hitler got rebirthed as a slug? Why should anyone believe that? Guess what happened to all the Natives on these lands. Tell them they had it coming. Think of just the corporate white-collar criminals that get away with it or even sick legal shit like the predatory lenders that goes unpunished that should be punished and the guy goes on to live a happy life. How many people have died from just sneezing in traffic? The world isn't doing any accounting Dave. It's random. It just is what it is."

"You don't have to armchair philosophize every-thing. My point is a bit more general," Dave said. "A person just doesn't always have to act like a dick and that's a better world. Could even be worth exploring a little what's causing you to speak the way you do some-times."

Jacob set down his beer and it wasn't finished. He touched a finger to it and pushed it away from him and it made a scratching sound on the table in a cabin where there weren't many sounds. He looked at Dave. "Ah. Okay. Well, for a general comment Dave that sounds like the audience is rather specific. We gettin' personal good buddy? Did I step on your tender toes?"

Dave turning his beer can didn't answer. Was turning something over in his mind too, it looked like.

Jacob reached for his own and finished it and then dropped it empty to the floor and stomped it flat. "Thought they'd be safe in your little glass slippers honey. It's okay. You be you, Dave. The world needs little soft things." He got up and grabbed a split log and opened the stove door then put it on the flames and the fire cast up sparks into the flue like little burning demons off to play in the night. Without turning back around and still looking at the fire, Jacob said, "Don't be afraid to get in touch with your tender parts Dave. Just give me a heads-up and I'll step out of the room 'cause it sounds messy." He closed the creaking stove door and looked back around. "Go on son, explore yourself, get in touch with your feelings." He got up for another beer. "It's one thing for women to talk like that. It's another for guys. All the emotions and feelings. It sounds like complaining from weak men I say. When shit hits the fan the world needs hard guys, not soft ones, not sobbing ones on the couch all wet and sticky." He reached over and pressed a finger to Dave's arm and lifted it like he was testing for it to stick. "Sometimes we need soldiers. You fight wolves with wolves. How you going to be that if you're just all soft on the daily?"

246

"You should listen to yourself. You sound like a drill instructor or something. It's cliché and outdated and it's oversimplifying it. And there's different types of strength."

"Dave did your therapist put you up to this? She giving you ten percent off for every guy you bring in? I want you to politely ask her for your money back if she's telling you soft is strong, David."

"Look, how is understanding yourself better a disadvantage in any scenario? You understand yourself you find your limits, both weaknesses and strengths. From there you can work on them. Improve one and build off the other. Maybe it takes some self-exploring to get there. Maybe comes with talking to someone. What does it matter?"

"I think people saying shit like that have too much time on their hands. And definitely too much self-concern. I say we're raising a generation of headcases and whiny little bitches. Sometimes you just have to man up a little. Give your balls a tug. Everyone's so goddamned self-concerned. Maybe that's our chief problem, actually. All this time spent talking about your feelings and micro-analyzing everything and putting everything on spectrums of disorders and then handing out all the prescriptions and Jesus fucking Christ. All of it just a product of people having too much free time. Just get to work. Just be a father already, be a husband, be a man. You know what that looks like. Stop thinking about yourself all the time. Suck it up and go about it and stop complaining and our dads did and so did theirs."

"Yeah. And look at divorce rates and suicide and spousal abuse and infidelity and depression and where all that nose-to-the-grindstone-bottling-it-up gets you. And I'm saying you can be a better husband and father, a better man if you know yourself better. Maybe that takes some self-reflection, and yeah, even talking to someone and that doesn't make you soft."

Jacob burped. "Tell yourself that, bud."

Dave shook his head.

"Get you another brew or are you about ready to switch to the lemon gins?"

"I'll take one."

"Or perhaps a hard lemonade would be your drink of choice as we move into these later hours?"

Dave didn't respond.

"Maybe if I look through the lodge kitchen I could rustle you up one of those little drink umbrellas for you." Jacob smiled, his eyes just starting to get a bit glassy.

Dave looked at him then looked away and didn't return the smile.

Jacob got up and opened and closed the door, still grinning a bit, then sat down heavy. Handed him one. "Cheers, good buddy. To shelter from the storm."

Dave met his eyes and they raised their drinks while the winds blew outside.

"Now what," Jacob said looking around. Then back to Dave. "I'd play you another round of gin rummy but seems like I got your number there. I have to imagine your ego must just be smashed all to bits, like your glass slippers, and can't take any more."

"I'm biting my lip here."

"Oh?"

Dave drank and lowered the can to the table and said: "Nope, not worth it."

"Nope what? Come on then."

"Nothing. Sure. Let's play rummy again. You deal." Dave picked up the card deck and gave it a short lob and it landed with a smack on Jacob's side of the table. He hadn't intended for the cards to splay out like they did. A couple fell to Jacob's lap.

Jacob picked them up and squared the deck. "But now I'm just plain curious, Dave. Sounds like you got something right ready to be said there."

Dave with tightened lips just slowly shook his head.

Jacob got up with his beer. He lifted his chair and walked it out from around his side of the table and set it down right in front of him. He sat down and their knees almost touched. They were staring and just one of them was smiling and that one said, "But now you've piqued my curiosity Dave. Now you just gotta say." He took a drink. "Ol' buddy."

Dave breathed out slowly and looked away to the sweating beer can on the table in its wet ring. Turned it. He looked back at Jacob. "I'm not so sure you want to hear it."

"Oh this is great. This is like first-rate theater here. Front row fuckin' seat. Let's go then. There's nothing I want more. C'mon I can take it, only one of us here is the wildflower." He drank. "Out with it."

"Alright then. Just this. *This*—" he nodded upwards to Jacob as he said it, "always bustin' balls, hey? Always the little shots. All the macho shit. It's your ego, man. And the negativity. It just gets old. Maybe it worked for you in high school Jacob. But c'mon. Christ it wasn't even fun to be around then. It's not now. You got this ego that fills a room. Suffocating shit, man. It gets a little old is all." He took a drink from his beer. "I'm saying that as a friend."

Jacob hadn't grinned wider that whole night. "Well, alright. Well done. That was great." He was nodding. "Thanks—friend. Good friend. My sweet friend Davey. I appreciate you delivering it so gently, handling me with the kid gloves there and all. I'm drinking to that," and he raised the can forgetting it was empty. "Seems maybe that was really eatin' at ya for a while. Hey? Burnin' a hole in ya. Maybe since we got here? Maybe even a long time before that. Shit, now I'm wondering. How long you been chewin' on that, brother? Must feel good to finally get that out. But was that really for me, or maybe you just did that for your own self. Well, how do you feel? Refreshed I bet." He leaned back in his chair. "That's nice that you're always looking out for me. Friend."

"You don't have to take it like that. That's not how I meant it. I shouldn't have even said anything." Dave looked away.

"Well," Jacob laughed. "Too late now though right? But no really, I appreciate it." His face went sincere-looking and he nodded. Then he spoke quieter than he had been. "But I say we keep this going. You know? Parlay this into a real self-development workshop right here. I mean trapped in the cabin just two buddies snowed in all bromance like. Fire fuckin' burnin' away there. Let's get some candles lit even. You probably packed a couple mocha vanniler lavenders some shit. Right?

Go get 'em out. Can't imagine a better place for a little personality-buildin' truth-sharin' session. So please. Tell me more of my flaws. And *you*," he slurred the word a bit while he pointed to Dave, "you from a state of such purity."

Dave just watched him. Was regretting this since it started. Any awkward silences were themselves filled by the storm whose winds let him know he couldn't even go take a walk.

"What day are we at anyways? 'Cause if it's January one, my resolution is to be more like you Dave."

"It's November."

Jacob looked for a beer to toast but only found the one he'd finished so he picked up the empty and ambled over to the door and his steps were heavy. When he opened it the winter wind funnelled in between the two snow-covered woodpiles stacked high on the porch. He shouted out to the night. "Hear this all you squirrels and bears and ghosts," he looked back at Dave and drew a breath trying hard not to laugh till his address was over, "you hillbillies and you lost wanderin' fuckin' beavers," he couldn't help it he laughed there, "from here on in I declare I will strive to be more like my good friend Holier-Than-Thou-Art Dave." He finished and looked happy then threw the empty beer can into the night. It didn't even clear the end of the porch given the wind. He took two more beers from the snow and spat into the snow and closed the door.

"Jesus," Dave said. "And the drama sometimes. You're taking it somewhere I didn't mean it anyways. Let's leave it at that. Play cards," he nodded to the deck.

"Woah now Dave. Hold up right there a second, good buddy. I think it's only fair for me to return the favour. Kindness begets kindness I've been told. Don't know about you Dave but that's my motto. I mean we've already opened the taps here why not work out the kinks in our longstanding friendship, friend." He put one of the beers in front of Dave but placed it down aslant and it took him a second to right the can vertical.

"I'm good," Dave said with little emotion and didn't reach for the beer.

"Oh you're good?" Jacob stared at him. Then still staring, cracked and drank from his own.

The storm blew louder outside like some huge wolf had found a couple little pigs in a stick house and felt like toppling it over.

"You, man," Jacob said shaking his head.

Dave waited.

"You talk like everyone needs to listen is what you do."

"I was only being honest. Felt like maybe you oughta hear it, that it might do you some good for the long-term."

"Ask me I think you coulda been a preacher. Always preachin'. The purity and the preachin'. And you know what," he said, "now that we're both feelin' all warm and fuzzy, I'll add this. I'm well aware I got my flaws. I know that. That's obvious. I'd be some version of retarded if I couldn't see that. But you, you Dave, you're worse off 'cause your own shit smell doesn't even register to your uppity ass. That's a worse problem to have. Blind to your own stink, my man. Bring that little insight up with your therapist 'cause there's enough work there you'll put her kids through college. Her kid's kids. Dave. Have a good look in the mirror bud. There's something needing some work there I guaranfuckintee it."

Dave laughed quietly. "Alright. Thanks."

"Bud. Any fuckin' time bud." He drank.

They sat there hearing the storm. Jacob wasn't going to leave it at that. He inclined his head to Dave, one finger pointing out with the others wrapped on the can. "And always so reserved. Subdued." He drank. "You're just so fuckin' bland. You know what you are? And I might be an asshole but yours is worse."

"What am I?"

"You. You're just fucking boring man. Really. You're dull. I'm not putting these beers back on my own behalf, my man. It's to liven you up boy. You," he pointed his finger from the can. "Not me." He pointed it at himself.

Before Jacob said that last bit Dave was gonna say we about evened things up there and let's just drop it. But when Dave looked up, he was smiling too. Smiling 'cause he must have felt that one. Then he said softly: "Hey Jacob, nobody's surprised she left, man. The only surprise is she stayed that long in the first place." Then he opened the beer in front of him and drank without dropping his eyes. "There's some truth-sharin'. How's that one sit?"

"There we go!" Jacob slapped the table and several empty beer cans bounced and a couple tipped over. "There we go! You levelled up there, my man. I respect that. Like that's the money shot right there. The kill shot. There's no topping it. Respect." He drank.

Dave knew his friend. Dave's heart rate increased.

"I always knew someone would say it. Didn't think it'd take this long, didn't think it'd be you. Did you know you're the first? Congrats." He nodded and raised his drink to him. "In my books that makes you a class-fuckin-act, buddy."

"Back at you bro."

Jacob had raised his beer to drink but it didn't make it to his mouth before he lowered it back down. Then he got up and stood with his hands by his sides in front of Dave. "Get up," he said.

"Fuck you, grow up."

"Nope. Get up. You took us somewhere with that one and now we're there."

"Go back to fucking high school Jacob."

"Alright then." Jacob swung an open hand heavy and hard and slapped Dave clean across the face where he sat. Not a play hit. The storm outside must have been between gusts as that slap sounded loud and sharp and stung the quiet of the cabin like it did his face. Dave half knowing it was coming still had his head cocked sideways and he stayed there a second as that throb registered to him. Then he lunged from the chair and drove his shoulder into Jacob's gut tackling him to the floor and landing him on his back. They scrambled there wildly and someone kicked a table leg and the rest of the cans fell around the men while playing cards flurried up. Dave tried to keep his weight centred to hold mount but Jacob put his hands on his chest and made some space to get his leg bent between them and drove Dave backwards. They both scrambled up and were panting and staring hunched over reeking of booze. They watched each other's eyes and chests for tells of a punch or takedown coming. Jacob feinted a left hook then shot for the tackle getting his arms around Dave's waist and driving him backwards, and just before they hit the floor again Dave's foot caught the stove leg bolted to the floor and it wasn't giving way so his ankle did. Jacob scrambled and got top position and was throwing a hard left hook for his stomach just as Dave let out a groan for his ankle. Jacob's punch forced the air from his gut and cut the rest of that groan right off. It was his ankle that hurt but he covered his stomach from the blow. Jacob seeing him cover up didn't throw again.

"My ankle," Dave groaned.

He looked down at him from mount. "What happened?" he asked not yet getting off.

"What happened? *You* happened." He was wincing as he said it and now he coughed a couple times.

Jacob got off him.

"I dunno," Dave said curled in a sit-up reaching for his ankle. "My foot got caught on the stove I think."

"Ah shit." Jacob looked down at it. "Does it feel broken?" He reached for it.

"Ah hell don't touch it."

"Look, let's see."

Dave had his teeth clenched and was squinting looking down at it.

"There's no bones sticking out. Ah shit man. Here," Jacob said, "let's get you in a chair." Jacob still sitting held out his hand and they clasped and pulled themselves up towards each other with Dave pivoting to stand on his one good foot. He wheezed then sunk in a nearby chair.

"Can you move it?"

He tried and was able to wiggle it slightly. "Yeah. A bit. I don't think it's broken."

Jacob pulled up another chair and sat looking at him. "Shit man. I'm an asshole. I feel stupid. Like really stupid."

Dave was massaging his ankle. "That's alright. I shouldn't have said that."

"Dude, I feel dumb. What are we even doing?"

"Yeah. I dunno. This is stupid, you're right."

"I'm just glad it's not broken." He got up and opened the cabin door for the snowbank and came back with a beer. Dave gave him a look. Jacob wrapped a towel around the beer and put it to Dave's ankle and Dave took it, holding it there.

"Well. I feel about as stupid as I've ever felt," Jacob said. "Or you know, this could give a few occasions in the past a run for their money in the least. I mean I guess I'd have to really think about that statement as I'm lucky to have no shortage of them." He grinned. "And starting from a very young age, mind you. But this certainly feels like it's made the running."

Dave choked out a short laugh. "It's alright. It's not broken. I feel like an ass too."

"Can we just chalk this up to alcohol-escalated cabin fever?"

"Let's do that."

"Hey," Dave said looking at him. "I'm sorry too. I mean it. I shouldn't have said what I did."

"No, maybe you should have. Maybe I did need to hear it."

"No, I mean it. I shouldn't have said it and I didn't mean it anyways. I'm sorry."

"Ahh it's all good man. I'm not so easily bruised." He put his arm around Dave. "You're the wildflower, remember?"

"Nice one. Alright a pair of assholes then. Go get us a couple nightcaps. Let's finish this night off proper with a drink to good company."

"Done." He got up and returned and they were partly frozen. Took the chair beside Dave and passed him a beer. "I asked the bartender to make you a Cosmo but this was all they had."

Dave shook his head. "You're a piece of work. You know that, right?"

"That's a roger, good buddy." He held up his beer and Dave tapped his own.

33

Not dead. Not exactly living. Three days the trapper lay on the floor of his cabin in a wasted state. There were sounds and smells without identifiable referents. Strange shapes and peculiar forms either in his mind or wandering there about the cabin—or both—as who could say which was which and they made curious movements and any of those animations that seemed recognizable didn't last. Though greatly dehydrated he still managed to leak out some piss on his pants and though he felt no hunger his body was starving and so the stains on his shirt must have been mostly bile. His head spun. He lacked discernable demarcation between the real world and a dreamt one, between the exotic hallucinations from a wrecked mind and those more familiar conjurings of simple nightmares. A vile wasting of time blended and blurred and the darkness awful in its suffocating weight. Chest hollowed, nerves shot.

Sleep was no safe place but sometimes he'd succumb to it. There his mind cast kaleidoscopic horror-dreams in the hazed theater of his skull. He sweat their vision. Images and scenes and soundbites like a Lynch or a Dali, some troubled visionary dipping a brush tip in various thick and oily vials of trauma to glob torment up on his mind's canvas, and within arm's reach of that deranged artist were towers of stacked and dusty glass jars filled with anguished tincture, so he could just paint up those painful scenes forever. He heard scrambled monologues of people from his past. Words mashed up and meanings indecipherable. There were cameos of the innocent, people trying to speak and possibly warn him of something, but their voices weak or taken. He heard sounds of trees snapping above the cabin and he waited for those falling tree tops to break through the ceiling. He saw the eyes of his enemy as well he saw the departed. Flames when it wasn't wind and waves and rain. Perhaps those images held some discernable meaning in either whole or in part that could be excised, maybe some occult artisan living at the end of a rumoured town in a shanty house with cut-out moons and suns on its walls could smith a key with wards and bits to fit every haunted image he saw these horrible days then slide it into the keyway of his troubled mind, turn that tumbler and set the message free.

When occasionally his mind would regain a few sparks of lucidity it served only to tell him this: Gone. All gone. Grandparents, parents, wife, son, blood-line dripped dry. So come, you too, it hissed. He felt himself being pulled. He closed his eyes and whispered to the dead air, No. But closed eyes had him fearing the visions that came with sleep and he reopened them. No better, as he would only see the painful sights of his wife's and son's tender belongings. So he tried one eye open and one closed and now surely whatever remained behind that mad-looking face was uniformly lost.

Though his torment was constant, his anguish surged in waves. And while some accusations of self-hatred and despair could be considered reasonable, having at least a plausible basis in reality—shelves hung too late, patience lost too easily—others were less so, and just his ailing body chemically warping his experience. As if continually waking in the morning of the type of terrible hangover that has you regretting things you did, things you wish you did, and those you didn't really do. These accusations prodded his mind like little pitchforks testing where he was softest. I should have gotten her to the hospital even one hour quicker. That could have saved her. Something I did could have even caused her illness. I failed her like I did the boy. *The boy*. The little bear boy. And there those little prodders found it like they'd skewered that very image itself and four of them pinned his eyelids open while the fifth, saying, *Raise that child in town*, served it up before him. Dangling from a pitchfork was a bear-fur cloak. As if somehow he'd missed the most obvious fact. "Oh god," he spoke for the first time since he had screamed ransacking the cabin. "Oh god," he croaked. As if some self-serving bias, some soldier in his mind had been shielding him, until at that very moment she let her guard down and the demons broke through the gates and ran amok for all reaches of his being. "*I* did that. Oh no." His voice like a toad. "*I* did that." And with that he lost it. He had very little energy after lying in this wretched state, and with what he had left he spent it writhing on the floor like a snake some menacing child had doused in gasoline and lit on fire then sat back to watch it curl and char. He twisted and spasmed on the cabin floor squirming from some horrible internal agony. Then he passed back out.

Time was altered, some minutes stretching other ones shrunk. Seemed he would close his eyes even just to blink and opening them again the light in the cabin had changed. He lay soiled in a place beyond sadness, a last locale on the long road of human misery so total in its gloom that there is nothing past it, just train tracks to a cliff's edge. Given enough trauma the brain may go unconscious like concussed from a bat swing, and at duress most extreme the heart can shut down too, the body switching off that life-beat if it's only pumping to prolong some terrible misery for its host. Death for someone at the brink of human capacity for what can be endured can become relief. A take me, God. A lift me up, my God. An I don't understand you, God. A how could you, God. A you don't even exist and you call yourself a god, God. Right then he desired his old faith for the sole purpose of cursing that being.

In the morning light of an uncertain day his face lay flat against the floor. He was very weak and he hurt so much. He'd never hurt so much before and wouldn't have imagined it possible. Heart hurt. Bone hurt. A hurt both dull and throbbing, at once specific while also total. Scalp even. And from that pain he knew he was not dead, or not entirely dead, and that came as something of a disappointment. But he figured he was mostly there. Had to be close. Wait a little longer and the hand would play itself out.

Golden light through the broken window shined onto the floor. Like it had come to investigate a crime scene. For over an hour his eyes tracked its leading edge, where light met darkness, the whites of his eyes widening beneath his rolling pupils. And then out of the shadowed cabin floor appeared a broken arrow-shaft tipped with a glinting broadhead. One that some mythic cherub once slayed an evil bear with. His memory was hazy but he remembered that story, thought someone had told him it once or he'd read it as some pagan legend describing a certain constellation in the night sky. There within arm's reach, the pretty broadhead shining like life's last little present for him.

He reached out an unsteady arm. He uncurled stiff and dirty fingers. He pinched its upright blade. The trapper rolled to his back and lifted his wrist high and pointed the arrowhead to a faint blue line and pressed its tip and pricked a vein. Just delicate. Don't rush this. This big mystery, he thought. That little hole, innocuous and tiny, blossomed one small beautiful dark bead of swelling blood. It grew. It hung. It fell.

The falling drop fell to the tip of his nose then ran down the bridge then down a side and made a small red pool in the corner of his eye. That made him smile. He again put the broadhead to the wrist-hole and pressed its razor tip in a little farther. The next drops fell softly to his nose like kitten licks. On his cheeks too. They ran down to his upper lip and he was happy and smiled wider in welcoming them. These blood drops like summer rain, warm and wet. He remembered lying on his back as a boy feeling cleansed from the wash of the sky. And who knows if that actually happened to him, as memory in the best of times is a contortion artist, a conman trying to sell you faulty replicas. Sweet drops softly falling. He remembered the rain. He closed his eyes. And there she was.

Her in the summer rain now too. Rain that made her dress cling tight against her skin and show the shape of her body whose sweet curves and contours he knew so well and knew were soft and so smooth to his touch and he'd always know her or he'd know nothing at all. Fundamental as colour, as shapes like circle or square. Her bare feet, her bare legs. He saw the dress above her knees against her thighs and she's smiling at him now. He sees it. She's smiling. God he's happy now. Wet hair to her shoulders in the warm rain, red dress damp clinging to her. And she comes towards him can you believe it she comes towards him and lowers to him and he feels her sweet weight laid on him now and her hair falls about him and he even smells her hair and it's falling around his face and it shrouds off the rest of the world—who needs it—and so it's just them two and her red lips part for him and he feels her breasts against his chest and his eyes looking to her eyes like the first time he ever did and my god. My god. And everything reddening like her dress.

Then she starts dissolving away like sugar in tea. Don't. And their embrace emptying. Please don't. If you could see his closed lids they'd show frantic movement from his searching eyes beneath them. And finding nothing and having lost her once again his emotions swing like a child's tantrum back to rage and his clenched fist so tight it turns white then shakes like his knuckles might pop and his veins engorge the more to turn those seeping drops to a trickle, and he swings that shaking fist for the floor fanning out a speckled blood trail up the cabin wall and his fist slams down hard on the floor. And in his fractured mind he hears: *End it!* The shadows weren't even whispering now they called out to him: *End it!* And there too from some other fold of his mind he heard: Get up! Just as loud.

End it! Get up! *End it!* Get up! Call something forth. Give it a name. What did you tell the boy? *What boy?* What did you tell the boy? *Did you believe that?* He lay on his side with his arm on the floor in front of him and watched a little red river seeping out. He was fading. *Let it all out and you seep out the pain too. Relief is so close. This is easy.* Get up. Take one single laboured step composed by every aching bone.

This tug-of-war fought in his embattled mind for an untold time 'cause the sun crept all across the cabin floor then up a wall then disappeared as night fell. Still his split mind argued back and forth along whatever bruised brain channels carried those cognitions. Then from out of the fog a word did come. A word like a life raft. It played over in his head like the tolling of a struck bell calling believers to prayer. He heard it clear, so clear: *Revenge.* He heard: *Revenge. Revenge. Revenge.* All around him, inside him, and he repeated back with eyes still closed that corrupted mantra. Then in that blood-soaked hellish cabin, his eyes snapped from closed to wide open. Wide open.

He wore a facemask of dried blood and some fresh too and he drew in the deepest breath he'd taken in three days, then choked on it, and that crusted mask cracked in spiderweb lines. The metallic flavour of it in his mouth, the iron of it on his tongue. He tasted it. It tasted sweet. He wanted more. Not his own.

With the broken shaft of the arrow still in his hand he stuck its tip in the floor then scratched that evil word into a cabin plank. Revenge, it read. Threw the arrow rattling away. Looked at the word while smiling red teeth, then fed that crazed smile the bottom of his shirt. Bit down and pulled the fabric to tear a strip and tie his leaking vein.

He put a question to himself, even said it out loud in the dark. "What to believe in and what is real?" Given all that had been taken and what had become of former sureties, what could be trusted? That others would be there for you was not one of them. That you would be there for them, also no. That the world would even rise tomorrow, none could say. But there are some trustworthy things. Things that stand on their own and can't be doubted. And he was aware of the concrete: pain. Pain exists. He was certain of that both in former times and now too. Pain's durable like that. Trustworthy. It can't be an illusion even if most other things can. He wanted to find the man who'd taken away his whole world and give that man something he could also believe in.

He rolled up to his knees and lowered his head. He clasped his hands and he whispered in the darkness to the shadows. "I only ask this: keep him safe. I don't ask much, only this: keep him safe, my enemy, watch over him. Don't let him leave these woods."

The idea fueled him enough that he began shivering cold in that frozen cabin and though he was so far gone from his right mind this mad trapper he felt filled and born anew with the zest of hatred and purpose of vengeance. He became the presence that visits the cancer ward, that lurks to the fallen in battle, the dark thing that stalks the woods.

He unclasped his hands. He unbowed his head. He rose in the dark.

34

The trapper lowered his mouth to the jug of creek water in the kitchen and drank from the spout, then he drank some more. He selected certain items from the shelves and some from their fallen places on the floor and put them in his backpack and for the remainder he went to the shed. When he walked out the door into the sparsely starlit night, no bow hung from his hand and no rifle slung his shoulder and he entered the forest quiet as a shadow stretching itself long and westward from a yet unrisen sun.

In the North that night blew a mean wind in the mean woods where trekked a snowshoed man looking for violence. Walk back the steps of how it grew up within him and eventually there'd still be the question of *why*. Because the boy, but the boy because the bear, but the bear because this, and this from that, and eventually we're back to a time we never knew and it's turtles standing on turtles all the way down. Some causal never-ending story of infinite regress, or some circular one like a world of Penrose stairs, or could be beginning-and-end and time itself are human constructs, or there are many worlds or one infinite one. Regardless of where it all started and who's guilty and who pushed whom first, he was pissed off and his intentions were cruel ones.

After some time trekking towards the lodge he had stopped and taken his snowshoes off. He was sitting and had been sitting for a long while, though it would not have felt like it to him as his mind was churning through its vast storehouse of ideas. Fragments of thoughts would emerge in his conscious stream and sometimes entangle with others: a person he'd not seen in years walked of their own volition into his mind and got paired with some abstract concept he'd not read in ages and you'd think had not taken hold but it turns out found purchase in some lonely crook of his mind—the two coming together had Gran speaking accounts of history, long-forgotten clients from guided hunts orating theories of ethics. Then idea and person would disentangle and recede back into some less-than-conscious level and a new pair would get their turn centre stage in his mindscape. Like the flickerings of strange films cast from a hundred projectors. He the sole audience with his frantic eyes moving from scene to scene as those film reels were swapped in and out by some manic operator.

At this hour of night a deer's eyes are fully dilated black discs and this one quietly pawed the ground for grasses and leaves, digging under the snowfall where others of her kind not far away were doing the same, just shapes in the night. On this quiet night she walked timid and wary and listened for predators, for steps that didn't sound like her own. She browsed in the dark forest at the base of a maple tree. She raised her head and swiveled an ear, then aligned the other. Must have heard something. She held her breath there listening. Somewhere in the night a cougar lurks. Somewhere a wolf.

There are places in humans softer than the down in their pillows underneath their lying heads. The trapper sat supremely still and wondered if he could take someone into the deepest most visceral state of terror. Suppose it's true the only fear is fear itself, then death neutralizes that state of dread. Maybe there is no such torment in hell as on the long road to it and anticipating the punishment causes psychological trauma more consummate than sulphur can burn. You can take his eye but once, you can make him fear that gouging for a long time. Could I instill a horror so severe it would haunt every day for the rest of his life that man behind the rifle? Could I return in kind what my enemy has given me? He considered the thought in that dark wilderness. Haunt, torture, kill. He had yet to decide.

The doe scanned her big black eyes searching for what she sensed in the night. But he made no sound dropping from the low maple branch and his fall was silent too and though his weight heavier than her own, when he landed on her back it did not break it. Her hindlegs gave out though and folded underneath her and she tried to step with just her forelegs but bearing his weight she only stamped in place in a useless march. His legs were wrapped around her body with his ankles locked together and he wrapped his left arm high up her neck then pulled that slender neck to his chest. And now she's looking up into the black sky watching a few falling snowflakes. He doesn't unclip his blade 'cause he dropped from the tree with knife in hand and he draws that cutting edge across her taut throat held tight in the bend of his elbow. The snow turns red. She tips to her side and he's still holding her neck against his chest like he's trying to calm her, them two lying in the snow together on their sides. Her legs slow their kicks and her big black dilated eyes start to soften, almost closed now. And then she's unmoving. And then her eyes the colour of the night are just as still.

He cuts a tiny incision at her paunch then inserts two fingers and spreads them in a V to make space for the knife-travel between the hide and the stomach lining. The blade in his right hand following behind his left he opens up her belly then onwards to her chest and her warm air rises behind his travelling hands like train steam in the night. He eases out the steaming gut pile then severs it where it clings to the cavity wall. In the middle of the offal mess is the heart still contracting from lingering pulses of its fading charge. He lifts it in one hand and frees it from its webbed matrix with the other. He lays the knife and cups her heart with both hands above her gaping chest that plumes up a great warm cloud into the air. As he brings her heart towards him, life-blood drips from the heart's cut valves and red drops pockmark the snow between his spread knees, like she's marking her way back home. That map won't be needed. His teeth in the living muscle. His beard red. This wolf.

35

There is still time before dawn. The trapper reshoed the snowshoes and continued on, now energized from the doe. Before reaching the lodge he made one more stop but it was brief and his knife not much bloodier and his pack only a little heavier. When he arrived at the forest's edge he waited, watched to see if smoke rose from their chimney beside the lodge. It didn't, or if it did it was only a thin spire too faint to see from a few last coals. He cut a small pine branch then left the cover of the forest and stalked to the cabin.

No movement through the windows and to be sure he watched awhile. He brushed himself clean of snow then took the flashlight from his pack, its lens covered in a thin red fabric, and held it unlit between his teeth. He took his time turning the knob to open the door so slowly that even had its hinges gone unopened a hundred years they still would not have creaked. Closed it the same way. The enemy now within. Stood a second inside the cabin listening. A snore from the farthest bedroom, heavy breaths from the other. He had entered carrying his backpack by hand and now set it on the floor then switched on the flashlight held in his mouth and it cast a dull red beam. He knew where the joists carried the floorboards, as he had helped lay them decades ago, and he stepped only along their lengths and in wool socks as he'd slipped out of his boots still strapped to the snowshoes outside the door. At the table his hands worked quickly: unclipped items, swapped some things, took others. He saw a headlamp hanging from a rafter. Rifles standing in the corner. Then shouldered up the backpack with its top open.

Two bedrooms opened to the large central room and he placed his steps to the closest as quiet as a fox hunting in the snow. Then passed through its open door. The room was sweet and heavy with alcohol saturating the air so thick it seemed moist and the man who perfumed it was lying on his back and breathing heavily. His sleep looking restless from an agitated mind. Maybe things the man had tried to leave behind or things he feared awaiting, the tenor of unease playing inside him like one arrived to new lands yet to welcome and so his mind yet to settle. Occasionally his head turning one way, then back the other. He mumbled out some muffled jargon to whomever he was addressing in his dream.

The trapper took the flashlight from his mouth and palmed its lens so the only light it glowed was a thin rim of pinkened flesh. He slunk towards the sleeping man, the trapper himself hardly more than a spirit in the dark of that room. Then he floated so brazenly close overtop the man in bed and the grim red glow of the palmed flashlight painted their faces with ever so lightened cheeks and darkened sockets. It was instant—that face clicked clear as a Geiger counter. *You,* his mind seethed. *Youuu.* The trapper's eyebrows bent in hate, his face grotesquely caricatured by the light's rose glow. The sleeper twitched a single shiver as if a cold shadow had moved over him. The trapper breathed in deeply, wanted to smell his prey. The man turned his head on the pillow making what appeared to be a motion of disagreement, while the head looming above mirrored that futile evasion. He stared so intently he seemed to be looking through the other's closed eyelids, false armor and faulty shields as they were, in search for the cowering eyeballs below. Then on past those eyes for something deeper still.

The trapper's face cut a small grin. The joy of encountering one's enemy and finding him helpless. The smell in that bedroom was something reckonable: drink mixed with grave digging and sweat and blood and death both ungulate and human all layered up together hanging heavy over the bed. Could be that smell toxified the dreams of the man and made whatever he was witnessing there ever more foul, as again he turned his head, and this time with his eyes and jaw clenched harder he appeared under even greater duress. And now when he spoke both there in his dream and to the one listening, him some medium connecting the two, his speech was clear: "No." That word just once.

The trapper watching, the trapper listening, a small grin between his lips. To find your enemy clinging by his fingers at the cliff's edge, the privilege to stand over him and decide his fate. The triumph of victory minorly tinged with the disappointment of the fight's end, especially if the fight gave the fighter purpose. And this one seemed so short-lived. The defeated waiting for a swinging club or final bear-stomp, bullet, arrow, or knife. Whether he lives or dies now entirely up to the advantaged. There is almost something paternal about it, between the trapper and what he's trapped, as the one is entirely in the graces, or the lack thereof, of the other. And within the trapper one single lost particle of the dove could almost compel him to stroke the man's head, like he would the boy's. Say to him it's okay. But the very mental glimpse of that paternal idea necessarily recalled his departed child to mind and that tiny and lost little dove that had so briefly flapped up somewhere within him turned to stone and her wings closed up and she fell like a rock from the sky. Any potential for mercy, gone as quick as it came.

But not this way. The knife still wet with blood remained closed. Draw this out like a lynx toying with a vole. Instill terror within this guilty man and give him something to carry, such as he gave you.

He lifted away from Dave then reached behind and over his own head into his open backpack without unslipping it from his shoulders. He lowered to one knee at the bedside. Seeing him there in this suppliant pose you might think him in prayer. You might think him some knight swearing an oath of loyalty before departing from his bedside lover, or crouched beside some dying king who was bequeathing him one final quest. He knelt down to lay what was still limp and warm in his hand to the floor. Then he rose and with a few sock-footed toe steps was out the cabin. He dusted his boots still strapped to the snowshoes free of their light covering of snow, laced up and set off for his cabin. He had things to do.

A pine branch dragged behind him, its needles raking his path smooth, merging his tracks with the land around under the falling snow that his visit might become one more secret kept by the North that keeps many secrets. And he's receding like a ghost gone back to its grave before the holy searchlight of the rising dawn.

36

"Gawd. Oh boy," Jacob with his dry throat half-spoke half-groaned from his bed. "Head's spinning over here. How you doing over that way, good buddy?"

He waited for an answer from the other bedroom.

"Daveyboy. Good morning how we doin' how's the ankle?" He listened. "I think we should reconsider our careers as cage fighters."

"Hey," he called, "Wake up!" He heard nothing other than the lifted storm outside.

Then Dave groaned. "Your head, my ankle. Woah. Actually. My head too."

"Then we're in this together pal. I'm on coffee. Have you your cup in a hot minute. Then maybe if we both hold on to the cabin walls together we can keep them from spinning."

"I'm getting up too." Dave took care swinging his hurt leg to the floor. Though the blood in the small pool had mostly dried it was still tacky when he set his good foot in it. He stared down. "What the hell. Jesus, what the hell is that."

"What?"

"Why would you do that?"

Jacob walked over to his room. He stared at it too.

Dave looked up at him. Then back down. "Why would you do that?"

Jacob was looking from him to the floor, then the bed, then back to him. Said slowly and looking puzzled, "I didn't do that."

"What the hell." Dave had lifted his foot out of the shallow pool that had welled in a small and circular shape, not unlike the cottontail's missing head. A dark-red stain from a headless rabbit on his bedside floor. A pool with perfect toe prints.

Jacob looked up to the cabin ceiling above where Dave sat like maybe it had fallen down, which didn't seem like the most absurd hypothesis. He looked back to the rabbit, then walked over and squatted to it. Poked it with a finger. Its cold body under its bristly grey fur was stiff. "Well that's entirely weird." He looked up at Dave. "I think you're prone to sleepwalkin'."

"No. I've never. Maybe you are."

"Most that do don't remember doing it." As he said that he was looking at Dave and then began squinting at what he saw. "I think there's blood in your hair."

"What?" Dave touched at his hair and what he found was dried and didn't come off on his fingers but he felt strands stuck together in matted hair-clumps of congealed blood. "What the fuck." He pulled trying to unknot the hair while tiny red flakes littered his finger-tips and confettied his shoulders and around where he sat in bed. He was looking down on the bed while doing it and watching little blood flecks fall to the sheets and pillow. He looked in total disgust over at Jacob.

Jacob was silent and stayed crouched and took in the strange scene while watching Dave pick at his head. "So weird," he finally said. "Okay, that's not sleepwalking. There'd be snow in the bed or on the floor if one of us had." He looked around the floor for signs of melted snow he'd already ruled out. He stood up and went back to his own bed and saw nothing strange. He felt at his own hair.

"This ankle would have woken me up anyways. And I'm even less prone to animal mutilation than I am to sleepwalking. What the hell is this, man?" Dave sounded distraught.

Jacob went to the table where their gear was and checked it over. Nothing looked out of place and he said so. Some cards and cans were still scattered on the floor from their wrestling match, but everything looked as they'd left it. Guns in the corner looking as they ought to, but he walked over anyways and picked his up and slid back the bolt far enough to see the brass cartridge in the chamber, not so far that the action would eject the round. Safety still on. He set it down then opened the cabin door and there was a small drift of snow on the porch and beyond that and as far as he could see were snowy lands pristine and bright. He slowly closed the door in thought.

"This is sick," Dave said. "What is this? What the hell?"

Jacob was thinking.

"This is so freaky. This is abnormal. Jesus. This is paranormal," Dave said.

"Don't say it." Jacob not looking at Dave dismissed the notion.

"Well, what else?" he raised his voice. "Those stories don't just come out of nowhere. You said yourself, every culture. And we were talking about it last night. Maybe we provoked it or something. Woke something up."

Dave's voice cracked. "Oh shit man. The dreams I had last night. Something was here last night." He looked wide-eyed at Jacob.

"Just take it easy. We'll think this through. The booze and your ankle were your dreams so just relax for a minute Dave. Seriously."

"No. No way. I felt something last night. I'm not just saying that. Like nothing I have before. A presence or something." Dave was shaking his head side to side.

"Dave. Just breathe. For sure this is messed up, I agree. But no ghost stories. Just chill for a minute. We'll think it through."

"Well how else do you explain it?" He looked white and his hand was back up probing his scalp. "Nothing missing. No snow in the rooms. No people out here anyways. No tracks. Just a dead fucking headless rabbit. My bed, not yours! We should not stay here." Dave eased out of the bed and hobbled to the nearest wall, mostly using his good foot that now tracked red toe prints. "Oh shit," he said seeing his tracks. He started dragging his foot on the floorboards to wipe off the blood and that left a smear. "They say these things can follow you home once they latch on. Christ, man. This is no good." He leaned against the wall.

"Look. Take it easy. We're okay. It's morning. Nothing else happened. You aren't dead, you aren't hurt any more than you were last night. So we think this through." He moved for the kitchen and said I'm making coffee then stopped on his way and started making a fire as the one last night had died.

"Why the hell is it in my room and not yours, hey? You tell me why. Tell me how. This is ghoul stuff. Ghost stuff. There were stories about this before we came. And now we see it. Okay. I think we should just leave. How could that be the wrong decision? Something's saying we're not welcome and saying it strongly and okay, I'm okay with that, we'll leave. No problem." Dave sounded shaky.

Jacob looked at him. "The lodge," he said.

"What?"

"The lodge. The hunting outfit. We've put in so much time and money to make this happen."

Dave hobbled to a chair by the fire. "I'll take my life over a job at a hunting lodge."

"Owner of a hunting lodge," Jacob corrected him.

"Co-owner of a hunting lodge," Dave corrected him.

"Hey. You're getting carried away though. Seriously. Just try to calm for a minute. There's an explanation." He poured then passed Dave a coffee and set the percolator back on the stove and went to the window with his own mug. The lands outside looking innocent. For a few minutes nobody spoke.

Then Jacob turned. "You know what this is?" He looked at Dave. "You know what this is?" He had a small grin.

"Yeah. A clear a sign as I've seen something is saying we're not welcome. The same thing I saw in my dreams last night. Pack up. No problem."

"No. I know what this is."

Dave was looking at him and waiting.

"Your face on the hill just got a lot more likely. Not otherworldly shit. Just backwater-hick shit. Maybe he's lost his mind and trying to scare us. This is just human stuff is what this is. Bet your ass it is."

Dave sat with that. In his panic he'd forgotten about the face. He said nothing and held his coffee without yet drinking it. "So why not take the guns? Why not light the goddamn place on fire in the night and make it look like an accident?"

"I don't know. Who knows. But for every ghost story up here there's a dozen more crazy human ones. Maybe he's just bushed-out bat-shit crazy. Maybe he wants us to leave their old lands like you said."

"I don't know. This all feels not right. Maybe we should just call for an early pickup, reassess back in town."

"Do what back in town? 'Cause of your ankle?"

"Because of *this* twisted shit." And Dave raised up his bloodstained foot. "We come back with the police."

"Like you said, no tracks. And what? Even if there were tracks what do we say to the cops? We think he killed a rabbit. Cut its head off."

"We don't even know it was him."

"It was him."

"Christ," said Dave. "Could be traps out there then if you're right. He could be out there somewhere waiting if you're right."

Jacob turned and looked back out the window. "If he was going to do something stupid makes sense he'd have done it last night." He set his mug down and got up and went to Dave's room and picked up the rabbit by a forepaw so as not to leak out more blood and held it up, then turned it slowly in examination. He couldn't tell how it'd died, that is if losing its head hadn't done it. Its body showed no bullet hole. He walked to the cabin door and opened it and lobbed it out where it made a small snow-splash. He sat back down. "If we're going to run this lodge, if we're going to co-exist with him up here, we have to figure this out now. No way I'm leaving from this. If you want we can call in the plane and I'll help you board and see you off and we'll get a beer when I'm back in town and I'll buy it and that's all good. There's no shame in it with your ankle." He nodded to Dave's ankle. "I mean that. No problem, I get it." He topped his own mug with the coffee and reached to fill Dave's and it was still full. "But no way I'm leaving. Fuck that." He brought his mouth low over the mug, lightly blowing steam and subtly shaking his head. "Given how much money we've already put down for this. The plans to run it full-on next year. This place is my dream. Nope. Not leaving. I'll go check him out. I'd rather go have a look and see what's up and try to talk to him. Rather that than call the police with nothing to say. I'll take a rifle like I'm hunting, and him and I will talk. Come to an understanding."

Dave looked at him. "I don't know."

"It's up to you Davey. But I'm staying. There's no shame in you leaving, I get it. You're genuinely hurt." He drank from his mug. "It's your call."

Dave was looking down, thinking. "You think it's him, hey?"

Jacob looked at him. "No doubt in my mind."

Dave reached up feeling for any remnant rabbit blood in his hair, fingered his scalp for any that might have seeped down to it. His face still looking white. He drank some coffee. Lifted his leg and moved his sore ankle around some. Sighed. "Well," he said. "It's not broken, I guess."

"My man," said Jacob.

37

Before he reached his cabin he lowered to all fours and dipped a cupped hand to a stream. The water freezing cold and he drank so much of the ice water his head would have panged terribly but for that it was already panging. When he got to his cabin the sun had well cleared the horizon and he unloaded the contents of his pack in the shed. He reached up high and grabbed the rump of the hanging bear hindquarter, its dried and blackened skin like leather. Made a deep sideways cut, then quarter-turning the knife, made two vertical cuts about the width of his hand apart, peeled and sliced off a thick slab red on its inside that he took to the cabin.

The cabin's ransacked state barely registered to him. He balled up old newspaper and split kindling and built a little square framework of tinder in the stove then lit the paper and layered in logs. The fire was slow to catch and slow to draw what with the pinched-in pipe, but it did take eventually and slowly began warming the pan he'd lifted from the floor and laid atop it. He sat on the floor and held the raw meat in one hand and the knife he'd butchered it with in the other. The curious theater of his mind must have been between acts as he just sat staring blankly at the flames through the open stove door waiting for the pan to heat. Finally seeing some old oil start to smoke he laid the meat to sizzle.

His eyes were heavy and he meant to rest them just a second and though sleep wasn't his intention it came immediately. He actually didn't feel all that exhausted but of course his body was and when the slightest opportunity for rest presented itself, it shut him down involuntarily for a little while. Straight away he sought her out like always. At first he just waited for her to come to him. And when she never showed he searched for her in that foggy dreamscape. Didn't know where he was going and his mobility laboured as he seemed to walk with a limp or was dragging something he couldn't quite see low in the murk about him. He called out her name but got no answer, same when he shouted for the boy. Seemed to have just dreamed himself into some hazy state lacking much for content, a present emptiness witnessing a cloudy void. He knew if you're lost in the woods you should stay where you are, but what if nobody's looking for you? he wondered.

The fog in his mind may have rolled in from the smoke in the room as when he opened his eyes he could barely see the meat in the pan. He reached out and lifted the charred bear then pushed the smoking pan off the stove and it banged to the floor hissing while it branded a plank with some half-legible name of a metal worker. That primal looking piece of meat was raw on top, bloody inside, and his teeth shattered its charred bottom. He tore off chunks swallowing them nearly whole. How to make seeds of fright root into your enemy? It has to be slow, he knew that part. He wiped his hands on his dirty pants and they came away streaked and no cleaner. Without getting up he moved about on his knees and cleared a spot on the cabin floor. Then got up and gathered all the candles he had which was several and placed them unlit in a large circle, leaving an open space in the middle. He repositioned the one chair still standing from his earlier rampage to be centred in the circle. He brought a length of three-quarter-inch rope from the shed then holding to one end he threw the coil up and over a rafter beam above the chair. On the end of the rope that remained in his hand he tied a noose knot, and with the other slack end whose excess dropped to the floor, he half-hitched to the nearest stove leg, such that the noose hung in the air over the chair at about head height of a seated man. He stepped back and took it in. It looked like a makeshift altar built for some crude ritual, as that's what it was.

Would they try for town? Would they come this way? Would they stay holed up in their cabin like mice? He knew he couldn't leave the hunters for too long and before noon he'd set back out.

38

"So, what are you thinking? Which way will you go?" Dave asked while seated watching Jacob gearing up.

"Not sure exactly, but he's somewhere east of here. I bet we coulda seen his cabin from the plane if we looked, or at least smoke. I'll try to find a way across the river, get to the hill. See if there's tracks or a trail there. See if the bear's still there or any sign of anything. If he uses that area a lot then maybe there's something showing down lower from that hill. Tree-blazes marking a trail, maybe flagging tape. You never know."

"Any cabin on that map?"

"Yeah no, I looked. Nothing."

"Why don't you take the sat phone." Dave was sitting by the fire.

"I'd say keep it here just in case something happens. It doesn't look like it's going to snow today so I can't get lost and I'll have the GPS anyways." Jacob was lacing up his boots. "If I'm not back by sunset, or say just after, phone it in for a plane just to be safe. But I'm not worried." He looked at Dave. "Really. If he was going to do something crazy he'd have done it."

"Well you and I seem to have different definitions of crazy then," said Dave. "Because if sneaking into a cabin in the middle of the night to lay a headless rabbit bedside after you drip its blood on a man lying there asleep doesn't check your crazy box, there's someone I'd like you to speak with when we get back to town.

She's a great listener and wears a white coat and has this padded table with buckles and straps. I think it'd fit you perfectly."

Jacob half laughed. "If he was going to do something violent, I mean."

"You should watch for traps under the snow."

"How do I watch for traps under the snow?"

"I don't know. Just be careful."

"I will. May as well play it safe and keep your eyes open and the door locked here."

"None of these doors lock up here."

"Yeah well, just the same he's not coming back after he's already told us he's here. Not in the daylight anyways. We'll sleep in shifts tonight. But it still doesn't hurt to keep an eye open and the rifle at hand today. Just in case."

"Yeah. Alright. I will." Dave's exhale was heavy. "Man this is messed up though. I hope this is the right decision."

"It is. And I'm not going to do anything stupid either. If I find him I'll feel him out. I'll try to reason with him. There's no benefit to us having this escalate further."

"What if you can't cross that river?"

"Well, if he crossed there's a spot."

Dave had found an old paddle in one of the closets and he used it as a crutch while he hobbled over to the window. He could see where the rabbit had disappeared in the snow hole. "What'll you say if you find him?"

"I'll play dumb about the rabbit. I won't even bring it up and pretend like we're not even suspecting him.

Tell him he won't have any problems from us and that we're looking forward to running the business and we're going to respect his property and we'll keep our clients away from his cabin. And really this all seems stupid 'cause there's no shortage of space up here. Tell him we're only running it for the fall months and not even until next year so most of the time we won't even be bothering him at all. Hell," Jacob said, "if it looks like him and his boy didn't just walk out of *Deliverance* they could even guide for us like he did way back then. Make a few bucks. Would be good for the kid too, right? Why not. Seems like that'd be good for everybody."

"And if he says no?"

"If he says no that's fine. Just the same I'll let him know we're not going away." Jacob's boots were laced and he'd put on his jacket hanging by the door and was shouldering up his pack.

Dave said, "You know what happened, hey?"

"Yeah. I think so. With the bear you mean?"

"Yeah."

"Yeah."

"You think you shot the bear he was hunting?" Dave said. "Maybe scared the hell out of him?"

"I'm starting to think so. It makes a lot of sense. Maybe. Maybe he thinks we just shot an animal for fun and left it. If that's the case I don't see what explaining things can't solve. He'd have to know we didn't see him and it wasn't on purpose and we weren't just going to leave it there if we didn't hit the river. Then the storm." Jacob slung his rifle over a shoulder. "I bet he understands."

"Alright. Well. Watch yourself. Seriously. Be careful."

He smiled at that, said you too brother, said he'd be back before dark.

39

With no snowshoes Jacob had to post-hole his way through the clearings, going even slower where the drifts mounded on the leeside of bushes and trees. He had hardly made a dent in the trek ahead when already he was sweating and so had to stop and drop a layer. At this pace he'd be hours hiking to the hill from where he had taken that fateful shot. Save for the odd sparrow and jay, the woods were mostly quiet.

When finally he did arrive to that rise in the forest, he climbed the short distance to the peak and stood there looking out at the other knoll off in the distance. Brought his binos up and rolled the focus knob and glassed for anything that might show in the texture of the snow. Nothing more than a snow-covered hill. He thought if any tracks had been made after the snow stopped that morning they must be too far to tell. He could just hear the flow of the river that separated the hills and scanned low through the trees trying to make out its rushing water, but he could not. So with no insights gained as to what lay ahead he walked down from the hill then eastwards towards the river and the rise of the next hill beyond.

He trekked the same route that he and Dave had last time. The sound of the river was different. When he emerged at its bank he was looking at a river now broader, faster. Some of the fallen precip was feeding its flow, as that flow was loud and frothy. It churned and roared and looked even less passable than it did cold. He looked to the north along its snowy banks for any sign of narrowing, and not seeing any, turned his gaze southwards. Appeared about equal. For whatever reason, maybe one single atom in his head spun right instead of left, he went south.

He walked the snowy bank looking for tree blazes or flagging tape or a place to cross. Other than his own that followed him, no boot tracks showed in the snow, no trees had been marked with a blaze. He continued on beside a cold and widening river. Then with his binos out he stopped and looked across into the forest and saw nothing and he looked farther on down his own side for any reason to keep hiking that way and saw none and so turned around heading back to where he had started, and once arrived, he continued north.

Mistake. There's a wildman in a jackrabbit suit white-camouflaged in this winter scene. He'd earlier crossed the river at a narrow spot to the north and he saw this man go south and knowing what was there knew he'd turn back around. He'd left hidden in the bushes what he was pulling over the snow, then started on a new path to intercept this hiker. He listened like a deer and he stepped like a fox and he watched like an owl, and when he'd finally seen his man coming back his way like he knew he would, he lowered his head like a wolf. He took care where he placed his tracks and walked in natural depressions and behind bushes and trees when the going allowed, and when it did not he smoothed them over with a needled branch. Put it all together, an apex predator—none greater: a man hunting another man.

Jacob hiked towards the trapper.

At certain places where the terrain constrains movement, well-travelled gametrails get worn deep enough into the ground that the snowfall doesn't completely hide away their concave contour, the snow subtly conforming to the trail's shape. Jacob was following one that snaked alongside the river. But where it's easier to travel it's easier to be ambushed, especially if one thinks he's the predator when he's really the prey. The trapper only moved when his man moved and his man was mostly moving.

Jackrabbits in the North are all white all winter, who knows what colour they are anywhere else. And so too was this old family suit the trapper's family had hunted with over the years. Same colour as the cut white shirt bandanaed across his face. He looked something like an albino bandit, a haunted snowman or an abominable one. His human tell was mostly just his eyes but even they're hidden behind a frosted lattice of closely set and unblinking lashes. Like his white brows above them. Like the white branches above him. You wouldn't see him, but seeing him you'd not be sure what to think of him. In some ways he fit so natural there in that surrounding, like it'd be hard to say who came first, him or the trees, and could be some of the environment just dressed itself to match. Yet in some regards he was out of place completely, like someone lost in time walking on homelands after centuries have gone by and where most ways of life except his own have long passed on. This timeless hunter or this anachronistic one. Regardless, every inch of him inside and out was aligned in predation and he stalked this lamb like not a single other thing was on his mind because right then there wasn't.

Most humans in the forest walk with the clumsy privilege of topping the food chain from such a height the details of their surroundings are lost on them. Jacob's preoccupied advance made the trapper's own silent. Jacob's focus on the river and what lay to the other side made him unaware of what was coming his way. What was close. Getting closer. What was awfully close now. What had now positioned itself just to the side of where Jacob was soon to walk.

The trapper sat concealed and still and didn't exhale often and when he did it was controlled and through his nose so that no mist rose from that veiled face. His narrowed eyes watched the man walking his way and with only a few steps to go the hiker's pluming exhales now came with sound too and the trapper listened to him breathe. In the gaps between those breaths he heard alternating commands: *haunt, torture, kill.* And of those three, all seemed reasonable and he'd still yet to decide. Now just paces away he scanned that approaching face. But the face did not fit the brand scored in his mind the day his world died out. Inside his head were loud calls for violence and demands for the infliction of pain. He considered them. *Kill for fun. Just cut him once and send him on his way.* Shadows whispering into the daylight. Occasionally a wolf will kill for fun even if some say otherwise and it doesn't make them evil, just staying sharp. Just their nature. Like the trapper's knife waiting to be drawn then drawn on flesh, its own essence crafted to sever flesh like predators' teeth shaped to tear it. But the trapper's hand doesn't move.

He's still, like fallen snow. Leaves his man by not leaving him at all, just closes those frosted lashes and lets the oblivious man continue on his way.

40

The face on the hill and the dream on his mind and the rabbit on the floor: *Dave.* Dave was not so well. His ankle throbbed under the ice wrapped in a towel he held to it. The presence he felt last night lingered in the day and a hangover didn't help and jitters from the coffee about the same. He tried not to think about it all, but mostly that's all he did, hoped Jacob was right and could find that face and somehow straighten this out. The rabbit. The rabbit sickened him. He'd already picked out the dried blood in his hair but he still caught himself reaching up to scratch at his scalp looking for more. All of it together was beyond unsettling. He'd thought cleaning up around the cabin might help set his mind at ease and so he'd washed his foot of the blood then scrubbed the floorboards too, but getting down low to cleanse the wood had him staring at those toes printed so clearly in that dried and dark red puddle. The sticky tack of it on his foot was stained in his mind. And he was alone.

He sat by the fire and read, or rather his eyes drifted over the words that didn't much register in his agitated mind. He held his fingers below the lines to steady his efforts. The skin around several of his nails was peeled back and he hadn't even noticed he was doing it. It wasn't a new habit but he hadn't done it in a while. Sometimes without raising his head he'd look around the cabin. Just looking. Corners of the room. He spun the wedding band on his ring finger with the thumb of his same hand. Fire dully crackling behind the closed stove door. Outside a bird cawed, one cackled.

He'd turn his head to look out the windows but with every passing minute their single-paned glass was gradually frosting closer towards their centres. So he'd get up using his paddle-crutch and hobble over to the windows, breathing hot air on the glass to melt sorry little spyholes. Saw one set of tracks heading out to the woods, and that's a lonely picture when you're the one they've left. Was looking forward to seeing those tracks retraced by the same person that made them. No one else. If the trapper was going to come back he wouldn't've left in the first place. That did make sense, he thought. It'd be a big risk him coming back to the lodge after he'd already made himself known. But. *But.* If he was crazy, and it certainly did look that way, he'd be capable of doing crazy things. So who knows. Dave looked to the rifle within arm's reach leaning against the table. He hadn't gone back into the bedroom since he had washed the blood.

It got to be past noon but he wasn't so hungry. He picked up the rifle and limped over to a window and scraped again with his nail its freshly crystallized and floral-patterned hole clear of frost then polished it with his shirtsleeve and brought his eye so close his lashes swept the pane. Stepped towards the cabin door and leaned his rifle against the wall. He opened the door a crack. Looked out. Saw a clear day and felt a cold one. His jacket hung beside the door and he put it on unzipped and boots on unlaced and limped out a step to the porch, then stopped. Squinted timidly at the sun. He took another step and that was enough.

The two woodpiles that bordered the door at either side were stacked tall and the snow had banked against them making the porch a little corridor. He looked at that clear field of snow with a single set of tracks leading out to the forest. Watched at the far end of them a second looking for Jacob, even though he didn't expect him back for a while. He scanned the forest's edge darkened by the canopy of evergreen boughs loaded with snow obscuring anything and everything beyond it. He quarter-turned his body and unzipped and bored a yellow hole that smoked in the snowbank among other yellow holes beside it. Standing there relieving himself with one hand on his hip he leaned back a touch in a stretch. The smell of fresh air. He closed his eyes and heard a few distant birds chittering. Felt the sun warm the side of his face, and that bit of warmth was all it took to just slightly lift his spirits.

Behind him a few silent flakes fell off a jackrabbit suit.

The trapper had risen from behind one of the woodpiles and slunk over its snowy top with his furred body making him so very quiet. But that wouldn't have mattered anyways with his injured and unarmed prey caught out alone in the snow. He stood there partially in Dave's shadow. The trapper hadn't seen his face and didn't need to—if it wasn't the first man, it was the second. For the initial split-second the fur wrapped around Dave's neck it registered to his mind as soft, even comforting in that split-second before the arm bone underneath the fur pressed so tightly into his neck that it started squeezing off his carotid artery and with it the blood to his brain. A hand on the back of his head wrapping him up like some huge furred white snake from forgotten lore, some storybook freak squeezing him out in a rear-naked-choke sending him off to sleep. Not even air enough to cough.

Dave reached up with both hands to try to pry those arms off but they were tight as a pulled wet knot. He swatted at them and to whatever they connected up to, but those swats were in vain with him getting weak while his vision reddened outside in. In the same moment he went unconscious, he went limp and fell back against the body behind him.

The trapper laid him down to the porch then took from a pocket like a roo's pouch two short ropes and bound his hands then his ankles. He untied the bandana still covering his face, and holding it outstretched by two corners, spun it—rolling it up tight. He squeezed Dave's cheeks with one hand and into that open mouth wedged the rolled shirt between his teeth then tied it behind his head. Zipped and belted Dave's pants. The trapper lowered down to one knee and grabbed Dave's jacket with both hands and pulled that limp body with its drooping head to sit upright on the porch, like some oversized stuffed doll, then pulled Dave's chest in to his own shoulder, and using the cabin wall as a brace, he stood up with the man asleep folded over his shoulder. Closed the cabin door. Swept the snow about the deck to hide the skirmish, but it didn't show much of a struggle anyways, there hadn't really been one. And he left with his captive the same way he came, carefully stepping into Jacob's tracks: one set in, one set out.

Not far inside the edge of the forest the trapper walking with the sleeping accused folded over his shoulder, split off from Jacob's trail and set off on the most direct route back to his own cabin, the same trail he had arrived on and where not far along his snow-shoes stood against the back of a pine tree beside an empty sled. He set Dave in the sled then bound him to the guardrails and if he woke he would have choked him out again, but he didn't wake. Leaving him there, he walked back to where they had diverged from Jacob's trail, and upon reaching that juncture he turned around, this time walking backwards to brush the snow clear of tracks.

When he returned to the sleigh his quarry was unmoving and there was no need to check for a pulse as he saw mist rising from the man's gagged mouth. The wide deerskin-leather tow-strap lay in front on the snow. He stepped behind it then brought it up to his stomach and leaned his weight into it to set the sleigh in motion and start trekking for the cabin, shuttling this captured man in the same sled that long ago he had shuttled her sick: one time to save a life, this time to ruin one. That former world now unrecognizable. As if he got tangled up in the wrong vibrating little string of some twisted physicist's mind, or coded into a cruel simulation by some deranged programmer, got sucked into a black hole lying under a tree root he never saw out there on the trail. Maybe there is a world where things turned out better for him. He the common inhabitant of these two disparate worlds was separated from himself not only by time but by changed, even distorted, personalities and beliefs and values. If by some bizarre occurrence a wormhole in the forest were to connect those two worlds and he was right then to encounter his former self, both of them drawing nearer to the other pulling a sleigh in opposite directions with opposite intentions in the dying light of the day, no doubt they'd stop where they met on the trail as two passing travellers in the isolate North always do. These two would pause confused like they had walked up to a mirror. Each with their frosted brows furrowed in disbelief, looking one another up, then down. So similar. Maybe they both raise up a hand. They'd start to say a greeting but would likely speak at once, so pause to allow the other go first, then simultaneously speak again. And if they somehow got past that awkward dance and did get to talking about something other than the weather, the referents to their important words like purpose and meaning and good and evil and love and hate could be so wildly different—even opposites—they might not have a workable language common between them. Each on the other side of a great schism preventing the imparting of meaningful exchange. Confused in their dialogue they might cease to talk and try for simple gestures, pointing to things at hand. But how much good could that be? Sun, tree, man. Then what? Both parties would inevitably stop their futile pantomimes and just stand there staring, thinking the other terribly confused, misguided. This sorry fool. And being incapable of communicating anything of substance and with nothing to share and nothing to transact, they might look off or away, ready to end this awkward interaction, embarrassed for the other knowing that their path leads them irrevocably lost. And so each at once steps aside and carries on to their own tragic ends.

It's too early for stars and neither will they come later, and in the twilight encroaching on a dying day the sleigh makes a sound of shush, shush, shush.

41

Jacob made his way farther north alongside the river. When he finally found a section narrow enough to attempt a crossing he left the bank, and the flow of the river brimmed nearly level with his boot-tops but not over. Had he walked on a bit farther still he'd have found it even shallower and with tracks of both snowshoe and sleigh leading to and from its banks. When he set foot on the virgin shore he turned back south bearing a path for the hill.

About an hour later into the afternoon with the sky starting to grey he arrived for the first time to the base of that hill where he'd shot at a bear back. They'd talked about it enough that even its small rise out of the otherwise level forest seemed charged with an aura. Jacob ascended looking all around as he went and there was an eeriness to it. Whether that sensation originated in his head or came up from the tingling land itself. Climbing the sparsely treed hill Jacob almost had the feeling eyes were on him. He spat in the snow and kept trudging upwards then thought he heard something and so took the vertically slung rifle and swiveled it forward, putting the butt of the stock into his shoulder with its muzzle pointed low, the gun not raised but now very easy to. The incline of the hill steepened enough that he trekked a couple short switchbacks the final distance to the top. That vantage point quiet, as if some ghoul had sucked in an enormous breath taking all the air off the top of that hill creating a momentary vacuum, and any second that air would come howling out in a terrible scream shattering thin ice and membranes of eardrums alike. A rounded untracked hilltop with several pillowed mounds of varying sizes that he assumed were covered boulders but hoped one was a dead bear. He turned and looked out behind him and about equal in elevation and some five hundred yards away was the other hill he'd recently climbed. Figured that about put him where he'd hit the animal— sow, back of a boar, cub—he was not sure. So where are you? Jacob began kicking at the shapes around him to test for a carcass. He unshouldered his pack to the snow then continued making sweeps with his boots trying to uncover a body or a blood trail.

Eventually one boot-sweep kicked up a hiding patch of red-crystalled snow. The day's cold air had made all the snow dry and light as powder and some of it swirled up in a thermal and was carried over the hill. He paused staring down at that patch of red contrast. Then he kicked around hurriedly in a circle trying to find more. Gotta be more, some drops in a line showing direction, he thought. Maybe when I hit it it bolted and the blood could be spread out, big gaps between the drops. He searched. He upturned the snow with his boots in widening circles where just outside that perimeter and unknown to him a small backpack lay buried. He went back to the blood patch and knelt down and first looked cautiously around him then unslung the rifle and laid it on his pack. Began shoving snow around by armfuls and lifting snow with his gloved hands to let it sift down between his fingers. Find a shard of bone or fur chunk or a piece of shot flesh. With his plot grown quite large in size he bumped something solid but not frozen in place. He started dusting it clear of snow, an odd shape emerging. He swept rapidly with his gloved fingertips acting like the brush of an archaeologist who just found first artifacts of ancient pottery or stone tools. When he realized the shape it was taking his jaw dropped. He kept clearing. Then his stomach dropped too. "Oh shit." He swept it fully clean of snow even though it was plainly obvious. A modern hunting bow lying excavated before him. He stared at it. "What the hell." He looked around him, then back to the bow, back to this puzzle piece with no place to put it. What in the very hell.

He lifted it from where it lay and turned it in his hand and snow fell from its crevices and some clung to its string and he saw the side-quiver held three arrows with one empty slot. He knelt there running through scenarios. Why leave a bow behind? Then suddenly from the corner of his eye he caught movement. He slowly swiveled his head. A wolf huge in size pitch black in colour had risen up from the other side of the hill. Big canine head. Its yellow eyes were on him. He froze. A chill ran down his back like cold mouse feet were running the knobs of his spine-bones. The animal stood some couple dozen feet away. A timber wolf capable of killing bull moose fifteen hundred pounds in weight and not just the sick or the old either. That dark head with pointed ears and cold yellowed eyes that hadn't yet bared its teeth just bared its teeth and lowered its dark head to the snow.

The adrenaline in his bloodstream was like a solvent sprayed on a stuck motor part and without taking his eyes off the animal that hadn't taken its eyes off him he laid down the bow and reached towards his pack and picked up the rifle. Slow is smooth, smooth is fast. He shouldered it. He put his eye behind the scope but he'd fogged that up when he raised the rifle through an exhaled breath so he unsquinted his off eye and pointed the gun wolfwards and he thumbed off the safety and jerked the trigger in a panicked shot. The firing pin hit the rifle cartridge with a dead bink, a sickening dull sound. His body flinched anyways, habituated to a kickback. The wolf prowled in one step. Then another. Its body low to the snow and its eyes unblinking. Jacob frantically cycled the action and ejected the old spent round and from the internal magazine chambered another and pointed the now fogless crosshairs on a target so close the entire lens was just a black blur. Pulled the trigger. Bink. Another dead round. Now his skin pebbled up from a single tremor shivering over his body and when that tremor arrived to his hands, the gun shook. He almost dropped it. "Shit." A profane cloud rose above him while a timber wolf stepped towards him. He cycled the gun again and expected no different and fired and it wasn't. "Fuck." He lowered that useless tool. The wolf, sized like it had wandered out of some folk tale, stalked towards him as if it knew its upper hand. Some few single digits paced them out now. He knew running would only make it worse likely triggering an instinctual pursuit. Adrenaline and fear and nowhere to spend it, that single tremor was followed up by outright trembles of fear. He looked down to the bow he'd never get up in time. Who knows if it would even draw back after having lain there all frozen. And that didn't matter now anyways. The big wolf who on all fours sized fully higher than the waist of a standing man now stood level to the head of this kneeling one. The wild dog its fangs bared staring straight at him so close he could almost reach out and touch it. Jacob lowered his head and looked down. Not a tactic. His shoulders rolled in and his back curved and he averted his eyes in a primal posture of submission and fear that begged mercy in any animal capable of displaying it. The wolf unblinking, its eyes like polished pyrite. The wolf stepping once more in his direction.

And then the wolf's head looking away. The animal moved onwards and continued to wherever it was going and didn't even turn its head as it passed. Just walked on like a solitary knight on some journey that did not concern this pathetic figure trembling in the snow. On some quest perhaps untranslatable beyond the language of its kind. Maybe it never gets there. Maybe always seeking never arriving forever trying to answer some wild calling. A calling sprung from within, not without. Having smelt the man's foul stink of fear, the wolf paid what was no threat no further attention.

Wolves rarely attack humans anyways. People just like to talk.

Jacob's sweat-drenched body still flinching with latent spasms of fear, he looked over his shoulder for the animal but the animal had already dropped off the hill and out of sight. He turned back around and just tried to catch his breath, tried to breathe slower. He took a few minutes to himself then drank water from the bottle in his pack and coughed some of it up. Then he just sat there.

With the bow strapped to his backpack he lifted it up, then remembered the gun in his hand was empty and so dropped the pack again and strapped it also. He hadn't packed extra rounds as the internal magazine's three had seemed plenty when he wasn't even out there to hunt, and now he was regretting that. He angled down from the hill shaken and more confused than he'd arrived. The bow. The wolf. The gun. Could be I didn't chamber a round after I shot the bear. Don't actually remember. No way I filled the magazine with two empty rounds though. No way. It would have been so obvious. They'd have been light and missing their bullets. Unless I was drunk. Don't think I was drunk?

He reached the bottom of the hill. Beside him an arrow stuck in an alder. But taking the shape of one more tree branch with the high side of its shaft holding a skiff of snow it didn't catch his eye. He took a few steps into the woods following what he thought could be a trail, and walking it a short ways it forked, then forked again. It was faint to begin with. Not without a gun, not after that wolf, he thought. Head back to the lodge and regroup. See how Dave's doing. Figure this all out. He turned around and this time passing the arrow its single orange fletching did catch his eye. With one finger he cleared its shaft of snow then eyed its angle to gauge its trajectory, his head turning back up the hill. Strange. Strange though not all that strange given the bow, he thought. Without dropping his pack he put two hands on the shaft and raised his boot up the tree, but he couldn't even see the ends of the broadhead, fully buried such as it was. He pulled but it was not coming out. Didn't see any point in snapping it off so he gave it up. Looked around for whatever else and what the hell. Figure this shit out. Just not without a gun. From his pocket he withdrew the GPS to mark the exact spot in case he needed to come back and search more tomorrow. Even having that detail to one day give the police didn't seem like such a remote idea now as this was all strange and getting stranger. He pressed and held down the power button and the grey screen remained unlit like the colour of the low hanging sky, and at first he thought it was just the cold slowing the batteries. So light it was in his hand, and he just realized that. Then he knew.

He slid open the battery cover anyways to confirm it. And those puzzle pieces began snapping into place. It all fits now. He was shaking his head. Now he was sure. He spat to the snow. "Lunatic backwater shit," he said out loud, maybe with the hope that vocalizing his disdain would help trivialize and subdue the feelings welling in his throat. Looked around. Pulled his hat down lower over his eyes. He thought he had just enough time to make the lodge before dark and not wanting to waste it he took his first step for the long walk, then bent over and put a hand on his knee and spat some salty bile up, gave it a minute in case something of more substance was to follow. Just shook his head there. Maybe just call for the plane. He thought that, he didn't say it.

In the receding northern light faint with the season's early darkness, the only thing he set his mind to was following his own tracks home. Just outside the edges of those bootprints was a no-man's-land of fear and uncertainty and doubt and shame so he tried to make his entire world the placing of steps. After he crossed the river he stopped and strapped his headlamp without yet turning it on. He hoped he wouldn't need to, 'cause when he took it from his pack its weight felt sickly light. He didn't even check for the battery, just strapped the useless headlamp there anyways in false comfort. But don't think about that now, he thought.

42

ave's head bobs in rhythm to the steps that pull him as he wakes to the lurching of a sleigh ride in a darkening day. He tries to raise his arms but finds he's bound to a sled. Tries to kick his legs but ankles tied too. Starts to squirm and can't barely wriggle and makes weak sounds from hyperventilating breaths and a constricted chest and what comes from his mouth are sorry whimpers, and had he been capable of anything much louder the shirt tied across his mouth would have muffled them anyways—*and what does it matter? Who'd hear it up there in that lonely North?* His eyes are wide though. God they're wide. 'Cause he's staring at the back of some freakish apparition pulling him deeper into the woods in a jackrabbit suit.

After dark the lurching stops and the tow strap drops from the trapper's waist to the snow outside the cabin. He turns around and though he hasn't yet taken any steps towards Dave he's still towering above him.

Dave looks up at that face for the first time since he's seen it through a riflescope. He barely recognizes it. This ghastly face. The same one but sunken, hollowed, grizzled. Like years of abuse have worn it out, some hard living that you wouldn't want to ask about unless you were on close terms with him—and if you were you'd have known what had happened anyways. They're looking at one another in a shared moment of those having a bond from things past. Things to be resolved.

Bound as he is Dave can't help squirming anyways. And then this silent man steps towards him. He doesn't reach for the cords binding Dave to the guardrails just walks on past to the back of the sled and kneels down. Dave tries to turn his head to see what he's doing back there and makes weak sounds of struggle and fright and his eyes move frantically side to side in his turning head. And then an arm wraps around his neck and no split-second of comfort this time 'cause this time he knows what that means. And those frantic eyes calm, then roll upwards, and Dave goes back to sleep.

43

Jacob emerged from the timber and saw no light in the cabin windows, no smoke rising from its chimney. The steps he retraced were a little wider in places than his original footfalls, but that's a detail lost in the faded light. He had no ace up his sleeve, no angles, no weapons, didn't know if anything was waiting for him either, but he just gave up his caution and headed straight for it. Stomped loud arriving on the porch then came in fast and sweating and opened the door and yelled for Dave in a small and dusky cabin you didn't need to yell for anything at all. Just a cold and quiet living room.

He reached up to power on the headlamp dangling from above but it hung dead. He lit a candle then unstrapped his load which thumped to the planks, reached for the satellite phone on the table hoping to get lucky and maybe the trapper had missed it. He hadn't. Jacob cursed. He picked up a cardboard ammunition box that should have felt full and heavy. It nearly floated in his hand. Sliding the Styrofoam tray out he did see brass and that surprised him. Pinched the end of one in two fingers and pulled it from its hole and saw the bullet missing and the cartridge empty of powder. A spent round like those in his gun. He dumped them onto the table and the hollow brass cartridges bounced and chimed discordantly then rolled about and some fell to the floor. In both rooms he saw nothing out of the ordinary, he even looked under the beds. Dave's rifle was by the door and he found that it also chambered an old round, as well those in the magazine. On the wall-mounted coatrack Dave's backpack hung empty, jacket gone. Beside the door there were no boots. "Shit." He paced the length of the cabin. "Shit," his cold breath said again. Seeing his breath gave him the idea to check the stove and see how long Dave had been gone. The vent and damper had been left open. The wood had burned down to a small bed of coals that with the opening stove door blushed like they were embarrassed about something. He stomped on the floorboards and listened for any hollow spot of a trapdoor or a tunnel and felt fairly stupid doing it but how else? How in the hell else? Shook his head pacing there.

He'd left the cabin door open and he stepped back through it. The edge of the woods dark and the woods beyond, darker still. He listened and listened to nothing at all—everything so quiet like the North itself was listening back. Standing there breathing heavily, confused and alone and looking off into a woods where the night had veiled its secrets. A land that didn't tell its own stories. His bottom lip quivered once, so together he pursed them.

With a match dragged on the iron of the stove he lit a second candle, leaving one in the cabin, and walked back to the porch. Holding it low he saw no signs, but he'd disturbed it all so much tramping back and forth he thought that examination was pretty well point-less. With a curved hand he shrouded the candle flame then started encircling the cabin perimeter looking for tracks. His movements were erratic from the snow and partway he tripped and the weak flame wavered and then it went out. He turned and went back for another match and now he was sweating even more than he had on his trek home, breathing heavier too. "Christ," he said. More careful now with the flame and searching low to the ground he saw nothing and the candle did snuff out again and so he relit once more before he finished his investigative circle. There were no tracks and that's what he saw.

Back on the porch looking off into the woods dark with no texture and nothing to tell and he knew his gun was unloaded and phone dead and headlamp dead and friend gone and himself alone in the North, this one lonely figure with one lonely candle leaked one lonely tear that would have frozen there on his cheek if it hadn't been followed by another. He still held a hand curved in front of the candle before him, which now mostly illuminated his piteous face and little beyond. He outstretched his arm as far as it would go to try and send that light out into the world, let him see anything at all out there. But that diffuse little glow barely brightened more than the small airspace it occupied.

He drew in a deep breath, held it a second listening. Then he yelled out his friend's name. "Dave!" he yelled. "Dave!" as loud as he could. That name leaving his lips snuffed out the candle. "Dave," he said in the dark with a rasping voice. And that name ran off all alone into the lost night.

44

No more dusk. No more sunset. No more twilight, demise of days, or talks of fading light. It's night now and a man sits bound and gagged surrounded by candlelight. His wrists are tied together, his arms to the chair. His head would've slumped to the side or forward but there's a noose around his neck taut enough to hold it upright, slack enough not to choke him. His eyes open just now. At first his vision is blurred, then it clears some, and then he jumps as much as jumping is allowed when you're roped to a chair as he deciphers out of that disturbed and murky room the figure seated opposite him. Wild long and dirty hair, a ragged face crusted with blood and grime that looks like it's been crying, but what streaks his cheeks are not tears rather ice water dripped from formerly frosted lashes like makeup running on a ruined night. Buried in dark sockets are bloodshot eyes burning out at him. Soiled hands with dirt far under the nails where nails there are. Shirtless and muscled upper body with a scarred chest. Then Dave looks down and sees he's shirtless himself too.

Dave's worried eyes search the disarrayed room and the pair opposite him don't even blink, never mind look away. The northern wind like a third party here wisps in through a broken window, but not one so interested and it comes and goes as it pleases. On the small table separating them rests the trapper's folded hands, two candles looking homemade with their dirty wax perhaps from deer fat poured into old tin soup cans, sometimes flickering other times steady and widely set apart. Between the candles, a bear hide. It's not very big and there's only a little blood on it. One end is stitched with two thin cotton ropes. It's laid out flat and you can see the hole.

Dave's looking at it. Bear hide. Bear hide cut like a cloak. Small cloak. He looks about. Where's the boy? You can almost hear the machinery of his mind snapping things into place. Small cloak. Click. The boy. Click. Oh god. Click. Oh no. *Oh no.* Dave stops breathing for a second. His eyes widen looking at the fur. And then they slowly, slowly lift upwards from the table. See a man's belly breathing in and out faster now, the bare chest heaving also, the grizzled face and narrowed eyes alight with candle flames, as if any burnt destruction thereabouts, forest fires and cremated things, smoking cedars and what all else, might just have those eyes at their source. Dave starts breathing noisily through his nose and his bare stomach is sucking in and out as he's looking down to the hide then up to the trapper, down, then up, hide, then eyes, and his gagged mouth makes a pleading sound of both suffering and whining pity, and then he tilts his head just slightly sideways in some mute empathic gesture of the other man's anguish— but only as much as the noose allows.

Wax is pooling at the candles' bases and still the trapper watches his captive. Dave's nerves now like melted fuses. That the man has not spoken seems worse to Dave than most words that could be spoken. He sits there feeling on display—he is. And all he can do is watch what's watching him back, or close his eyes and try to wish it away. It almost feels like he's onstage in a play written by a troubled mind and it's been going on for a while now and he's only just realized it, only now understands he'll be in the final act and that seems not so far away. He's got the lead role in this play and of course it's already been written but he's only going to know his lines when it comes time for him to speak them. He'll be acting it out whether he wants to or not. That makes him both actor and spectator. Participant and witness. He swallows and it's hard going with the rope cinched around his throat. He looks upwards along its length searching for its end, but the rope just twists on up into the obscurity of the dim heights. But he's sure if this madman pulls its tail end, he'll be kicking his legs and dancing for his audience.

The candles draw further down and in the long silence Dave calms enough that he takes a chance to meekly gesture at his captor. He tilts his head a bit forward and grunts through the gag. A suggestion, it seems, for the man to hear him out. The trapper watches. Dave repeats this gesture a couple more times. Finally the trapper shows his first animation. His eyes don't move but his right hand unclasps from his left where they rested on the table and lowers out of sight. A click and it returns with the blade locked into place. He places it beside the bear hide and its steel tip points at Dave. Dave watches the candlelight dancing along its bloody steel, as if the foundry that hammered it to shape ingrained within the metal the fire from its forge to forever lick its blade. The trapper reclasps his hands. The captive inhales deeply, then shudders exhaling. Makes no further suggestions, and just closes his eyes.

Wonder if what he saw there was any better.

45

"This is bullshit." Jacob sat by the stove and lowered his empty glass once more and ran a cloth over the bow limbs to dry their weeping condensation. "Ghosts." He drank. "Nope. No way." He drank. "Bullshit." At his feet three arrows were laid out on the cabin floor. One by one he checked that each broadhead was fully threaded into its collar, that the vanes were not cut or peeling, that when he lightly flexed their shafts they showed no splinters. Each in turn he set their blades sideways on his thumbnail and tried to shave downwards but every edge held their place like the razors they were. All nine edges from all three arrows the same.

He opened the cabin door and reached up to an icicle hanging from the porch roof and this time he didn't look around outside and he didn't yell anything he just snapped that crystal root and put it in his glass and closed the door and refilled the glass. Sat back down in the chair by the stove with the ice clinking in the glass of his chilled whisky. The cold whisky smoky on his tongue as he rolled it in his mouth. "There are tracks and I didn't see them. That's it. That's a sure thing. Didn't float down from the sky, he just stepped in mine. No other way." The ice tinked against the glass. "They're there and I'll see 'em. First fuckin' light. I betcha."

He lifted the bow and gripped the string and drew it back unloaded, watched the string travel and the cams rotate and that it pulled smoothly all the way to full draw. Turned it a bit as he held it loaded to look at it from another angle. Seemed sound. Then he gently drew down the string without firing. Slid the cleaned and dried arrows back to their side quiver and laid it on his backpack he'd already packed for the morning. He opened the stove and laid in two quartered logs but he did not stack it full as there was no need to keep the cabin warm till noon. He'd be setting out early. Very early. His legs were stretched out in front of him with his arms crossed on his chest and the fire burned brighter and his eyes squinted looking into it and not because it was bright. "I'll see you tomorrow, Hillbilly."

46

"We saw each other that day."

Dave opens his eyes at these the first words from his captor sitting across from him in the candlelight.

"We saw each other that day," he says again.

Dave entirely tuned to the trapper: no movements, no thoughts.

"You saw my face," he says. "And I saw yours."

Dave slowly shakes his noosed and gagged head.

"Yes, you did. Don't say you didn't. We both know you did. And what did I see in your hands?" asks the trapper.

Dave makes weak and muffled sounds.

"What did I see in your hands?"

Sounds that further whimper.

"That's right. A gun."

That last word sends Dave's chest heaving.

"You," the trapper whispers. "*You*," he seethes. He nods downwards at the bear cloak. "You did that. And not just that. Other crimes too. You stole my compass. You stole him from me. Stole him of his future. You abducted him from me. You killed what was holy to me. Destroyed my stars and my moon." He leans in from his chair between and overtop the candle flames burning from mostly just wax pools and their glow below him makes his hollowed sockets all the darker. "You ended a bloodline. Whatever future lives he would have had and his child would have had you prevented their living. A crime against humanity, a future one."

He leaned back. "Shed blood so shall be shed your own. Codes written as far back as there is history of law. But is that justice? There needs to be punishment that fits the crime. That's justice. Your crimes are stealing, abduction, murder, genocide, destroying worlds." He speaks calmly delivering these facts.

"Do you have a son?" the trapper asks.

Dave listening to all being accused of him was already shaking his head no and that lagging gesture befit the current question. His eyes catch the glinting polished triggers of rifles hung on a wall.

"No. No son. But who knows. What father in your position wouldn't lie. Regardless. If he exists he isn't here and you don't have the currency to square your debt."

Sweat beads roll down Dave's temples. The trapper without breaking his stare lifts his hands from the table and moves them outwards in unison, then with two fingers from each hand pinches the two candle flames that hiss then curl like thin grey serpents rising in the dingy room. He watches Dave from between those wavering strings of smoke and now the only lighting comes from the candles on the floor and one of those guttered nubs sputters and pops then dies out altogether and with its own hiss joins the two that went before. The trapper brings his eyes to Dave's bare chest. Sees his heart beating through his skin—he may have been listening to it, his hearing is very good and the room so quiet.

Dave realizes what the trapper's doing and that only makes that worried muscle pound the harder.

To every heartbeat the trapper starts saying, "Thump, thump, thump." Says it like he's the one conducting its tempo, and given the terror he's instilling in this man, you could say he is. The trapper's mouth cuts a kind of cruel smile or leer and his dried lips, not used to that shape, crack. Blood seeps from the small fissures. He looks up to Dave's eyes, then back to his chest and watches that pace further quickening. "Thumpthumpthump," he says through his bleeding lips. The trapper uncurls a single finger. Points it at Dave. Stretches his arm out slowly, crossing the gap between the dead candles and over the sleeping bear, until finally he touches the tip to Dave's pulsing chest. Holds it there feeling his life beat. Looks into his eyes. And that crude smile, his lips wet and red with blood, widens a touch. Maybe from the satisfaction that he can set the pace of this man's pulse and excite his life before he takes it. He looks back down to Dave's chest. Then he traces on that bare skin a circle the size of a fist. "I have not decided yet," he says as a drop of blood hangs from his lip. "I may eat your heart." The blood drop falls.

At those words Dave's face twitches. His nose pantings are shallow and lack sufficient oxygen and he feels like he's losing some of his faculties and his eyes flutter, but he does not faint. His bladder lets go. Just a small puddle of urine on his chair seat but mostly down his leg where it trickles to the floor to form a larger puddle. His toes wet and warming and he now realizes his boots have been removed.

The trapper gets up and walks for the door and Dave watches his bare and muscled back, sees him bend to pick up a shovelhead. Dave's unsure how long the trapper's gone, because when his pulse slows from being jacked to heart-attack pace it nearly flatlines and his exhaustion brings sleep. Or something like it.

47

Jacob woke in his chair by the stove in the dark holding an angled tumbler unspilt of its whisky. He looked out the window. Dark. He had no clock but felt dawn could be close. "Fuck it." He set the tumbler empty on the floor then slapped himself once on the face. He lit a candle he packed another he grabbed his things and set out searching.

Methodical and slow. Figure it out. The porch was the only place to start regardless if that prior investigation had showed nothing. He looked at one woodpile mostly buried under snow. Piss holes, some his own. He made another. Turned and looked at the other woodpile behind him and saw its snowy top had been disturbed. They had brought in wood from it and Dave likely brought in more while he was gone yesterday, and scrutinize as he did it was hard to say if there was something there or not. He left the porch and walked to the backside of that pile and saw that though some snow and ice had fallen from the roof, the texture of that snow patch did sorta look differently than the snow around it. Just subtly peculiar. It gave him pause. Still, nobody just flew up and away, he thought. He went back to the porch and turned and with the candle held low began following his yesterday's tracks. "Go ahead and snuff out I'll relight your ass every minute till sunup," he promised the flame with words soaked in whiskey. One candlelit step at a time Jacob scrutinized his route to the forest. This being his third time on that snow trail it was now a tracked-up path rather than distinct steps, so kicked about from his own return home last night with toe drags and booted snow. He stayed on it. Find a blood drop. A piece of fabric. Find a step that doesn't look like my own. Anything. He relit the candle often. Eventually he did see a shadowed hole just outside the main track. He stepped over to it and couldn't see any treads so reached in. Like some magic trick gone awry he pulled out a headless rabbit. Right. He dropped it back in its hole.

By the time he'd finished the short trail through the clearing and reached the forest's edge he'd gained no knowledge but he'd lost no conviction. If someone came, if someone left, this is how. He stayed stooped and scanning, bent low over the tracks, and hadn't gone far into the woods—*there it was*. "Ha." The same peculiar surface to the snow he'd seen behind the wood-pile. A subtle brushing like a swept path. Leading east. He stared and took it in like he'd been searching for raked snow all his life and now finally found it. Now it was obvious. He stood up smiling to himself. Reached to the inner breast pocket of his jacket and withdrew a metal flask and unscrewed its top. Wiped his lips. "Hillbilly," he said.

48

Dave wakes to the bang of the shovelhead hitting the floor. Sees the trapper walking towards him looking like some sort of soot worker, more so a body raised from the ground than one digging into it. The cabin has further dimmed as some candles have burned or blown out and it is not yet dawn.

Before the trapper retakes his seat he picks up the knife on the table then pushes the table out from between them. Its dragging legs screech uncomfortably. He sits down putting his elbows on his knees then his chin on his wrapped fists that hold the knife pointed outwards at Dave. Eyes, knife, intentions—everything about him daggered. And those eyes that hadn't much colour before were now like portals to the remorseless night itself, as if part of him had stayed out there and part of something else came back. The trapper looks down at the small yellow puddle on the floor.

"Are you suffering, man? I can't even tell. I see you shake." He looks him up and down. "I'm looking right at you. It just does not register. Your suffering simply does not register." He leans back and crosses his arms on his chest with the knife now held sideways.

Dave watches it and though it's pointed away from him it looks no less menacing with the flames licking at the dried blood on its blade.

"You're an insect in a web. That rope on your neck," he nods upwards, "keep trembling 'cause you're calling what spun it."

The wind blows outside. The wind blows inside. The draft coming in through the broken window finds its way to the stove vent and the fire inhales. "Keep trembling, you're ringing the dinner bell calling the spider to feed."

Dave makes pitiful sounds that might have been words had the rag not prevented their shape.

"What could you say? What could you possibly say?"

The gagged man moaning inarticulate.

The trapper reaches towards him and sets the back-side of two dirty fingers against his captive's cheek, pauses a second like he hadn't anticipated that feeling of life from the warmth of living skin, then he slides those fingers under the shirt-rag tied across his mouth and forces it down to his neck. His fingers leave a swipe mark of streaked mud on the man's cheek. The trapper sits back in the chair.

"Speak."

Dave yells, "I didn't kill your son!" He gasps for breath and says, "I'm so sorry. But I didn't do it."

The trapper listens to that. Then he shakes his head. "I saw you, I saw the gun. That's a terrible lie. Do better."

"I swear to God I didn't shoot that day. He passed it off. The gun."

"The gun," the trapper says. "He passed off the gun. Why would he pass off the gun? Imagine how you sound to me now. I saw you with it. Not him. I didn't even see anyone else that day. Not then I didn't." He grins. "But yesterday I did."

Dave's face goes blank as he sits with that. "Did you do something to him? What did you do? Oh god."

"Right now we're only concerned about you."

Dave says in a pained and weak voice, "I told him we should get closer. I said it didn't feel right. And after the shot he passed off the gun, I swear he did."

"Listen to yourself. Put yourself in my position. You're insulting."

"It's true, though," he says, nearly in tears. "I'm so sorry," he almost sobs. "It was a mistake."

"Okay. There you are correct. It was a mistake. One you can't take back. And some mistakes are still crimes that have to be punished. I'm sure you get that. I'm sure in other circumstances that would be easy for you to see. What kind of world would we be living in? The world's a better place when people who have proven they can make the worst mistakes possible are prevented from making them again. Maybe you have a tendency for terrible decisions. Maybe horrible misjudgments are part of your makeup and your offspring are predisposed to the worst kinds of errors that ruin things for other people. People minding their own business. Of course you can't go free." He unfolds his crossed arms and with the knife pointed low, gestures a circle between Dave's legs. "In the least…"

Dave watches that ugly motion. He shakes his head like he forgets the gag was gone. Then he pleads out different combinations of sorry and that he didn't do it, that this is all a terrible mistake.

"You've said all that already."

Dave pleads on.

Maybe the trapper's hearing him out or could be he's just in the depths of his own mind as his eyes do occasionally skitter about the room, sometimes staring into the cabin corners, at an upside-down framed picture, at scattered pieces of the shattered past. He returns to Dave. "Stop talking. Mistake or otherwise you can't go free. But to keep you captive till the end of your days would only punish me. To feed and care for you. To see you and be reminded of what you took from me. From this world. Maybe someone tries to come for you. No. Can't have that. Send you to the police in town? Who knows. You could be freed on a mistrial, some technicality. That won't work either. We settle our own disputes up here. Your actions make it clear the world can't risk your existence, and so I owe that world your ending. There's no other options. Then it's burial." He shook his head. "And you'll be with company far better than you deserve."

"Please don't do this."

There are no clocks but sunrise is not far off and the trapper says so then walks over the messy floor—pots and pans, broken glass, firewood—and goes out the cabin door again. Dave stays awake this time and hears him out there digging. Sitting there tied to a chair listening to the flat sound of soil landing from out of a high arc with the predictable rhythm of some dull and bedeviled metronome counting off the time he has left in this world. He occasionally hears mumbled words sounding like a troubled man in either counsel or feud, maybe both, his embattled self fighting different wars out there while he pitches up earth in the bleak dawn light.

The sun crests over the eastern horizon of northern landscape and begins navigating that forest maze. Backs of trees start to brighten and some few first rays find the cabin walls, then its windows, then shine through the glass, bringing an impartial grace to the ransacked cabin's mad squalor. Dave's shoulders rise and fall softly at the break of day. On his otherwise cold body, sunlight warms his face.

The door opens. The trapper sees his captive's face bathed in the tender light. Stands and watches it a second while holding a shovelhead. "How about that. How does that feel?" he asks. "What a light to die in." He closes the door and takes a step then stops. "Tell me. Would you say it's beautiful?"

Dave says nothing.

"Would you?"

Dave nearly catatonic stares at this grim figure across the cabin.

"Say it. Go ahead," he says mildly, encouragingly. "Say it's beautiful." He walks towards Dave and passes before a window, returning the seated man to shadow, then sits down opposite again. Sweating, filthy, looking head to toe all crazy, never mind what corrupt ideas may have been rotting his insides. Like he's dug up something out there better left undug and then proceeded to both ingest and drape himself with it.

Dave watches nervously the shovelhead in his hands.

The trapper whispers and smiles invitingly, not unlike an operator of a carnival game of chance, "Say it's beautiful."

Dave neither moves nor speaks nor gives any sign he might.

"Okay. Okay. Good. Because you are in no position to say that. You are in no position to say life is beautiful." His smile recedes. "Nobody can. Not until they've outstretched their arms and put all the suffering on one hand and all the beauty on the other. Until you've scaled that up, do not speak." He throws the shovelhead aside and Dave jumps at the bang. "Just be quiet because you do not know what you are talking about." He reaches out and covers Dave's closed mouth. "Beauty," he says. "Beauty," he says quietly. "Each curve shaping its letters should be written in all the blood ever spilt in cruelty. In violence. In all the pain of common hardship. It wouldn't drip off the page, it'd soak through any paper ever printed as high as you could stack it." The trapper tilts his head upwards like he's looking at some tower of account. Slowly follows the rope back down returning his gaze to the face of the man noosed. "The *u* alone should be a grave that holds all the poor dead babies and it would sag so deep you couldn't see the belly of it." Holding Dave by his face he tilts his head down for him allowing a look into that grave. "Can you hear all the screaming mothers begging for their child to be spared? Can you? Play those sounds in your head, boy, all of them." Dave's looking down and doesn't see the trapper reach out his other hand, and with index and thumb flicks the lobe of one of Dave's ears who nearly shatters into a thousand pieces like cracked-up ice. "If you could hold all that in your head at once it would take you straight to hell. So don't you call it beautiful until you've weighed it all up accordingly." The trapper isn't speaking loudly but his words charge the room. He returns Dave's head to level.

"Have you lost a child?" He's squeezing Dave's mouth harder and the eyes of the face held in his hand are large, fearful and confused. "I have. But you know that. That's what brought us here. And that's not even what I'm talking about. You need to lose all the children before you can speak on this, then hold it all in your head at once and talk to me of beauty, of meaning," he whispered, "of God. No. You couldn't do it. You'd convulse and drool and go insane. Horror that would snap your brittle little mind in two." The trapper now slightly shaking while he speaks and so Dave's held face quivers too.

"Want me to go on?" He nods Dave's head up and down. "I want you to dam up the edges of this entire continent from coast to coast to coast to coast," the trapper without raising a hand points a finger up, down, left, right, "then play the last millennia over on quick-time. Do it now, I'll wait." He stares at Dave. "Now look to the ground. We'll see the blood flooding your ankles. Look," he pointed, "I can see it already." The trapper was either pointing to the urine puddle or to a red mark on the side of a toe where Dave must have missed cleaning off some rabbit blood. "On this land tribes raided other tribes. Men and women tortured, enslaved, murdered. On this land whole villages wiped out by disease from colonizers. On this land families torn apart, children taken and abused in schools run by the faithful. *Don't look away,*" he seethes at Dave who is just staring back. "Feel that. Put it in your belly then say have faith, say all suffering is growth, say it all happens for a reason, and you are either ignorant beyond imagination or a sadist. Both some version of broken. Don't you dare try to dismiss or justify with your pretty and empty words the utter immensity of all the misery. Have you lost your mind?" He waits for a response from the man whose mouth he covered.

Dave makes a short and muffled moan.

The trapper's eyes lower to the back of his own hand. "My hands are not clean. If life other than humans can feel significant pain then loosen that noose I'm coming in beside you and we'll atone together." For a minute or two he watches his own hand holding Dave's face, whatever scenes were playing in the trapper's mind. "Maybe my day will come." His eyes return to Dave. "But today it's you on trial. Accusation: murder of a little boy. Verdict: guilty." He finally releases Dave's face leaving a bloodless imprint of the grip across his mouth.

No words come to Dave as if that phantom hand continues to silence him. He's thinking how to argue his case or apologize or just ramble with the hopes of prolonging his life, and he starts to speak but the trapper shakes his head and says, "Don't. Don't speak, we don't have much time now. Look. You were raised to hunt by your family. Maybe the gun was even passed down. You went in the forest. You saw a bear. You shot the bear. The bear was a boy. Things were set up from before you picked up the gun. There's no getting outside of what came before—are you so arrogant to believe you stand outside of cause and effect? But the fact remains, you've proven yourself someone who makes the world a worse place. So this is justice, not malice. Don't mistake it."

The wind blows. The fire burns.

Dave risks speaking anyways. And maybe he means it or maybe he's just trying to buy time, but he says in a weak voice, "If it couldn't have been otherwise, then what you're doing here isn't your fault either. I'm sorry for your pain I never caused. I forgive this."

The trapper returns his chin to rest on his fists. Appears to reflect on it as he does take a bit of time before he lifts his head. "That's fine. I wasn't asking. All you need to do here is die."

The bound man searches in his captor's eyes, looks at this troubled man operating from the colder regions of humanity's wide borders, tries to find a speck of warmth, some single spark of connection. A search that comes up empty.

"Believe this," he says to Dave. "This is important. Listen. At sunrise you will die. And I already feel my back warming. Those aren't words. I mean that as much as I've meant anything. Put that truth in your skull. *Hey.*" He reaches out and taps a finger on Dave's forehead and Dave's whole body spasms from that touch as he sits listening to these ravings. "Very soon I will kill you. I promise. You have very few breaths. Few words to speak. So few memories to recall. So tell me. I want to know. What's inside you right now? Your last minutes of life. Account for it. For all the wasted others. For horror and beauty. For all the misery including yours in this moment. Speak to me of truth and meaning. Is there something worth telling here? What's inside you? I want to know."

Dave pauses before speaking waiting for the disturbed man to tell him not to. Then he draws a shaky breath. "There's something."

"What? A God?"

"No."

"Then what?"

"Something."

"What something?"

"Just what I know," Dave says meekly, hoarsely. "I've felt it before."

The trapper shakes his head. "You know it. Listen to you. You sound like a child. Actually you don't know that. Because someone else believes otherwise with the same felt conviction. Round up a table of believers—Christian, Muslim, Jain, Jew, Buddhist, Wiccan, some nondenominational spiritualist, some New Age proselytizer, a crystal worker, an energy healer—they're all sitting at the table, all knowing their personal relationship with a god or gods or a living universe or whatever each one calls it. That their version is truth. But all their convictions are based on feelings from their belly. Or holy texts with dubious pasts. Beliefs that contradict one another. Mutually exclusive. One god or several. Afterlife or no. Hell or forgiveness. What is sinful and what permitted. So only one is right or they're all wrong. Fairy tales and superstitions.

"Do you think you're different than a deer dying of hunger in the woods dragging about in pain until eaten alive by some wolf? You're not. I'm your wolf. If you live old enough life ends in dementia, disease, decay.

There's nothing beautiful about that. Nothing divine either. What you say you know, your inner truth, those are the convictions of a child. That feeling inside you corresponds to nothing outside you. It's an illusion. And for you it's one that ends now."

The man in the noose lowers his eyes and the trapper lowers his own head to keep within his gaze, bobs it down low like an owl. "The universe hears you? No. God saved you from bankruptcy? No. Your ancestors watching above protected you when the plane crashed? No. In a world with infinite events it's a statistical certainty that unlikely outcomes will happen all the time. Some good, some bad. When they happen to animals that like stories they tell a story and here's how that story goes: It's a miracle and I'm special." He leans in towards Dave and grabs the rope just above his hair and brings their faces so close together that Dave no longer sees the guns on the wall or the books on the floor or any other items painted with that haunted lighting, just sees two black portals to a place he doesn't want to go. "You're not." He sways the rope like he's stirring a pot causing Dave's head to circle. Releases it. "Open your eyes," he says.

Dave's eyes are already open and he just sits there in horror-struck terror.

"You've just washed up to the shores from out of the unknown reaches of some anonymous dark and you're groping at the pebbles like they're runestones and feeling the bumps on the rocks for braille. But they're just dead fossils of the confused before you. You're looking for signs and symbols that tell a story but there's no story, there's just dumb existence, and bound and

341

strung there as you are, it looks to me like you're failing at it. Fill in the gaps, make your own meaning. In fact there's no other way. But that's all liable to get buried in the garden when a bad man comes to your woods." His lower lip starts bleeding again as if those last words were sharp.

The trapper stands and kicks away the chair where he sat and it tumbles into the candles. "Let's give your Unnamed Something a final chance." He folds his hands together low on his stomach. "I'm open to anything that wants to make itself known here." He bows his head and closes his eyes, then opens them back up and rolls his eyes upwards to stop just under his lids. "But failing that we'll take the silence as your condemnation." He closes them again.

Dave does shut his eyes too. Why not? Them both listening there in the risen dawn. Both hearing the faint seething of the northern wind. The stove's slow burn of the coals. Two bodies breathing. Nothing else.

After this minute of silence the trapper opens his eyes and looks at Dave. "I'm sorry. No one spoke on your behalf."

Dave is shaking and breathing faster.

The trapper speaks with a raised voice. "Your existence, man, all you've felt, all you've believed, all you've loved and been loved back by was the bouncing around of predestined and meaningless things and your feelings of connection are just strange manifestations of your futile and isolated mind." His bare and scarred chest is heaving. "You're a glorified insect. One more that dies along with an unknown multitude in the same instant. And that's exactly how much sorrow

342

you're worth to me." He moves with the knife to Dave and cuts the strings lashing him to the chair then grabs the rope coming down from the rafter in one hand and severs it where it's anchored to the stove leg with the other. He puts two hands on the rope and pulls hard, standing Dave up to his feet by his stretching neck, then kicks away the chair.

"What's inside you!" His voice so loud in the cabin.

Dave makes a choking sound and just stares at something he's never seen before.

"Don't waste this! Do you have anything to tell me? Do you feel the presence of the sacred? Draw your last breath and speak, puppet!" The fire is still smouldering in the stove but the cabin must have turned colder with the start of day as those words smoked coming out of his mouth.

Dave's panicked eyes search the room: window, guns on the wall, bear hide on the table, burning candles, the trapper. He sees a man who's bare arms and chest glisten in sweat, blood at his fingertips and lips, a sunken and dark face, someone wholly changed from that face he first glimpsed over the distance of the hills that day. He grimaces, nearly squeaks out with his jaw hardly moving, "You don't have to do this."

"Then you're not listening! That's my point! I already have!" The trapper leans his weight down on the rope and hoists the standing man up to his toes. The rope inclines Dave's head like he's staring off to where he's going.

The tightening rope starts to constrict the blood flow to his brain and the oxygen to his lungs. Dave isn't twisting, he's still. His neck hurts and his ankle and most other things too. His wrists are still tied together in front of him and his fingers are laced. Like he holds something within them, some offering for whatever awaits him. A small rare bird held between his woven fingers, or a bit of gold, perhaps. Some paltry gift to appease the vulgar gods awaiting him on the other side. Him hanging stretched out there with just his toe tips on the ground, like a dancer nearing her finishing pose of the final act. His head feels light and his vision narrows. He looks down to the man hanging him. Two men with terror for common ground—one receiving, one inflicting—staring at one another in reflective horror like funhouse mirrors.

The trapper sees in those dying eyes the fading life like others that have gone before: deer, boy, woman, all the rest, all told from the same black pools like bottomless inkwells.

Dave shuts his eyes. Then he hears music. Singing. Wherever it is coming from. The words are perfect. He can't understand the words and there aren't any. Maybe just the song of a dawn bird, some trill of a mourning dove coming in through the window. Maybe he actually thinks he holds it in his woven fingers—there is less blood and oxygen flowing to his brain. He touches his thumb to his wedding band. The trapper pulls on the rope and Dave's head jars and a tear is shaken from his cheek and one of his feet lifts into the air. He bends those airborne toes and sweeps them looking for earth. One inch may as well be one thousand. Dave chokes and spit dribbles through his tight lips.

Then Dave speaks and who knows if he says it to his wife as goodbye, or as some prayer for his version of

God, or perhaps he has some rare capacity of love for those who do cruel things and is saying it to this poor and wayward human being that stands before him, but these words slip through his constricted neck and come out as a choked whisper you'd have to listen hard to hear.

"I love you."

Words like a vessel carrying meaning across time. None more sacred ever said. Those words resounding inside the trapper.

On the cabin floor a shadow grows. It came in from the window and appeared on the sill like a stain that poured across the pine planks and filled in the etched word scrawled upon one. A shadow from a man who stood beside a hollow grave and a fresh mound. Who before looking into that empty pit prayed his friend was not lying at the bottom. Who carried on towards the broken window where he heard sounds of raving and pleading, talk of violence and death and torture. He had crept up in the northern dawn and seen his friend about to die hanging with one foot off the ground.

I love you. As though released by Dave's weakening hands, those words flap like doves' wings inside the trapper's head. Those words entering the trapper without his invitation or permission, but without trespass or violation either.

Like the rifle-clap that sounded the death of his boy, those three words thread across his cut mind as if that sweet witch is reaching down kind and gentle to suture up a gap formerly cloven. And pathways that former trauma had closed off flood their backlog of dopamine and endorphins and whatever other mind-elixirs juice a brain to feel wonder and joy and awe and he feels a rush of loving kindness like a tide raised from a super-moon washing him over and carrying his wife and boy back to him along with every other joy he'd ever had. Things he'd lived but so far never recalled, even early sweet impressions more like felt shapes than mind pictures, even things he'd lived inside the belly of his mother and maybe further still and transferred from her mother and her's before as a flower whose endless bloom forever pushes out petals like a wellspring.

Right then the trapper hears everyone who has ever said those words to him. Then in some expanded state of consciousness, he feels everyone who's ever said those words to anybody, and all the feelings of those receiving those sentiments. Every single one held in his head at once.

A hunting bow is drawn back. A broadhead shines in the morning light.

Those three words ringing bells inside the trapper, his healing mind at once baffled by and drawing upon them. In those words he hears many words. He hears family words and nature words. He hears the loon sing and the wolf howl and the geese honk and the silence of snow falling and the thunder of iced lakes cracking and rain tapping on the roof and the gentle rumble of coffee boiling and he hears the woman he loves breathing in bed and the little boy laughing. Big love things ineffable.

And the trapper got to live all that. He got to exist. And to exist is very rare. Very rare. And if one thing always causes another and there's no getting outside of it, then the border of the skin is hardly border at all.

Perhaps acting out some grand legacy of everything that came before, even if only as a witness. A present that holds within its code all things prior and maybe all to come. And he was a piece of that code.

Like a long idle lightning rod that in some one-in-a-thousand-year storm got struck and lit up, his insides were nearly sizzling under the load of boundless love and his mind was scorching up in neuronic fury and all but on fire and his glowing eyes so wide and bright.

Almost as bright as the shimmering broadhead tipping an arrowshaft nocked to a string on a bow at full draw.

And from the top of his scalp under his dirty hair all the way down to the skin around his callused toes, all of it made from the same tissue as his inflated heart. That little heart-artisan inside him unsheathed and now sized fully to a man, now one and the same— look to his hand where once held a rope perhaps now a hammer—and this mystic might just go on to tap at the walls of the loving world to size them ever larger.

Dave opens his hazy eyes and looks downwards to see why the toes on his one grounded foot had not yet joined the others airborne.

The arrow now loose on its fated path, the bowstring that propelled it vibrating behind like a plucked guitar string.

The trapper's face encrusted with dried blood and dirt, papery like an old husk of corn, was streaked with tears as what had upwelled ran free and streaming. His hands that were gripping the rope slowly raised higher and the hanging man's single sweeping foot touched back down. Not like an angel lowered from heaven, not like a cherub or saint or anything fantastical either, as there is no supernatural here. The trapper would ask this man for forgiveness. He who had lost a son would kneel down and ask the one he'd thought taken him for forgiveness—but the arrow.

The arrow so pretty and dazzling in the morning light there. The arrow that had come in through the window broken by a shovelhead. Its broadhead blades sharp and polished slicing through that spectrum of northern morning light, radiating shards of severed light that filled the cabin as it raced with the brilliance of a shooting star burning at dawn. It shined like the sunrise behind it shined, like kindness and birdsong and laughter and effort and romance and beauty and sacrifice all shine.

The broadhead now so very close flooded the cabin with shimmer like starlight.

If you enjoyed Immortal North please rate and review it. That goes a long way for a new author. Thanks.

— Tom

Tom Stewart was born in 1982 and grew up near Winnipeg, Manitoba, Canada. He attended University of Manitoba taking literature and philosophy for two years, dropped out, and worked across the North as a fishing and hunting guide, oil-rig roughneck, bush pilot, and he backpacked internationally in the off-seasons. Tom now lives in Tofino, Vancouver Island.

Sign up at LuckyDollarMedia.com to hear when the next novel by Tom Stewart is published.

Manufactured by Amazon.ca
Bolton, ON